A Folk Tale Journey

THROUGH THE MARITIMES

Helen Creighton

A Folk Tale Journey

THROUGH THE MARITIMES

EDITED WITH AN INTRODUCTION

BY MICHAEL TAFT AND RONALD CAPLAN

Breton Books
Wreck Cove, Cape Breton Island
1993

The Cover Painting is "Lobster Pots in the Wintertime" by Joe Norris, Lower Prospect, Nova Scotia, from the Collection of Dr. Philip J. Brooks. Quotes from Helen Creighton's *A Life in Folklore* are published with permission of McGraw-Hill Ryerson Ltd.; and those from *Eight Folktales from Miramichi* with permission of Dr. Edward D. Ives. Some of the tales have appeared in *Eight Folktales from Miramichi* (Northeast Folklore Society) and Pauline Greenhill's *Lots of Stories: Maritime Narratives from the Creighton Collection* (Mercury Series, National Museum). The tale told by Lillian Crewe Walsh and Rory MacKinnon's tales numbered 47 and 48 first appeared in *Cape Breton's Magazine*, Number 40.

All photographs are from the Helen Creighton Collection, Public Archives of Nova Scotia, with these exceptions: Wilmot MacDonald courtesy the Northeast Folklore Society, and Lillian Crewe Walsh and Rory MacKinnon courtesy the families. Helen's photographs of Mrs. Laura McNeil, Mrs. Sephora Amirault, and Mrs. Henri (Hermance) Pothier are taken from printer's negatives prepared for *La Fleur du Rosier*, courtesy Penny Marshall, Director, University College of Cape Breton Press. Thanks to Margaret Campbell, Head, Photo and Print Collection, PANS, who was our guide to Helen's photographs.

Production Assistance: Bonnie Thompson
Typesetting: Glenda Watt
Darkroom: Eric Boutilier-Brown, PANS; and Grant Young

Canadian Cataloguing in Publication Data

Creighton, Helen, 1899-1989

A folk tale journey through the Maritimes

ISBN 1-895415-28-4

1. Tales — Maritime Provinces.   I. Taft, Michael, 1947-   II. Caplan, Ronald, 1942-   III. Title.

GR113.5.M37C73 1993   398.2'09715   C93-098697-0

Breton Books
Wreck Cove
Cape Breton Island
Nova Scotia
B0C 1H0

Introduction to the Journey

IN A TYPE-WRITTEN NOTE among the papers she had isolated for this collection of folk tales, Helen Creighton wrote: "I had been collecting for many years before I realized how much the characters I was hearing about meant to the storytellers and ballad singers. The song of 'The Dreadful Ghost' is about a man who had betrayed two women, one of whom in despair took her life. Her ghost made his life on land so unbearable that he was forced to sea, but there is no escape even though it is an old belief that ghosts can't cross water. She then forced him into her boat and the boat sank in a flame of fire. Not a cheerful love story, but dramatic. Mr. Hatt loved to sing it and being a compassionate eighty-six-year-old man he must have felt sorry for the participants. Consequently, he had no sooner finished his song than he turned towards me and remarked earnestly, 'He was a fine man, he was, and she was a good girl. She didn't go out on the roads on Saturday nights but stayed home with her father and mother.' They were his friends and he pitied them."

As we read Helen's book of folk tales from the Maritime Provinces, the characters in these stories become our friends, our responsibility. And, like Mr. Hatt, we pity them, love them, are amazed and amused by them. This is true of the tales and of the storytellers, and perhaps even of the folk tale collector herself. They all gave a part of their lives to these stories; the passage of these tales from the storyteller to Helen re-created them and kept them alive. And reading these Maritime folk tales (whether we read them silently or aloud), they are now *really* ours, as essentially they have always been ours—ours to remember, to tell, and to re-create as we pass them along.

"Others must have done the same," Helen goes on. "I think of Ben Henneberry who lived on Devil's Island at the mouth of Halifax

Harbour. He fished alone, tossing in his small boat on the restless waves of the Atlantic Ocean. When he sang 'The Courtship of Willie Riley' with its seventy-eight verses, he must have felt he was telling of a personal friend as he followed him through his trial, courtship and marriage. He sang entirely from memory and without hesitation, showing that he must have sung it time and again. So for a solitary fisherman or one living in isolation, he would find companionship here. Today he would simply turn on his radio."

The characters who live through these tales come to us from a time when people depended on one another for entertainment and education, to keep the other world—really the rest of *this* world—alive. The heroes and villains of modern media are the great-grandchildren of Jack the Giant Killer, Cinderella, Bluebeard, and the card-playing devil. Whether we turn on the radio or read these folk tales, to ourselves or aloud—that's up to each of us.

And these are not ordinary tales. They display a bizarre quality, often a gruesomeness, sometimes a sexuality, which marks them as coming from another time. They are not the tales found in modern-day children's books, nor do they resemble today's adult fantasy literature. As an introduction to this collection, Laura McNeil's "Cinderella" is a tale that cannot be confused with the Disney version, nor even with the older Cinderellas of Charles Perrault and the Brothers Grimm, reprinted over and over in storybooks. The vitality and inventiveness of Laura McNeil's version suggests a long and rich tradition, only some of which has managed to come down to us.

Once aware of these tales, their future is a responsibility we can choose to assume. Whether these tales live and die is up to each of us. There is no getting around it. They depend on our breath....

AND THIS BOOK is a folklore collector's journey, with the mix of what might come of each day of such a journey. Helen's work was to put herself in the way of stories and songs. It was not so much science as a way of life. There were no guarantees. In the quest for stories, Helen Creighton was never sure what she would get. It was part of what she did with her life, and like a wanderer in one of the tales, she set out on journeys pretty much open to what she would find. And she got wonderful full stories. And she got jokes and summaries and riddles and even elements of current events—an extraordinary mixed bag of other people's delights, things that they wanted to share.

In preparing this book, we could have selected only the finished, obvious folk tales. Or we could have had two sections, something like "The Well-turned Tale" and "Fragments along the Way." But, clearly, that is not what Helen wanted, or how she valued these tales. She knew that even the very short versions were worth our time and offered some pleasure: they spoke for the places she had been. And she also knew that the mix of stories gave a more real picture of the folk tale collector's story, her own story, the way of her life.

There were of course the personal qualifications that inform anyone's work. For instance, "They know not to tell you certain things," Helen once said. She meant, in her case, the ribald tale or song, which she did not want to hear. "They size you up." It was an autumn afternoon in her apartment in Dartmouth, a few years before she died—orange light through the window, time for a cup of tea. Helen said this with some pride. "They know not to tell you certain things." She told of collecting among men in a fish shed and how, during the taping, another man came in. He wanted to sing something onto her recorder. She pretended to record and let him sing—a song that clearly embarrassed her other informants, that he would sing such a thing to her.

After the man left, Helen assured the others that the song had not been preserved and the song session continued comfortably. At that point, telling this, Helen stood and mentioned "tea" and started for the kitchen. In the middle of the living room she suddenly spun on her heel, an arm in the air and her fingertips at her breastbone, a wonderful smile on her face. "But of course," she said, "it was a pity not to get the tune. The Devil has all the best tunes." Pause. Spun away. And off for our tea.

SO THIS IS HELEN CREIGHTON'S COLLECTION of folk tales picked up along the way. It cannot be anything but a personal story. Her notes reflect her relationship with the storytellers. No great attempt has been made to place these tales in an academic context. She included some type-indexing, which we have supplemented with type- and motif-numbers at the end of each tale. We have used Aarne and Thompson's *The Types of the Folk Tale* and Stith Thompson's *Motif-Index of Folk Literature.* This is a scholarly way of showing that these stories are part of the folk literature of the world. Further annotation is left for others. As we understood Helen's manuscript presentation, this was to be a book for the rest of us, for now.

While Helen was still alive, Memorial University of Newfoundland's Dr. Herbert Halpert gave her provocative queries and suggestions which helped Helen shape the manuscript. As editors, we have corrected obvious typographical errors in Helen's manuscript, and we have worked to maintain the sound of the storytellers as revealed in Helen's transcriptions. Because Helen did not complete her introductions and paragraphs of additional information, we have supplied a few quotes from her diaries and her autobiography, *A Life in Folklore.* In the case of Wilmot MacDonald, we have drawn on Dr. Edward "Sandy" Ives' remarks in *Eight Folktales from Miramichi.* In every case, we have made clear which passages were not part of Helen's original manuscript.

Finally, our thanks to Carman V. Carroll, Provincial Archivist, Public Archives of Nova Scotia, for encouraging the development of these tales as part of Breton Books. The staff of PANS have maintained the extraordinary combination of carefulness and openness one hopes for in an archives.

Ronald Caplan
Michael Taft

A Folk Tale Journey...

• PHOTOGRAPHS AFTER PAGE 76 •

PART ONE

Because you have to begin somewhere...

1. Cinderella (Souillon)

AS TOLD BY LAURA MCNEIL, WEST PUBNICO, NOVA SCOTIA

HELEN CREIGHTON: I don't remember other women expressing favorit-ism for particular tales, but Mrs. McNeil had no doubt of hers. This was "Souillon," a longer version than the "Cinderella" known to most of us. The great attraction came in the singing of two little songs. Mrs. Mc-Neil must have told this *conte* to many schoolchildren over the years and she described their anticipation as they waited eagerly for the music.

THERE WAS ONCE A LITTLE GIRL who lived with her father. Her mother was dead, and she was a beautiful little girl and everybody loved her. They were very happy, she and her father, but he began to be lonely and married an ugly woman who had a daughter named Cat'line. The woman was ugly and disagreeable, and the daughter was as ugly and disagreeable as her mother.

When they saw how well-loved the little girl was, they be-came jealous of her, although for a time they treated her well so that her father wouldn't notice. But after a while they couldn't keep up any longer so they began to ill-treat her. They dressed her in sackcloth and had her do all the hard work around the house and made her stay in the corner among the ashes around the hearth. Because she couldn't keep herself clean, they called her Cinderella. But in spite of everything, she kept on being beautiful and good, and that made the stepmother and Cat'line hate her still more.

Now the king of that country had a son who was a prince

and he was beginning to think that his son was old enough to be married, so he announced in all the country that at a certain night he would give a grand ball. Of course everybody was all excited, and Cat'line and her mother decided that they would go to this ball. For days they sewed and made all sorts of preparations while Cinderella was in her corner doing all the chores and hard work around the house. She was wishing that she could go too, but of course she had to help them and she knew she couldn't go.

When the day of the ball came she helped them get dressed, and she pleaded with them to let her go too, but they laughed and told her where she belonged and that she couldn't go. Then when they were ready they made fun of her because she couldn't go, and she felt very badly.

After they had gone she didn't know what to do, and she was digging among the cinders when all of a sudden she touched something that was hard and shiny, and when she picked it up it was a little golden key. Then she kept on digging and she found a little chest. She opened it right away and found it full of beautiful clothes and a dress trimmed with silver. Horses and a coach were in the ashes too. She couldn't think what it all meant until a fairy appeared and said to her,

"Wash yourself and leave your sackcloth covering, and dress yourself in all these beautiful clothes. Then get into the coach and hurry to the ball, but be very careful to be back before twelve o'clock. If you are not home before twelve, you will fall back into your old state as you are now."

Cinderella did as she was told and then got into the coach and drove the horses. She had never seen such horses before. When she arrived at the ball everybody turned to look at her because they had never seen anyone so beautiful.

When the prince saw her, he was dancing, but he left and came to her and asked her to dance with him. After that he would not dance with anyone else all evening, and she was so lovely he fell in love with her right away. The other ladies were not very happy about it and, like the rest, Cat'line and her mother were staring at this beautiful girl.

The prince tried to find out who she was but she would not tell, and first thing he knew she slipped away and nobody knew where she went. She hurried to her carriage and drove quickly home and got back into her old attire and tried to make herself look as she had before. When the clock struck twelve the horses and the carriage and all the beautiful clothes disappeared.

At the ball the prince was very unhappy, and he wanted to know more about this beautiful lady, so he announced that the ball was over, but would be continued the next evening. Everybody went home then, and all they talked about was this mysterious stranger, and they wondered who she could be. When Cat'line and her mother arrived home they started telling Cinderella about her and how the prince had danced with her. Cinderella listened for a while and then got tired of their talk and said,

"Oh, she was no more beautiful than I am."

"How dare you say such a thing," they scolded. Then they told her that the ball would go on the next night.

The second night she had to help them get ready again, and even though she knew what would happen, she asked if she could go with them and was refused. After they left she dug again in the cinders and she found things as she had done before except that everything was more beautiful and her dress was trimmed with gold. The fairy appeared again and told her she must be back before the clock struck twelve. Then she took off her sackcloth, washed herself clean, and put on her beautiful clothes. She put the harness on the horses and went to the ball.

When she went into the ballroom the prince was waiting for her. In fact all the people were expecting her and looking for her. This time he had a guard on the door to watch where she was going, but she went so quickly that they couldn't follow her. He had tried to find out who she was and where she lived but she wouldn't tell him anything, and before twelve she slipped out of the ballroom and got into her coach and drove home. She took off her beautiful clothes and dressed herself in sackcloth, and everything disappeared in the ashes and looked as it had before.

The prince was very much disappointed and he announced

that there would be another ball the next evening. Of course everybody was talking about it, and when Cat'line and her mother came home they couldn't talk enough about it because she had been more beautiful than before. Cinderella was quite amused and said again,

"Oh, she was not more beautiful than I am." Her stepmother and Cat'line scolded her and said,

"How dare you say such a thing, and you, dirty in the ashes."

So the next day Cinderella had to help Cat'line and her mother again to get ready for the ball. Again she asked to go with them but they only laughed at her, and when evening came they left her and went alone.

After Cat'line and her mother were gone she was playing in the cinders and she found the little key and the chest and the clothes and this time they were trimmed with diamonds and were still more beautiful. She found the coach and the horses, and again the fairy appeared and told her to wash herself clean and dress herself up in these wonderful clothes, and to be sure to be back and in her old clothes before twelve. Then she disappeared.

When she got to the ballroom the prince was waiting again and he found her more beautiful than ever. Everybody was looking at her, and they all thought she should be his bride. He danced with her all the evening, and he was sure then that he loved her and wanted her for his wife. When it came near twelve o'clock she made her excuses. The guards were at the door waiting for her and they tried to hold her, but she was too quick for them and all they could catch was her slipper. She hurried and got into her coach and went home and took off her beautiful clothes, and when the clock struck twelve she was in her corner again and everything was vanished.

When Cinderella disappeared from the ballroom again everybody was disappointed that the guards hadn't been able to hold her, and that they still didn't know who she was. They took the slipper to the prince and he said that the next morning they must start and go all over the country and find the lady it would fit.

The ball was over now, and when Cat'line and her mother got home they told Cinderella what had happened and about the slipper and how beautiful it was, and how the prince was going to send his men all over the country to see who the slipper belonged to, and again Cinderella said,

"She was no more beautiful than I am."

Now in the country there was a great commotion because all the girls were hoping they would be the one to fit the slipper. The men went everywhere, and at last they came to the house where Cinderella lived. They came in and asked if there was anyone to try the slipper on there. The mother tried first, but she had a great big toe and it didn't take long to see that the slipper didn't fit her.

Then Cat'line tried the slipper, but she had a big heel, so her mother started whittling on the heel and then it hurt and she cried out,

"It hurts me. It hurts me. It hurts me." Her mother would say,

"Endure, endure, endure, and you will marry the king's son," but endure as she would they couldn't make her heel small enough and they couldn't get the shoe on her foot at all.

Then these men said,

"Isn't there anyone else you know of that we could try this shoe on?"

"Oh," the stepmother said, "there's my sooty Cinderella in the corner over there, but there's no use to try her."

"Well," they said, "it doesn't matter who she is. The prince said to try every woman and every girl." So the stepmother told Cinderella to come out of her corner and try the slipper on. She put out her foot and the slipper fitted exactly. They were all greatly surprised, and the stepmother and Cat'line were angry with jealousy because the shoes fitted Cinderella.

"Well," the men said, "the king has said that the woman the shoes fitted would be the prince's bride."

The guards went back to the prince and told him, not thinking he would really marry her, but he said it didn't matter who she was, he would marry her all the same. So he went and got her and everybody was invited and they had a very big wedding. When she was dressed as a bride she was so beautiful he knew she was the same girl he had met at the ball.

They lived very happily for a while, and then war broke out in the country and the prince had to go. He was very sad at leaving her but, before he went, he gave her a little golden bell and told her to go back with her stepmother and Cat'line and, if she ever needed him, she could go to a certain place with the little bell and ring it and he would come to her. Then he got on his white horse and rode away.

After he was gone she went back to her stepmother and took all her beautiful clothes with her. It wasn't long before her stepmother had taken them all away from her and hidden them, and she also hid the little bell, but not before she had rung it a few times when he came back and talked to her. Cinderella was put back in sackcloth and she was given all the hard work to do; they even sent her to tend the sheep. Poor Cinderella hunted everywhere for the bell then but she could never find it, and she couldn't go to the place and ring it anymore. After the prince had waited in vain to hear it he thought Cinderella didn't love him anymore, and, as the years went by, he thought she must have died.

Poor Cinderella was obliged to obey her two mistresses. Every morning she would go along, her head low and her heart heavy, through the fields with her sheep which she tended all day. She always worked with her spindle and she thought that some day the prince would come back and deliver her from all this misery. The only happiness that was left to her was to keep the sheep because with them she could at least live in peace. The sun's rays and the songs of the birds consoled her a little.

Then one day when she was going to tend her sheep she had to cross a little brook, and as she was crossing it she lost her spindle in the stream. She was frightened because she knew something would happen, and that she would be punished if she didn't get it back.

While she was looking in the water and wondering what to

do, an elf appeared and asked her if she wouldn't go down to the bottom of the brook and they would give her the spindle. So she went down with the elf and found a nice little house with three fairies living in it. One of the fairies asked her if she would cook the breakfast for them and she said yes, and cooked them a nice breakfast. When they asked her if she would make their beds and she said yes and she did all the work they had to do that morning. When she was all through the eldest fairy approached and gave her the spindle and said,

"I wish that you will become more beautiful day by day."

The second fairy approached and said,

"I wish that when you go home tonight you will sing and it will be so lovely that everyone will come out of their houses to listen."

The third fairy said,

"I wish from now on when you speak that pieces of gold will fall out of your mouth."

Cinderella thanked them and took the spindle and climbed up out of the brook. Then she went on and stayed all day with the sheep. When night came and she started for home she began to sing. The people heard her and it was so much more beautiful than anything they had ever heard before that they came out of their houses to see who it was.

Cat'line and her mother heard it too, and the mother said to Cat'line,

"Go out and see who is singing so beautifully." Cat'line went out and saw Cinderella, so she went back and told her mother that all she could see was Cinderella coming home. Her mother said,

"That can't be," and she went out to see for herself. At that moment Cinderella was coming in at the door.

"How is it that you sing so well?" her stepmother asked in an excited voice. Cinderella began to tell the morning's adventure, and as she was talking, gold fell from her mouth. Cat'line and her mother were confused and grew more jealous and envied Cinderella this wealth.

"Cat'line," said her mother, "tomorrow you will go to tend the sheep in order that you may see the fairies and obtain their good wishes. Cinderella will stay at the house with me."

The next day there was a great commotion getting Cat'line ready for her day's work. She took all her nice clothes and a nice lunch and started out with her provisions in a basket in one hand and her spindle in the other. She went straight to the brook and threw the spindle into the water. The elf appeared and asked Cat'line if she would go down into the brook to get the spindle, so she followed the elf and soon found herself in the strange home.

"Would you," asked one of the fairies, "make our breakfast and help us with the morning's work?" Cat'line stared at the fairies, and in an unkind voice answered,

"Do you think that I am here to be your servant?" However she prepared the breakfast, but when the fairies sat at the table they found dishes made of toads and frogs and snakes. After breakfast Cat'line went around and tidied a little, but she didn't do it well. When everything was finished the first fairy handed her the spindle saying,

"I wish that you become uglier and uglier every day."

The second fairy advanced and said,

"I wish that toads and frogs will come out of your mouth every time you speak."

The third fairy approached and said,

"I wish that tonight when you go home you will start to sing and it will resemble the bellowing of an ox and everybody will come out of their houses to see what it is."

Cat'line was very angry and grimaced and climbed out of the brook. She spent a lonely day, not attending to the sheep at all. At last to her great joy the day ended, and she started to go home. Without thinking about the fairies' wishes she began to sing, and the echo of her singing spread all around the village and the people all thought it was an ox bellowing and they were really frightened. Cinderella and her stepmother heard it too and were also frightened.

"Go to the door and see what it is," the stepmother ordered.

Cinderella opened the door and saw Cat'line coming. She told her stepmother who did not believe her and went to see for herself. At the same time Cat'line entered.

"Why are you making such a noise?" asked her mother. Cat'line began to relate the adventures of the brook, and toads and frogs and snakes began leaping out of her mouth. Her mother was horrified, and blaming Cinderella for all this, she heaped insults upon her. This was the beginning of new tortures for Cinderella who was growing more beautiful every day while Cat'line was getting uglier.

One day however Cat'line and her mother were absent and Cinderella was left alone in the house. She had been awaiting this chance for a long time, and as soon as she was alone she began looking for the little golden bell the prince had given her. She hunted and hunted and finally she found it in the attic. As soon as she got it she rushed out and ran to the place where the prince had told her to go, and she rang the bell. After a little while she saw his white horse and the prince riding at a gallop towards her.

When Cat'line and her mother arrived back at the house Cinderella was not there and they were very weary. Looking out the window they saw her coming with a strange gentleman on a white horse. Then they were surprised and wondered who he could be. They wondered too what Cinderella could have to tell this stranger because they could see her talking to him. Little did they suspect that it was the prince and that she was telling him everything that had happened to her during the last seven years while he had been away.

When Cinderella and the prince entered, Cat'line and her mother received them very graciously as though Cinderella was very dear to them, although really they were very jealous of her. They brought the best chair for the prince, but they forced Cinderella to remain behind it as she had always done. Then they took charge of the conversation and the prince didn't let on who he was. When it came time for supper the prince asked,

"Which one of your daughters, Madame, will you place at the table with me?"

"Oh, Cat'line, if she wants to," replied the mother with her best smile.

"Oh," said the prince, "I would much prefer Cinderella." The mother swallowed her disappointment as best she could and, turning to Cinderella, said in a brusque voice,

"Go and wash your hands to eat with this gentleman." Cinderella obeyed, and as she was washing her hands she sang,

> Monsieur my gentleman
> You will excuse me,
> Seven years have passed
> Since I have eaten at a table.

The prince understood what Cinderella was trying to tell him. After supper the evening passed in conversation again between Cat'line, her mother and the prince. When bedtime came the prince asked,

"Which of your daughters, madame, are you going to give me to sleep with?"

"Cat'line, if she wants to," replied her mother.

"Oh, I would much prefer Cinderella," said the prince. This was another disappointment for the mother and, turning to Cinderella she said, looking as though she would strangle her,

"Cinderella, go wash your feet to sleep with this gentleman."

Cinderella went aside, and while washing her feet sang:

> Monsieur my gentleman
> Please excuse me,
> Seven years have passed
> Since I have slept in a bed.

The prince understood what Cinderella meant.

Cat'line and her mother could not sleep all night. They didn't know who this strange man was, but they were afraid that something was going to happen to them. The next morning they got up very early and waited and waited for Cinderella and the gentleman, but they were in no hurry to get up. Cat'line and her mother got tired of waiting, and they began to look through the keyhole and they saw Cinderella dressing in her beautiful clothes.

At first they couldn't understand what that meant, and then it dawned upon them that this stranger could be no one but the prince. They were struck with fear.

When the prince and Cinderella came out of the room he led her to the table and Cat'line and her mother served the breakfast. After it was over the prince stood up and addressed them. He reproached them and made them recall all they had made Cinderella suffer during the seven years he had been gone.

Without giving them a chance to reply he grabbed the two of them and dragged them out of the house and put them in a puncheon which he headed up but from which the bung hole was left open, and he threw the puncheon in the sea. Poor Cat'line and her mother saw what was going to happen to them and the mother cried to Cat'line,

"You that have a big heel, glub, glub, put it in the bung hole to stop the water from coming in, glub, glub." Cat'line tried in vain to close the hole with her heel. Little by little the water rose in the puncheon until it was full, glub, glub, and she and her mother were drowned. The current carried them far away and they were never seen again.

As for Cinderella and the prince, they lived happily ever after and spent the rest of their days in the palace.

[Types 503 Gifts of the Little People, and 510 Cinderella and Cap o' Rushes]

EDITORS' NOTE: The song from "Souillon" can be found in *La Fleur du Rosier: Acadian Folk Songs/Chansons folkloriques d'Acadie*, collected by Helen Creighton.

PART TWO
On the Atlantic Shore...

Enos and Richard Hartlan

HELEN CREIGHTON: I knew nothing about folklore until I met these kindly men.

When I first visited the Hartlan estate at South-East Passage (Halifax Co.) in July, 1928, it was no time before I was introduced to the family Ghost House. There it stood, empty and forlorn, in need of paint and signs of habitation. "I am part of this family's past," it said. "They are proud of me." It was this sense of pride that aroused my curiosity. Perhaps they cherished it because it provided a stock of stories for them to tell, visitations from another world and activities of witches who drove them out with threats of using their black art upon them. For the Hartlans were known as the best storytellers in the surrounding country. Accounts of the supernatural had been handed down through their German grandfather and uncle. These were popular subjects in those days and the family made the most of them.

Their property was on a bluff which overlooked the western entrance to Halifax Harbour. The sea below them tossed against a pebbled beach and surf pounded over the sands of nearby Cow Bay Beach. On the fine summer evening that I am thinking of the atmosphere was serene and the soft sea breezes drifted over us like a caress. In a storm this could be frightening, and in fog it could be eerie. Strange shapes would appear and you could imagine almost anything. The German grandfather had come to Nova Scotia's western shore with the founding of Lunenburg in 1753 and had brought his folklore with him, creating the situation under which succeeding generations were brought up. It was from their maternal English ancestry that their wealth of folk songs was inherited. Mr. Enos fished, farmed, and in later life, did odd jobs while Mr. Richard worked as a labourer at Dartmouth's Imperial Oil Refinery. Mixing with other men, there was a great exchange of stories and songs which added to their repertoire. Everything was committed to memory because they were illiterate. Yet I look upon them as my finest teachers because folklore in all its forms dominated their lives.

Balmy as the weather was on this visit, a fire in the kitchen stove was welcome in a house so close to the sea. Actually I was looking for stories of people who sang pirate songs so I could write an article about them. But as so often happens in the experience of a collector, there were much more precious items to recover. One ancient and beautiful song was our reward for this evening, but it opened the door to a new career for me.

Meeting Enos for the first time I could see that something was bothering him but he soon explained his hesitation, and said, "I used to be a pretty singer but me teeth is gone and me voice is rusty." We usually sat around their kitchen table with only his wife as audience and family support. He would hold his spare figure tense. His eyes were very blue and alert and he made every word tell. When his voice gave out for singing he would regale us with stories of ghosts and the witches his grandfather had kept out by nailing a board over the door with nine letters from the German Bible. A witch could go over that board, but not under it. Translated it read, "And the word was made flesh and dwelt among us."

Many visits followed and everybody cooperated, agreeing readily that this material so precious to them should be preserved. So pleased were they that this unexpected recognition was viewed with such respect that they would often walk to the Osborne house two miles away when sand blown across the road made it impossible for me to drive through it. And their payment? I took one of my father's cigars down one evening for Enos and I took photographs and had prints made for them. Otherwise it was the shared enjoyment of a priceless heritage.

Picture the Osbornes' roomy kitchen with our hosts, members of their family and their friends, and any others who had come knowing they were in for a rollicking evening. Enos' stories were profusely sprinkled with expletives, and at the story's end he would declare, "That's as true as I'm settin' here." Or, "My father told me that not once but a dozen times." Then just as he seemed to be running down the sparkle came back to his eyes, he faced his attentive audience and announced, "Now I'll tell you a real story." As soon as he felt assured that everyone in the room was listening, he began. This was "Jack the Serving Man." Words in brackets are from another telling in my *Folklore of Lunenburg County*.

2. Jack the Serving Man

AS TOLD BY ENOS HARTLAN, SOUTH-EAST PASSAGE, N.S.

THERE WAS A MAN ON A FARM who couldn't keep a serving man. Every one he took, in the morning he would be dead. Well one day a feller came along and said, "Don't you want to hire a man?" The farmer said, "Yes, but it's no good. Whenever I hire a man he's always dead in the morning." "All the same," said Jack, "I'll try."

So he slept in the room where all the others had been killed. This man was a sailor.

So when the farmer went to bed, Jack he didn't go to bed. Instead he made a fire in the hearth and sat down by the fire. At midnight he was settin' there when one snooky *(smoochy)* little cat came in through the keyhole all hunched up and sat by the fire. *(Pause for effect.)* Till twenty-five come. *(The "twenty-five" was fairly thrown at us.)* Twenty-five, mind you. They all sat alongside of the fire all drawed up and the last cat was the biggest. Then the last one said, "You've got a *(a German word which seemed to mean "some work to do")* in your hand." The sailor couldn't understand what was said, but all at once the big cat said *(to the little ones),* "Pack an"—and they all jumped on him. "Pack an"—that's Dutch for "lay a-holt and kill him."

Fortunately Jack had a knife with him and when they

jumped on him he cut the biggest cat's left paw off, and when that happened all the cats run away. *(He examined the paw he had cut off and saw it was a hand with a ring onto it)* and went to bed. In the morning the boss come in and saw him alive.

"What?" he said, "you alive?" and the man said yes and got up and went to work.

Through the morning the man's wife was sick so they sent for a doctor. He come and he reached for her hand for to take her pulse. She had given him her right hand and he wanted the other one. She wouldn't show it so he hauled out the other one by force and it was cut off. Jack, the new serving man, come in just then and when he saw what had happened he brought the paw in. He says, "Whatever *(whosoever)* that hand belongs to, that's the hand that was going to kill me last night." So the farmer turns to his wife and he says, "So you're the one who's been killing all my men," and he bundled her out of the house and put straw around her and he built a fire and he burned her up. She was a witch, she was.

[Motif G252. Witch in form of cat has hand cut off: recognized next morning by missing hand]

HELEN CREIGHTON: Enos sat back, well satisfied with his performance. He lived to the age of eighty-four and, according to his obituary, beloved by all. Courteous, but never hesitant about expressing his own thoughts, I bless this family that started me on my life in folklore.

I must have taken the tale of "Jack the Serving, or Servant Man" down by hand in the late 'twenties or early 'thirties and that must have happened twice. It is always the same story, but not always the same words. I had no recording equipment at that time, but in 1943 the Library of Congress in Washington provided me with a Presto machine and I recorded on discs. The items were later put on tape which made it possible to take the words down exactly as spoken. My longhand had not always been as fast as the speaker's words, and even with tape a few words were difficult to make out.

EDITORS' NOTE: The version of "Jack the Serving, or Servant Man" offered here was one of the stories Helen took down by hand.

3. Enchanted Washing Woman
AS TOLD BY ENOS HARTLAN, SOUTH-EAST PASSAGE, N.S.

THERE WAS A WOMAN OUTSIDE the house and she was a-washing and there was a sailor come along and fell in love with her, and he went up and spoke to her and asked her what she was washin' there for, and she said, "I'm going to wash here till you see that tree growin', the pine tree growin', and that pine tree that will be cut down and sawed in lumber and," she said, "the first child that rocks into the cradle that that pine lumber is made of," she said, "will be able for to release me, to release me." But it don't say whether it did or not. It don't say. I never heard whether it did or not.

[Motif D791.1.3. The deliverer in the cradle]

4. Woman with Keys
AS TOLD BY ENOS HARTLAN, SOUTH-EAST PASSAGE, N.S.

THERE WAS ANOTHER WOMAN A-WASHIN' and a feller comes along and he finds out where it is *(the preceding five words are uncertain)* so he went up to her and he asked her what was she doing there. She said, "I have to wash here," she says, "to eternity." So she took him in the house and she showed him every room into it and she showed him the room what she would come out of. But she told him, she said that she'd come ugly. She'd come ugly, but not to be frightened. Not to be frightened. So he went through the night, he went and she come back that ugly that scared him and he dropped everything and he started out of the house. Started out of the house. She frightened him to death, she come out that ugly from the room that she told him that she'd come out of. So she must have been ugly. And three weeks after that he went to his grave. Frightened him to death. Yes, frightened him to death and it killed him. He took it so to heart that it killed him. In three weeks he went to his grave. So, what did she do? What did she do to *(words are uncertain)* him?

She said that she was out and had a bunch of keys into her mouth when she'd come, and he was to take them keys. He was to take them keys out of her mouth and then go into the room. But it frightened him to death. He went home and in three weeks he went to his grave, frightened to death. That's an old story, an old story. I learned it when I was first knockin' around and I picked it up.

[Motif D759.1. Disenchantment by taking key from serpent's mouth at midnight] *Recorded for Library of Congress in 1943.*

HELEN CREIGHTON: Another folk tale told by Enos Hartlan is in my *Folklore of Lunenburg County*, p. 145. It is called "Jack and the King's Daughter," and seems to be a garbled form of no known story. It is listed there as coming from Lunenburg which place was the first Canadian residence of the Hartlan family.

Mr. Richard Hartlan favoured hunting stories, treasure expeditions and tall stories. He always began the latter with a twinkle in his eye, and the warning, "Now I'll tell you a good lie." His rosy cheeks grew a little rosier, knowing that he could count on the new audience facing him. There are many tales of "The Wonderful Hunt" not only on this continent, but in Europe and Asia as well. This is the way Richard tells it:

"There was a fellow went out duck shooting and he went to a river and my George, there was any amount of wild geese there. He said, 'I'm going to have a shot at them,' but he couldn't get a sight without bending his gun around a tree. Then he fired at the wild geese and he went out to see what happened. He got two carloads of wild geese, and when he come ashore his boots were full of eels. He made a good shot, eh?" See *Folklore of Lunenburg County*, p. 136.

Then, pleased with our response, another story came to mind and he was off again. He spoke more quietly than Enos, and didn't make so many repetitions for effect. Yet each in his way was superb in his presentations.

[Types 1890E Gun Barrel Bent, and 1895 A Man Wading in Water Catches Many Fish in His Boots]

Dan and John MacPherson

HELEN CREIGHTON: In the thirties I had stayed at the home of the John McNeils in Guysborough County, and we had kept in touch through the succeeding years. Mr. McNeil, who contributed many songs, was familiar with the whole county, and often suggested people I should visit, and sometimes he or one of this family would go with me. In 1961 I was in that county again, and one day when I was talking with their daughter Margaret she told me excitedly about two storytellers I hadn't heard of before. Guysborough has many lonely uninhabited spots and the men we were to visit lived so far in the back country that there were no telephone poles. Neither was there electricity at the home of Dan MacPherson, so his stories had to be taken down by hand.

Dan and his brother John were lonely men because no woman would live in such remote surroundings. Dan said he was longing for a woman, but this was not said in any way suggesting that we might oblige. Knowing Margaret's family they were at once disposed to listen while we explained why we were there. The result was the tale of "The Minister and the Pot," and "Big Claus and Little Claus." Dan's brother would add a line now and then, and in one story he simply took over and finished it. This didn't seem to bother Dan; but John was apologetic. He said it wasn't right for storytelling, meaning they'd had no time to work up to it. I can't describe the men except that they were kind and courteous. I believe they had a room or two in Halifax where they spent the winter. Thinking it over, I realized I had less fear in visiting them in their secluded surroundings than I would have in visiting the sort of accommodation they probably had in the city. They were of Irish extraction, and great talkers.

One thing surprised me in my diary where I note that in conversation they said, "I be's" and "I has," which they don't do in their stories. Since my tape recorder required electricity I could not record them. I would then have kept them talking to get a sample of their speech. As John suggested, their stories would have been better told if they had been given time to think about it.

5. The Minister and the Pot

STARTED BY DAN MACPHERSON AND FINISHED BY HIS BROTHER JOHN WHO GOT IMPATIENT LISTENING AND JOINED IN

THERE WERE TWO STUDENTS going to college. The college closed and they were on their way home and there wasn't much way to go in those days but on foot. They were pretty tired and thought they'd like to get up somewhere, but they couldn't get anyone to take them. There was an awful rainstorm coming. They went to a house off the road and seen a light quite a ways off and they were just about giving up but one fellow rapped at the door and the other dropped back at the window, and he could see in. There was a table set, and brandy and everything on the table.

One fellow rapped at the door and the other saw what was going on, and he saw the woman grab the brandy and put it in the cupboard, and she put everything else in the table-cloth and put in another cupboard and then came to the door.

The fellow asked if she would put them up and she said no, but he put his feet in the door and they got in. This woman was a truckman's wife and there was a minister who was coming to see her when her husband was away trucking. They were supposed to be poor. There was a big pot there and the woman took the corner off the pot to hide the minister before the students came in. They got in, so she told them her husband was away and he was pretty rough if he came home and found anybody in the house. They said they wouldn't mind that, and it would be better than being out in the rainstorm. They might as well die one way as another.

They got in and they were sitting around and after a while they heard a rough step coming to the door and the old truckman came in. He was all soaking wet and sat down and never spoke. He just looked at the fellows and took his big boots off. He fired them to one side and asked what they were doing there. They told him they were travelling and wanted to get in for the night as they were coming from college.

"What's the good of college? Here we are tonight and not a bite of food to eat." So he said he couldn't see any good in this college business. This fellow who'd been at that window said,

"I don't know, I might do something." The old truckman didn't believe in any religion or anything. They told him they were studying for clergymen and they said they were no better off than he was. They said there was a hereafter, and he said no. The student that had been at the window said,

"If you keep quiet a while I'll read and we'll see if any good will come out of it." So he read for half an hour. So he told the old fellow to go over to the closet. He didn't want to go, but he did, and there was everything there he wanted to eat. The old fellow said,

"Well, there is something in this going to church and going

to college as well." He said he didn't believe in drink, but he'd read again. So this time he sent him over to the other corner and when he opened that cupboard he got the brandy and they had a fine supper.

The student asked the old fellow then if he'd like to see the devil. He said he never believed in such a thing, so he said he'd just give him a glimpse of him. So he lifted a lid off the pot after putting a fire under it, and he just got a glimpse of the minister as he jumped out of the pot and ran out of the house. So he said he did believe, and next Sunday he was going to go to church.

The next Sunday he went to church and the minister was there coming out with the crowd. He didn't know who he was, but he said,

"I don't know who you are, but you look more like the devil than anyone I've ever seen."

[Type 1730 The Entrapped Suitors; Motif K1571.1. Trickster as sham magician makes adulteress produce hidden food for her husband]

HELEN CREIGHTON: Their stories were learned from an old man in a blacksmith shop in Guysborough County. Story taken down at East Erinville, September 1961.

6. Three Feathers
AS TOLD BY DAN MACPHERSON, EAST ERINVILLE, N.S.

THE TWO OLDER SONS WERE very proud of themselves and the younger one was simple and was left to do the chores. They dressed up and expected rich girls to like them. Their mother died and they were left three feathers. The two older sons took their feathers and one went east and the other west and then they dropped them and nothing else happened.

The simple fellow looked at his feather and wondered what

to do with it and a hatch opened and a little old man in a green cap etcetera came up. Three tasks were set aside for him and they were impossible and dangerous. One was to go straddling from the house and face winds for so many days. Another would be to walk so many miles like the furthest point north and he had to fight a ghost. Or to climb a mountain of glass and get an apple. Every time when he was nearly at the top something would happen and he'd slip back again.

[Motifs D1021. Magic feather, and L160. Success of the unpromising hero (heroine)]

Told September, 1959. This story must have been in an old school book but was told differently here. In the book these are sons of a king, and his wife died and left the three feathers. The school book version is evidently well known here, and it was assumed we knew it too. The school book was probably the old *Royal Reader*.

John Obe Smith

HELEN CREIGHTON: Occasionally I have gone in a house where the grandfather sat in his chair looking glum and lonely. All the family had heard his songs and stories and made it clear they were through with "that old stuff." They belonged to the modern world; his day is over. But that was not the fate of John Obe Smith of Glen Haven in Halifax County, who lived with his grandson and family. In my diary written in 1950 I describe them as a pleasant, happy family and full of fun. At first I thought they would be straight-laced but after singing a temperance song, Mr. Smith admitted he didn't go to temperance meetings to uphold their cause (he usually had a bottle in his pocket) but because the pretty girls were there. Even yet at ninety he was not above chucking me under the chin; it was mischievous but never offensive.

The striking thing about the Smith household was the devotion of the children to their great-grandfather. When I went there for an evening they would seat themselves around the long dining table and listen with rapt attention, never interrupting. Even though I took ice cream or some other treat along Mrs. Smith, his granddaughter-in-law, always ended the evening with a cup of tea or cool drink all round, with cookies and cake to make it a festive occasion.

Mr. Smith was delighted when I suggested taking his picture and immediately put on his Orangeman's sash complete with medals. This he was to be buried in even though the Lodge had not functioned for twenty-five years. And when I returned with the prints he asked me to get him a dozen for other members of his family.

I asked him one day if he knew any "once upon a time" stories and he surprised me with three shortened versions of well-known tales. But singing was his main contribution. Being a jolly man, he particularly liked the comical ones and he must often have sung them to himself as he sat on the verandah and looked out upon the lovely waters of St. Margaret's Bay. His ancestry is Welsh and German and he used to sail on schooners, coasters, and fishing vessels to Newfoundland and Labrador. Anyone who waved when passing their house would be sure of a friendly response.

7. Little White Bull

AS TOLD BY JOHN OBE SMITH, GLEN HAVEN, NOVA SCOTIA

A FELLOW WAS TRAVELLING and he was so hungry he didn't know what to do for something to eat, and he was settin' down cryin' when along come a little white bull, and the little white bull says,

"What's the matter?" he says. The boy says,

"I'm hungry."

"Unscrew my horn," he said. So he unscrewed his horn and took out a white tablecloth and spread it, and first thing, here was everything he wanted to eat. He put it back again and screwed it on and the little bull said,

"What do you want?"

"Well," he said, "I'd like to have some money."

"Well," he said, "unscrew my other horn; you'll get all the money there you want," so he took off the horn and he took out a couple of thousand dollars in gold and put in his pocket, and then he wanted some more, and he said he'd like to go home. He said,

"Oh, that's nothing, I'll take you home. Get on my back." So he got on the bull's back and it wasn't long before the bull took him home, and he got home and he hadn't a place to go, and he told the bull,

"I ain't got no place to go," so the bull says,

"Oh, I'll soon have a place for you," so he built him a fine house and everything that could be into it, and Jack went in and he got married, and I guess they're livin' yet.

[Type 511A The Little Red Ox]

8. Jack and the Old Woman

AS TOLD BY JOHN OBE SMITH, GLEN HAVEN, NOVA SCOTIA

JACK STARTED OFF for to seek his fortune, and he told his father for to bake him a cake. He met an old woman and she was very hungry. *(Here he must have given her some of his cake because....)* The old woman give him a kind of a little book, and whatever he wished for he could have.

He wished for something to eat first, and first thing he

knew there was a table with a turkey and a goose and everything like that, and that was all right. Then he wished for a suit of clothes and a pony so he could go home. She said all right, and first thing there was a suit of clothes and a pony.

Then he wished for a castle on his way home so he could go and have a nice place full of servants and everything, and when he got home there was his castle and servants and everything, and he had a great time and he got married to a fine little girl, and I guess they're livin' yet.

[Types 513, 514 The Helpers, and 515 The Shepherd Boy]

HELEN CREIGHTON: Compare with "Little White Bull" in this volume, page 28. Recorded June, 1950. Mr. Smith doesn't know where he learned the tale, but it was not from his mother.

9. How Salt Water Got Salt

AS TOLD BY JOHN OBE SMITH, GLEN HAVEN, NOVA SCOTIA

ONE TIME THERE WERE TWO BROTHERS. One fellow was rich and the other was very poor. So the poor fellow didn't know what to do so he guessed he'd go to sea and look for his fortune. He travelled along and he was very hungry and he had a piece of bread and an old fellow came along and he said, "Oh, I'm so hungry."

"Well," he says, "I ain't got much but I'll give you what I got."

And he says, "Where you going?"

"I'm going to look for my fortune."

"Well," he says, "I'm going to give you a little mill to grind. All you got to do is to turn it. Whatever you want you can get." So that was all right. So he ground himself a ship, oh a fine ship and he went to sea and he had nothing to put into her so he guessed he'd fill her full of salt. So he started to grind and he ground and he ground and he got her full and then he didn't know how to stop and his ship sunk and it made the ocean salt and it's been salt ever since.

[Types 513, 514 The Helpers, and 565 The Magic Mill; Motif A1115.2. Why the sea is salt: magic salt mill]

Edward Collicutt

HELEN CREIGHTON: Edward Collicutt lived in Canaan (Lunenburg County), a remote lumbering village north of Chester on Nova Scotia's southwestern shore. Most of my collecting had been done in fishing villages, so it was a change to go inland. Back country roads were bad in 1947, and this was no exception. However the trip was well worth the discomfort. Residents largely of Irish stock were friendly and had been prepared for my arrival, except for two men who were building a house. They recalled my first Paul Bunyan yarn and after we went on they thought up stories for my return. They had a tall story which they "hollered" down from the roof where they were working, and there was much merriment in the telling. Never before had I taken down a story from a rooftop.

The steep road to Edward Collicutt's house had to be taken on foot and it seemed endless. Mr. Collicutt was ready and waiting, and while we were getting acquainted he told me he had been a guide, and gave an example of a moose call. Then we talked of stories and he said he had one that took half an hour to tell. I had no recording equipment, so it had to be taken down by hand. I could write a quick longhand; even so it was an hour and a half before I had it all. He had learned it in the Maine lumbering woods where many a song and story were exchanged in leisure hours. Being illiterate he had to commit it to memory. Compared later with the Hans Christian Anderson story, it is almost identical. This often happens and it never ceases to amaze me. He said I should return in the evening, for this is the time all over the province for singing and storytelling. The fruits of this one afternoon are in my *Folklore of Lunenburg County,* and Mr. Collicutt's version of "Little Claus and Big Claus" is also there and in Edith Fowke's *Tales Told in Canada,* published in 1986.

It was thirteen years before I returned to Canaan. A daughter had gone ahead and told him we were coming. We were kept waiting while I suppose he was dressing for the occasion. After a while we saw a window go down which meant he was planning to leave. He came out beaming and leaning on a homemade walking stick on the same lines as my shooting stick. He was dressed in light cotton beige trousers, a red checked shirt and sweater, grey woolen socks and dark shoes. When he put out his hand to be shaken, I recalled warmly my last visit. At that time I had no opportunity to observe him as he talked because I couldn't take my eyes off my notepaper, but I remembered the relish in his voice as the tale went on. His was a great art and he knew it. Now all I had to do was listen, for tape recorders had been invented and I was well equipped.

Rev. Allen Gibson of Chester had said we could use the Baptist Church, Mr. Collicutt's small house not having electricity. The skills in his earlier performances had not been lost with the advent of radio and television, and he was fascinated by the machine, so there was no trouble in getting him started. It seems best to assume they will. As my diary reports, "He was soon off and at first I was disappointed thinking his story was the familiar 'Jack and the Beanstalk.' I soon realized this was a tale I had never heard before."

10. Strong John

AS TOLD BY EDWARD COLLICUTT, CANAAN, NOVA SCOTIA

THERE WAS A WOMAN LOST HER HUSBAND and she had one child, a boy, and they called him John.

"Now," she says, "I'm going to keep my boy and raise him up to be a giant." She wouldn't part with him, so she took him in. She nursed him till he was seven years old, and out on the front lawn was a willow tree growing all this seven years, and she told him for to go out.

"Come here." She stood in the door. "Jack," she says, "pull up that willow tree. See if you can." He went and pulled and yanked at it and he couldn't bring it. So she took him back in the house and she nursed him till he was twenty-one. The morning he was twenty-one she took him to the door. She says,

"Come out the door again, Jack. Now see if you can pull up that willow tree." He down and he got hold of the willow tree and he give it a few yanks and it went up over the roof of the house, the ground did.

"Now," she says, "that's all right, Jack. Now I want you to go—I want you to go and make a fortune for yourself. I've kept you all along as I can keep you, but," she says, "before you go I want you to up to the farmer's and see if you can't get straw enough to fill my bed from him." So he started, and he went to the barn and he got a rope and he started up to the farmer's, and he went up to the farmer's, and the farmer was up on the field. He went up, and he said,

"Would you mind giving Mother straw enough to fill her bed?"

"Oh, sure I'll give you straw to fill a bed, Jack. How are you going to get it down?"

"Oh," he says, "I'll take it down."

"Well," he says, "pull around that stack by the corner of the barn." That was all right. Jack laid his rope down and he went down and pulled a couple of handsful out, and it was a pretty slow way of getting straw to fill a woman's bed. He grabbed the stack and chucked it on his back. *(Narrator laughs heartily, enjoying this part of the story.)* He brung it down and he fired it down in the yard and the stack busted open and he put the straw up agin his mother's door.

"Now," she says, "I can't get out."

"Well," Jack says, "hold on a minute I'll let you out." He shoved it away and she got out.

"Now, Jack," she says, "I want you to go and make a fortune for yourself. Your suitcase is already packed, and everything." So he got the suitcase and he started on. He travelled that day till coming round sundown he heard something tinkle tink, tinkle tink, tinkle tink and he went over to the building and looked in and it was a blacksmith, you know. So the blacksmith said,

"Are you looking for work?"

"Well," he says, "I was, yes."

"Well, how much wages would you want?" the blacksmith said.

"I don't want any wages at all," he said. "I'll tell you what I'll do. I'll work with you a whole year," he says, "if you'll make me a sword at the end of the year that will split that old anvil in two," he says.

"Well, all right, I'll hire you," the blacksmith said. "We'll have to go and have a little writings done up." So they went down the next morning and had a little writings done up, downtown. Jack worked away till the end of the year and when the end of the year was up the blacksmith got the sword ready and he says,

"Here's your sword." And he handed it to him, and he took

and looked at it and he went off and went up to the old anvil and he give it a couple of turns, around over his head and it come down and it broke in two.

"Well," he says, "I'll have to kill you. The bargain was I'd kill you if you couldn't make it."

"Oh, give me a chance," he said. "Give me a chance." So he give him a chance, and he made another one, and he had it all ready the next morning. The next morning he handed him the sword and he give it three clips around over his head and he split the anvil in two and it went right down through into the bottom of the cellar, and stuck in the clay down there.

"Well, that's all right," Jack says. So the time was to leave there, and he went upstairs and got his suitcase and they give him a lunch for to travel on, and he travelled that day—went out travelling, hunting for a place to make a fortune. So he seen no one till coming along towards night he come along to a great-looking farm and he says, "Here might be a good place for to make a fortune," so he went to the door and he asked where the man was, and they said he was up on the field. So Jack went up to see him, and he said to Jack—the farmer said to Jack, "What are you, hunting for work?"

Jack says, "Yes," he said.

"Well, what wages would you want?"

Jack says, "I don't want any wages at all," he said. "I'll tell you what I'll do. If you'll give me as much land as I can chuck you off of one of me toes," he says, "in the end of the year, I'll work with you a year."

Well, the old farmer thought that would be easy. *(Narrator laughs gleefully.)* Well, the old farmer says,

"We've got to go down in the morning and see the lawyer and get things fixed up." So they went downtown and got things fixed up and come home and Jack went to work, and he worked a good man's work. When it was coming along to the end of the year, the old man told him, he says,

"Take and harness the horse up and go up across the pasture and get a load of wood today." He said, "Mind, don't go through the other gate." So Jack got ready and started and went up and he took one look and took the lock off of their gate and the wood was too scarce and he went up to the giant's land and he seen great wood. He took his sword and took a hack and hacked the lock off. He went in and went up and turned his horse and give him a bite of hay, and he went to work chopping a load of wood and he was up there chopping a while and first thing he heard, "Rhur! Rhur! Rhur!" and "By gosh," he said, "the old man told me not to get through here or I'd be killed." What should roar up to Jack but a big two-headed giant. He said,

"What are you doing here?"

Jack said, "I'm getting a load of wood, sure."

"If you don't get out of here I've got to kill you." He made a hack at Jack and Jack snipped off one of his heads. He said,

"Oh, let me live; let me live. If you'll let me live I'll give you a black horse and all the gold and silver you can haul."

Jack said, "I'll have your horse and gold and silver too," he says, "and you too." So he cleaned that up and fired it on the load and he went to work chopping again. He heard a great roar, "Rhur! Rhur! Rhur!" and what came roaring up to him was a big three-headed giant.

"What are you doing here?"

Jack said, "I'm getting a load of wood."

"No wood here and I've got to kill you," and he made a hack at Jack and he hacked Jack a little in the leg, that time. *(Narrator laughs and mutters to himself, "There she goes," meaning his memory.)*

He was working away and he begin to think that he must have pretty near a load enough on for that little horse, on the wagon. So he knocked off chopping and he went and he harnessed up his horse and put it into the shafts and he was going to start for home. He put the bridle on the horse's mouth. He threw the bits underneath and he says, and he went to go, and *(makes clicking noise with his lips),*

"Come on, come on. Get up, come on, get up," and the wagon was settled down into the hard road clean to the hubs, "Come on," he said, "get up. Oh, my soul, now what am I going to do? I've killed the old man's horse. Pulled his whole head off." Jack pulled the whole head off the horse. *(Narrator laughs.)* So Jack took and fired the horse on the wagon and the harness on the load, and he had the giants what he killed, the two giants. He jumped in the shafts, and the first jump he made he jumped them right out of the ditch, out of where she was in and away he went. He didn't bother shutting no gates and when he come down around by the corner of the house with his load of wood, he had so much on he struck the house and he drove it three feet around off of the underpinning. The old man come and he said, "You've ruined me," he said, "you've ruined my house."

"No," Jack says, "that's all right; I'll put it back where it was." So Jack he went down and he fixed the house all back up where it was. Now he says,

"It's the same ain't it, old man?"

"Yes, yes, yes, that's all right." So now, be darned, the old man wanted to get clear of the man. He was frightened; now fright come onto him, so he knowed an old witch woman down in the pasture. He went back in the pasture that evening to see her.

"Now," he says, "if you can tell me—I've got a man out there I got to get clear of him. I got to get clear of him. Can you tell me any way—anything that he can't do?" He used to do everything he told him to do, you know.

"Well," she says, "have you got any grain to grind?"

"Well," he says, "I've got some but it ain't thrashed."

"Well," she said, "you thrash it tomorrow and when the sun gets about half an hour high you send him down to the mill to get it ground." There was nobody could get anything ground after sundown; the devil lived in this mill. So when it come the sun about half an hour high he told Jack for to take the horse and take the grain to the mill and get it ground. Jack harnessed up and started out with it and went down to the mill and before he got up to the mill he seen the miller come out and turn the lock on to cut off his path to the house, his place. He hollered, and said,

"Hold on, hold on; stop there, hold on. I got some grain that's got to be ground tonight."

"Oh," he hollered back, "you can't get no grain ground there tonight," he said. "No, by no means." Jack went up and turned his horse around and attached it to the hitching post and took his sword and clipped the lock off and walked in the mill and hunted around and,

"Well," he said, "there's the place the flour comes out, must be. Now what drives this thing?" He went in the back part of the mill and he pulled down a lever, and away the water rushed in onto him. The mill started. He went out and he took the corn and his grain and the flour come out ground. He worked there till twelve o'clock that night. Well, he went home, when he got it all finished, at twelve o'clock in the night, and he drove right in to the old man's house. He come to the door. He said,

"Where do you want this flour and feed put?" he said. "In the house or into the barn?"

"Oh," he said, "drive it right in on the barn floor and let it set on at night," the old man said. So Jack took it over and put it on the barn floor and that was that. *(Narrator whispers to himself, having got a bit mixed up here, "Now, my golly." He pauses and then says, "He left it settin'." Then he continues.)* Oh well, he went into the house and they got his supper ready and he got something to eat and he went to bed that night, and early the next morning the old man he went over to the witch woman again, and he said,

"Ain't there nawthin' you can tell me?"

"Well," she says, "give me twenty more dollars, and I'll tell you something that he can't do." He give her the twenty dollars.

"Now," she says, "you go home and tell Jack for to go to the devil and get that letter from him what I sent him some time ago." So the next morning the old man says to Jack,

"I got something I want to do. I want you to go to the devil," he says, "and bring me that letter back I sent to the devil here a bit ago," he said. Well, Jack started on, he walked with his head down a while, and by and by he pricked up walking. He thought of the old mill where he got the flour ground where the devil jumped down on his shoulders.

Question from Helen Creighton: Did the devil jump down on his shoulders when was grinding the flour?

Mr. Collicutt: I had that mixed out, you see.

Helen: What did the devil do when he jumped down on him? On his shoulder?

Mr. Collicutt: He grabbed him. He was only supposed to be a small devil and he drove him down through the hopper is where the story went. *(Narrator chuckles.)*

Helen: How did he get rid of the devil?

Mr. Collicutt: When he jumped on him, he didn't pay no attention to devils. Jack didn't. Everybody else was frightened. *(He hesitates again and says, "Now I thought of it just a second ago, great strip of it.")*

When Jack was going into the mill he saw this here devil come out from under the mill, little devil, and Jack took after him as hard as he could run, and the devil got to there, to the devil's den ahead of him. There was a big square door, stone door, thick stone door you know. So Jack went up to the door and he says,

"Let me in."

"We can't let you here," the devil said. "You can't get in here."

"Well, I got to get in," he said. So Jack took his sword and he picked, and he picked the lock off and the door fell down in hinges and in he went and there sat the devil, chained with a big chain, links three inches through, and he looked at him and he says,

"Are you the devil?"

"Well, I'm supposed to be," the devil said.

"Well, I come here for to get a letter from you. My master sent it some time ago."

"Oh, your master didn't send me no letter."

"Yes he did," he said, "and you get it quick."

"Well, I can't do it because your master never sent me no letter."

"Then you've got to go with me," Jack said.

"How am I going with you, and here I am chained with this big chain? See these big links?"

"Haul out of the way." He cut it off and fired the chain over his back and away he went with the devil to the old man's home. And when he was coming in through the yard the old man run out the door *(narrator chuckles as he tells it)* and put his hands up and says,

"I didn't send the devil no letter. I didn't send the devil no letter."

Jack said, "That's what I wanted to know." He says, "Come here," and he took the old man and he placed him on his toe and he gave him a sending like that and went off with the whole farm, and Jack married the daughter. He had a daughter, and he kept the old woman along for a servant girl, and they've been living happy there ever since.

(Going back to check up on one point where he had made a mistake he recalled that Jack was to "have what land he could chuck him off on his toe, you know? He'd got it drawn up by the lawyer.")

Helen: You make gestures, don't you, when the sword is being used; make the sign of the sword. And when you throw anything?

Mr. Collicutt: Yes. This story tells that when he kicked the old man he went off with the whole farm and Jack had the whole farm and the old man's wife and daughter and what money and everything he had; he made his fortune.

Helen: And what happened to the farmer? Did the devil go off with the farmer?

Mr. Collicutt: Oh, there's one little bit I forgot. Jack asked the devil before he put the old man on his toe, he says, "Can you go back home alone?"

"Well," the devil says, "I'll try it."

"Well, so long," Jack said to him, and he took the old man out and placed him on his toe and away he sent him and he went off with the farm. The devil went back alone, back to his den. I don't know who put the hinges on. *(Narrator laughs heartily.)*

Helen: Do you know where you learned that story? I never heard that story.

Mr. Collicutt: You never heard that story in your travels? That's a good story; it takes half an hour or more to tell. Jim Church told me that story.

Helen: Did he live here in Canaan?

Mr. Collicutt: No, he lived over on the road; go out the Canaan road and then go up in the field there. He was a cousin of mine, first cousin.

Helen: Mr. Collicott, the first time the farmer went to see the witch woman, did he have to pay twenty dollars?

Mr. Collicutt: Yes, he had to pay twenty the first time, too. He paid twenty the first time and he paid twenty the second time.

[Type 650A Strong John] *Recorded in May, 1960.*

HELEN CREIGHTON: Apparently part of the story is missing. Mr. Collicutt told it well, making gestures of cutting with a sword and laughing gleefully at parts which amused him. His enjoyment at the playback was a joy to see. He followed every word and said afterwards he didn't know he was so good. Then he sang a few songs and told a few riddles, one the questionable kind that embarrasses the listener but turns out to have an innocent answer to the amusement of the narrator. We delivered him a happy man to his own door, the road having improved by this time. His daughter told us that she composed songs and had put the tale of "Little Claus and Big Claus" in rhyme.

As we left, Mr. Collicutt asked a question which had seemed to puzzle other informants. He said, "You're not a married woman? You have no man of your own?" When I shook my head negatively he thought it over and then turned to my companion with the same question. He must have thought we were very odd.

Cottman Smith

HELEN CREIGHTON: Cottman Smith belonged to a family who had made a name for themselves in the farriers' trade. Innovative and dependable, they not only did the usual shoemaking and repairing of shoes for horses and oxen, but branched out to more artistic endeavors. Living in the beautiful resort town of Chester (Lunenburg County) on Nova Scotia's southwestern shore, their forge has produced articles of wrought-iron that have graced local homes and have also been carried to the distant homes of summer residents, a perpetual reminder of this lovely village.

I was told that a visit to him would be rewarding. Now at age ninety I found him full of energy, intelligent and friendly. He had read my *Folklore of Lunenburg County* and said he could add many items to that collection, including stories. For the moment he couldn't bring them to mind and he busied himself about his property until I mentioned one about a line fence (and) sparked a thought and he stopped being busy, but once that was told he stopped himself again until something else came to mind and so it went for two rewarding sessions. I could imagine him in his smithy in younger days exchanging stories with customers from the surrounding country, for that is how so many tales have been preserved. His only folk tale was "The Miser's Barn" recited earnestly by one who cherishes a prized possession.

11. The Miser's Barn

AS TOLD BY COTTMAN SMITH, CHESTER, NOVA SCOTIA

AN OLD SEA CAPTAIN NAMED HATT kept a store. He was well read, but outside of nautical education he hadn't much. He said this story had been told him by an old German and that would be over 100 years ago.

A German who was a miser had money and he just kept it in its own box. But he had to have a new barn and he gathered his lumber to make it and piled it up. He could get that himself but he needed a man to help build it and he didn't want to spend the money. He enquired where he could get a man cheap.

One evening a well-dressed man came to the door and said, "I'd like to see you. I hear you want to get a man to build your barn. I can build barns quickly. I can have it done and it will be reasonable and good."

"What will I have to pay?"

"All you've got to pay is to sign your name here and nobody will disturb you for twelve years, and they won't disturb you then. I'll have your barn in good time for you to get your hay in." He hummed and hawed but finally signed his name. The next night at bedtime they heard considerable racket and there were dozens of men and the building was going up and they were just finishing the last board on the roof and his wife went out and hollered and the rooster crowed and they disappeared. The barn was complete, all but one board.

He got a man to go up and put the board on and finish the shingling. The next morning the board was gone and the shingles, and he never could keep one on.

In twelve years the man came back and said,

"I've come for my pay."

"What do you want?"

"You!" It was the devil. The old fellow died and he took him.

[Related to Type 820B The Devil at Haying; Motifs G303.9.3.1. Devil hires out to a farmer, G303.14. Devil's unfinished work cannot be completed by human hands, and M211.2. Man sells soul to devil in turn for devil's building house (barn, etc.)]

HELEN: Told at Chester in 1952. The storyteller said she came out and hollered, so I presume it was his wife.

Mrs. Caroline Murphy

HELEN CREIGHTON: Until the building of the Causeway in 1949, Cape Sable Island (Shelburne County) was an isolated place. Lying on the southwest shore of Nova Scotia it could only be approached by boat, and the run by ferry between the Island and mainland could be rough indeed. That was the Island where Mrs. Murphy was born, and which she knew for most of her life.

She was an amazing woman and one I could never forget. She was a gracious hostess and probably never happier than when telling stories to children. Her manner was gentle and her voice soft and pleasant. Like all Cape Islanders she spoke with a New England accent, for that is where most of the population came from.

Mrs. Murphy grew up outside the Island's only town and that is probably why she was never privileged to go to school. Yet she could read and she wrote a good legible hand. When she became a telephone operator people would call her for help in spelling a difficult word. She couldn't remember how or when she learned to read. On my all too few visits to her home in Clark's Harbour she was always cheerful and anxious to share the treasures of her mind. She was of an enormous size. In fact after meeting her I wrote that she looked and walked like a balloon in motion due to an over-active thyroid and when this disability made her depressed she wrote verses about interesting events that happened on the Island. These included my unexpected visit, and many years later a folklorist from Newfoundland's Memorial University collected them as part of the Island's folklore.

It took several visits to get Mrs. Murphy's tales, because so often she wasn't well enough to talk. She was probably in her thirties in 1949 (when these stories were recorded), and didn't live for many years after that.... On my last visit, she was recovering from influenza, and said her legs were weak, and she wondered what would happen if they gave out when she was walking on the road.

Children must have loved her and I can imagine her pleasure in telling them the cumulative tale about "The Old Cat Spinning in the Oven." It served as a lullaby (as did "The Ducks"), and she told it in a sing-song voice so that the children will be asleep by the time the story is ended. It is much the same as "The Mouse with the Long Tail" told by Mrs. McNeil of Pubnico, in this volume on page 147.

12. The Old Cat Spinning in the Oven

AS TOLD BY CAROLINE MURPHY, CLARK'S HARBOUR, N.S.

ONCE UPON A TIME there was an old cat spinning in the oven and along came a mouse and nipped off a thread and she said,

"If you do that again I'll nip off your tail." So when she came out with her thread he nipped her thread off again. So she turns around quick and she nips off his tail and he said,

"Pray puss, give me my long tail before it comes cold weather," and she said,

"You go up to the cow and get me some milk."

So first he hopped and second he run, and to the cow he quickly come.

"Pray cow, give me milk. I'll give puss milk and puss will give me my long tail before it comes cold weather." And the cow said, "Well, you go to the barn and get me some hay."

So first he hopped and second he run, and to the barn he quickly come.

"Pray barn, give me hay and I'll give cow hay and cow will give me milk and I'll give puss milk and puss will give me my long tail before it comes cold weather." And the barn said,

"Go to the locksmith and get me a key."

So first he hopped and second he run and to the locksmith he quickly come.

"Pray locksmith, give me key. I'll give barn key, barn will give me hay, I'll give cow hay, cow will give me milk, I'll give puss milk and puss will give me my long tail before it comes cold weather." And the locksmith said,

"Well, you go to the mines and get me some coal."

So first he hopped and second he run and to the mines he quickly come.

"Pray mines, give me coal. I'll give locksmith coal, locksmith will give me key, I'll give barn key, barn will give me hay, I'll give cow hay, cow will give me milk, I'll give puss milk, and puss will give me my long tail before it comes cold weather." And the mines said,

"Go to the raven and get me a feather."

So first he hopped and second he run and to the raven he quickly come.

"Pray raven, give me a feather. I'll give mines feather, mines will give me coal, I'll give locksmith coal, locksmith will give me key, I'll give barn key, barn will give me hay, I'll give cow hay, cow will give me milk, I'll give puss milk, and puss will give me my long tail before it comes cold weather." And the raven said,

"Go to the sow and get me a pig."

So first he hopped and second he run and to the sow he quickly come.

"Pray sow, give me a pig. I'll give raven pig, raven will give me feather, I'll give mines feather, mines will give me coal, I'll give locksmith coal, locksmith will give me key, I'll give barn key, barn will give me hay, I'll give cow hay, cow will give me milk, I'll give puss milk, and puss will give me my long tail before it comes cold weather." So the sow said,

"Well, you go to the cheesemaker and get me some swill."

So first he hopped and second he run, and to the cheesemaker he quickly come.

"Pray cheesemaker, give me swill. I'll give sow swill, sow will give me pig, I'll give raven pig, raven will give me feather, I'll give mines feather, mines will give me coal, I'll give locksmith coal, locksmith will give me key, I'll give barn key, barn will give me hay, I'll give cow hay, cow will give me milk, I'll give puss milk and puss will give me my long tail before it comes cold weather."

So the cheesemaker said,

"Go to the well and get me a bucket of water."

So first he hopped and second he run and to the well he quickly come.

"Pray well, give me water. I'll give cheesemaker water, cheesemaker will give me swill, I'll give sow swill, sow will give me pig, I'll give raven pig, raven will give me feather, I'll give mines feather, mines will give me coal. I'll give locksmith coal, locksmith will give me key, I'll give barn key, barn will give me hay, I'll give cow hay, cow will give me milk, I'll give puss milk and puss will give me my long tail before it comes cold weather." And he hopped up on the well and saw his reflection in the water and he went to turn around to see how he looked without his tail and he tumbled in and was drowned.

[Type 2034 The Mouse Regains its Tail]

13. The Ducks

AS TOLD BY CAROLINE MURPHY, CLARK'S HARBOUR, N.S.

ONCE UPON A TIME there was a family of ducks. There was a mother duck and she had nine children, and one day the mother duck got ready to go to market.

She took her little sunshade with her basket on her arm and in came one little duck and she said, "Quack, quack, quack, quack, quack, Mother where are you going?"

"I'm going to market."

"May I go too?"

"Yes, wash your face and comb your hair and you may come too." So then in came the second little duck and all this was repeated. It varied by the ducks forgetting and saying, "Can I?" instead of "May I?"

[Type 2300 Endless Tales]

14. There Was a Man Who Had a Double Deed

RECITED BY CAROLINE MURPHY, CLARK'S HARBOUR, N.S.

THERE WAS A MAN had a double deed,
He saved his garden full of seed
And the seed began to grow
Like a garden full of snow,
The snow began to melt
Like a garden full of hemp,
The hemp began to peel
Like a garden full of steel...

... began to roar
Like a lion at the door,
And the door began to clap
Like a stick upon your back,
The back began to fail
Like a ship without a sail...

The ship began to sink...

Sounded like six hundred horses underground.

[Type 2014 Chains Involving Contradictions or Extremes] *Fragments of a piece that used to be told to children at The Hawk, Cape Sable Island.*

PART THREE

Along
the Fundy...

Hedley Doty

HELEN CREIGHTON: It wasn't in his home town of Yarmouth, Nova Scotia, that I met Hedley Doty, but in Annapolis Royal on the Fundy shore. He was a government photographer and was evidently well-known here, for he had many friends. He is remembered in Halifax for stories of wartime experiences and adventures in sailing, but when I found him he was in a group who either lived or dropped in for an occasional meal at the fashionable Queen Hotel. I never had to sit alone at a table because the atmosphere was friendly, and everybody seemed to have a good story. Small towns usually had at least one outstanding character notable for some idiosyncrasy whom people loved to take off. Major Whitman, a resident, was very good at character sketches, and there were hunting stories and tall tales, and much good-natured laughter.

It was a surprise then when two Arab tales turned up, told by Mr. Doty. I don't remember whether they were told in the dining room or the comfortable lounge where a number of us gathered in the evenings. I can only say that wherever he was, in a car or the hotel, he was always a good teller of tales. My diary says that he described these two short stories as Aesop fables.

15. The Arab's Legacy

AS TOLD BY HEDLEY DOTY, YARMOUTH, NOVA SCOTIA

AN ARAB DIED and left a great fortune. He had two sons and, instead of leaving money, he left two stallions and stipulated that the sons were to race and the one whose horse lost the race would get the fortune. They tried to race but couldn't go slowly enough and one day they went to an Inn where a wise Arab was sitting. He saw they were in despair and asked them their trouble so they told him. "Well," he said, "I think I can help you," and he whispered something in the ear of each.

The next day the two sons began their race riding as fast as possible and each one trying to win. What had the Arab said?

Answer: He had advised them to change horses. Then each wanted his own horse to lose.

[Motifs H1050. Paradoxical tasks, and L148. Slowness surpasses haste] *Collected in Yarmouth, 1947.*

16. Shake Hands with the Donkey

AS TOLD BY HEDLEY DOTY, YARMOUTH, NOVA SCOTIA

THERE WAS AN OLD ARAB who kept his fortune in a cave. He had several servants. Somebody stole the treasure. Nobody knew where the treasure was but the servants and none of them would admit to having stolen it. So he went to a wise man and asked him what to do. He said,

"You have a pet donkey. Tie the donkey in the cave." He whispered something else to him. "Then line your servants up, tell them that your donkey is well trained and can always distinguish a thief and that whenever his tail is pulled by an honest man he will remain quiet. If a thief pulls his tail he will bray."

He then told the servants to go in the cave one at a time and pull the tail. The men all proceeded in turn and came out again and there had not been a sound out of the donkey. The old Arab said,

"I can still tell who the thief was, but to show that I am just a man and am not nursing any hard feelings, I will shake hands," and he went down the line and shook hands. After he had done this he selected one of the servants in the group and told them it was all a trick, that this particular man was the guilty one and he had him executed. How did he know?

Answer: He put paint on the donkey's tail and all touched it but the guilty man which gave him away.

[Motif J1141.1.16. The thief is tricked into betraying himself in supposed ordeal] *Collected in Annapolis Royal in 1947.*

Norman McGrath and Horace Johnston

HELEN CREIGHTON: If you think of Victoria Beach (Digby County) as a place to go swimming on fine summer days, you will be disappointed. But if you are looking for folklore, you will find a treasure at every turn of its wandering road. It is situated on the north shore of Annapolis Basin and its rocky coast is the home of fishing shacks and wharves. The terrain is hilly and as you approach Digby Gut sheer cliffs fall steeply and blue iris grows on swampy ground. It is often shrouded in fog which creates fantastic pictures. Visitors gather to view the setting sun for this is one of the few places in Nova Scotia where you see sunsets over the sea.

In 1947 Norman McGrath and Horace Johnston were approaching their eighties, or perhaps had already reached them, and their commercial fishing days were over. Now they fished for fun. Mr. McGrath looked as though he would tell comical stories. Instead he was the one who remembered long folk tales. Mr. Johnston had a quick wit and confessed, "Sometimes I tell the truth and sometimes I don't," like the day two young men sailed past their wharf and called out, "Did you have a good catch this morning?" "Yes," said Horace although everybody knew they hadn't been out. He turned to me and explained, "I might as well say yes; it don't cost no more."

One day a friend and I went to their shack and in no time Mr. Johnston told us a good but weird ghost story. It seems that there are more ghost stories on the road from Annapolis Royal to Victoria Beach than anywhere else in the province but while most believe the stories they tell, Mr. Johnston's are more likely to be "yarns." Then Mr. McGrath had his turn. I had no recording equipment that year, but could write a fast longhand. "Seven Years Before the Wind" took nine and one-half pages of my writing which I had to do without ever asking him to stop and let me catch up. If he was interrupted, he might lose his train of thought and not be able to pick it up again. My wrist was so sore it was almost useless.

17. Seven Years Before the Wind

AS TOLD BY NORMAN MCGRATH, PORT WADE, N.S.

THERE WERE A MAN AND HIS SON used to go a-coasting between New York and Boston. The man kept his son with a vessel while he went farming himself. The young fellow lost the vessel, but he was anxious to go again, so he said to his father,

"If I could have another vessel I could make a go of it." So his father bought him another vessel, but one day he got off his reckoning and he got blowed about, and pretty soon he got dismasted and his sails were gone. He was adrift for many months, but at last he drove ashore on an island handy Scotland, and he was the only one saved. It was dark that night and there was thunder and lightning. He crawled up a mountain and looked up and saw a great big animal. He thought it must be a wild animal, but it proved to be a black dog and it spoke with a human tongue. The dog said,

"Don't be frightened; I'm not here to hurt you, I'm here to save you, and, if you'll do as I tell you, you'll be saved." So the dog led him up and took him to a big cave, and it was comfortable there. When the captain got dry the dog said,

"Now I'll tell you what to do. Not far from here there's a large shipyard. I'll take you in the morning on my back and swim you to the mainland and you'll find a big shipyard there and you'll order a ship so many feet long, so many feet wide and so many feet deep." But the man said,

"Where can we furnish the money?" The dog said,

"Don't you worry. Whenever you come ashore I'll be there and I'll give you a cheque to get all you want." So the man went, and he found it just as the dog had told him. He was a rough-looking fellow himself to order such a wonderful ship, but it was finally finished. So he went back to the dog and the dog told him the ship was ready and the crew, probably fifty men. He said,

"Sign them on for the round trip. Launch the vessel, put her in the stream to anchor and at a certain night at ten o'clock I will arrive. I am not to be seen by any of the crew. I'll come as a dog and won't be known as a man, but I'm human."

The dog came alongside and was pulled aboard by a rope. He was put in the cabin and the captain went down and says,

"What is the next?" He says to get under way, so they got their anchors up and got under way and went out of the harbour. He goes to the dog and says,

"What course will we steer?" He says,

"Before the wind." The wind changed after a certain time and they couldn't take the course. The captain asked the dog what to do now. The dog answered,

"Before the wind; swing her off." Every time the wind would change the dog advised him to swing her off, and this went on and they sailed for seven years before the wind. After a year of this the crew got discouraged and refused duty. The dog says, "Pay 'em off." So the captain goes and pays them off. He gives them a pack of cards and charged them so much for their board and so much for their lodgings and gave them all the rum they wanted to drink, but they had to pay for the rum also. It was only a short time before they had no wages to pay their board and gamble, so they became broke and had to ship over again. This continued for seven years, and they were paid off seven times.

At the end of the seven years the ship struck on the shore. The captain goes and tells the dog and the dog says,

"We're right where we wanted to go. We're to our destination. Now you've got something to do and, if you do not fall through, you'll be an independent man. In the morning you take the crew and they'll set you ashore in the boat. Let them come back here. You will find this an island very richly decorated with gold and silver. There is a mansion there with many rooms in it. You can go in any room, but you must be alone and you must stay all night. In the night you will find everything very rich and very costly and decorated with gold and silver ornaments." The dog told him he wouldn't sleep; he would like to, but something would keep him from sleeping. But in the night there would be a very pretty girl appear to him in that room, and whatever that girl wanted him to do, to refuse everything she said, and in the morning the boat would be ashore and he would come aboard.

"Now," he says, "after getting aboard I've got to be hid, because that girl will be here on the ship in her natural shape and she will look everywhere for me, and I've got to be hid." So that first night the girl came and she tried to tempt the man, but he refused all questions asked him.

The next day they take down the casings of the pumps and put the dog between the casings and fixed them up again so the ship looked as natural as before. The girl appeared at a certain hour, and only had one hour to stay. She looked for the dog and she said,

"You've got a dog aboard," but it couldn't be found. Next night the captain had to do the same thing and, instead of one girl there were two, and the second was more tempting than the other. But he refused all question asked by the girls, and in the morning he came aboard the ship and the dog told him the two girls would be there searching and there would be no use hiding him in the same place, so they hid him in the topsail aloft and the girls looked everywhere but couldn't find him. The hour expired, and the girls were turned into birds and flew away.

The third night the captain had to do the same thing over again and, instead of two girls there were three birds, and they lit as ladies. He refused all questions asked by the three. He went aboard as usual in the morning and the dog said he had to be hid in a new place as they would look now in the places he had been, and they would search but he musn't be found. So they made a big canvas bag and put the dog in that, and had a long hose made of canvas leading through the rudder post to give him air, and they put him under the ship. The birds came, and when they hit the deck they were ladies. They looked for the dog but he was under the ship's rudder. When the hour expired they were birds and flew away again. Now the dog tells the man,

"This island is worth all kinds of money, and everything you can get off in a certain time is yours. Load the ship." They practically loaded the ship with a very valuable cargo and, when the ship was loaded, the birds came aboard and they were three young girls. The dog was a natural man. They proved to be a very rich family that owned that island, and they were a brother and three sisters.

Now the ship took her cargo to New York, and the son had left as a farmer, thought he'd like to go home and see his father. The papers were full of this costly ship. When the son got to his father's house he found him a poor man because of the ships he had bought and lost for his son. The father was very glad to see him and, after a while, the son said,

"Say, Dad, did you hear about that costly ship that's in New York?"

"Oh yes, but what's the good to hear of it? It's of no benefit to us." He said,

"What do you say if we go to the city to see this ship? You don't go to town very much."

"Nonsense," he says, "I'm not interested in that ship. It's of no benefit to us." His son kept coaxing him until he consented to go to New York to see the ship. When they got to New York the captain walked right through the guard at the dock and the watchman paid no attention. They stood on the wharf and the old man's eyes stuck out. He had never seen such wealth before. The son says to his father,

"What do you say we go aboard?"

He says,

"Go aboard? You'll have me run in jail. You've made me a pauper, and now you'll have me in jail," but the captain coaxed and he went aboard with him. The son says,

"Let's go down below in the cabin." The father didn't like to go because he thought he'd be arrested. Finally he went and saw a very fine furnished ship. The son rang a bell and a waiter came. He said,

"Dad, what'll you have to drink?" mentioning several different kinds. In came the waiter and they drank.

"Now," he says, "Father, this ship is mine with all the belongings. I made a trade with your ship and got this one instead." He said,

"Son, you've made a great trade. You've got a lot of wealth."

"Well," he says, "this is nothing to what I've got. The most valuable article I've got I'll show you her." He had married one of those girls before he went to his father's house. He went to one of the staterooms and called for his wife and she came out. He introduced her to his father as his wife and says,

"This is more valuable to me than the ship with all its wealth." The other girls and their brother had put ashore in England, so he was clear of them.

"Now," he says, "you'll have to sweep the streets no more or stay on your farm. You can live in luxury for the rest of your days."

"Well," he says, "Son, I'm pleased with you. The vessel I got you, you made a great trade."

Now to go back—in olden times of witchcraft, everything that happened was called witchcraft and there were old witches. The man that owned the island formerly was a widower with his son and three daughters, and he married a woman who was a witch. He died thinking he left them all right, and left these girls there. But the old witch didn't want them to have any part or parcel of his property, so she put a spell on each of the children, and the boy was to be a dog all the days of his life. But the witch couldn't make twenty-four hours of the day all a dog or, in the case of the girls, she couldn't make them birds all the time. There had to be two hours out of the twenty-four when they could be themselves, one in the day and one at night. So the dog had a theory of knowing what would break that spell. He had to find a man that had the will power of going seven years without seeing land or a human being, and being tempted by the three sisters would break the spell on the girls. As for him, he had to find that man who could carry all this through.

[Type 410A Enchanted Princesses and Their Castles; related to Type 545 The Cat as Helper]

HELEN CREIGHTON: Their shack was in a picturesque spot beside the sea, and they must have enjoyed the sound of waves at night lapping the shore. Although their habitation was small, it was spotless. They offered us a place to sit but the day was fine and we assured them we loved to sit outside. The men sat on a wooden bench and I on the wharf at their feet where I could write better. Mr. McGrath explained that this was the sort of tale told in a vessel's forecastle and was called an old forecastle yarn.

When I arrived the next day, in typical fashion they didn't apologize for not having shaved, but said with a straight face how busy they were all morning shaving. I had a chance then to look at their sleeping quarters. Mr. McGrath slept on a camp cot and Mr. Johnston in a bed with a thin mattress on boards. He glories in its hardness and says this is the best way to rest. Some men come in from fishing and sleep on the floor behind the kitchen stove.

On my next visit the men were tired for they had actually been fishing but a neighbour woke them up and soon they came outside. The fog spun curious designs. The sky was clear one moment and clouded the next, and the water ranged from blue to green. Rain came and we had to "step inside," but that did not stop the flow of storytelling. I sat on the one camp stool while the men sat on their bunks. When we left they called out an invitation to come again and I think they passed a few jokes between themselves which it might be just as well we couldn't hear.

Accepting their invitation, my companion this time was an artist and while Mr. McGrath waited for her to adjust her equipment, he told me the tale of "The Girl with Three Lovers."

18. The Girl with Three Lovers

AS TOLD BY NORMAN MCGRATH, PORT WADE, N.S.

IT SEEMS AS THOUGH there were three brothers keeping company with one girl, and these all four being born in that neighbourhood, they liked one another very much and were much attached. As they grew up into manhood and womanhood they all three thought an awful lot of this one girl. Consequently they all escorted her home at different times, John, Joe, and Steve, but John being the youngest she loved him best and he kept company as often as he could.

The other two fellows got a little jealous, so these two brothers told the other fellow if he didn't keep a little more scarce they would be likely to ill use him. But he couldn't keep away, so one night they caught him and beat him terribly, and they told him that if he was ever saw ketched up with her again they would kill him, because one of them had to have that girl.

Being a young fellow he went away and he stayed seven years, and during those seven years he became a very rich man. During that time his mother had died, and she thought a lot of that son. The most she had to leave for him was three valuable rings with very costly settings.

When the seven years was up he decided to return, and after arriving at his home he learned that his brothers were still living and neither one was married to the girl. He learned from his aunt about these rings being left for him, and he told her who he was, but she was to keep the secret. So she gave him the rings his mother had left him if he ever returned.

So he disguised himself in plain clothes although he was quite wealthy when he returned, and he went out a-gunning, and he put on one of those rings. He heard the story that one or the other of those brothers was to marry that girl, but they didn't know which. Neither did the two brothers know. But the one that could tell the best story was the one she was to have, and they were to be married on a certain night in the week.

When he went a-gunning he hunted around that house mostly, and finally saw her looking out the window. He knew his brothers' circumstances and also hers, so he was displaying this very valuable ring and he was dressed as a tramp very rough. She thought,

"Why should that old tramp have such a valuable ring?"

She thought, "He's a beggar and looking for something to eat, and why would he have on such a valuable ring?" She went to the door and asked if she could help him to anything, and wanted to know where he got that valuable ring, and him dressed as he was. He told her it was his and he came honestly by it, so she says,

"Would you sell the ring?"

He says yes, so she says,

"What would you ask for the ring?"

"Oh," he says, "money can't buy that ring. There's only one thing can get it."

She says, "Can I buy it?"

He says, "Yes, you can."

"Well, what is it? If there's anything I can do I will if it's reasonable and right."

He says, "If you will let me kiss the back of your hand I will give you the ring." She thought it was a terrible thing to let that old tramp kiss her hand, but she held it out very shy and he kissed it. He took off the ring and gave it to her and went away back home, and the next day he went a-gunning again, and he went over the same grounds and he saw the same lady, but he had the second best ring on that time but he was dressed very rough.

She spied this same tramp back with his gun and his rifle and with a far prettier ring, so she goes to the door and hails him and says,

"I see you've got on a much prettier ring. Is that for sale?"

"Yes," he says, "but money can't buy it."

She says, "What would you want for that ring?"

He says, "Nothing more than to kiss you on the cheek."

She thought that was terrible, but she wanted that ring so she let him kiss her. He took off the ring and gave it to her, the second ring.

Now he had one more ring which was more costly than the other two, so he goes again a-gunning over the same grounds. She saw him and said,

"There is that tramp again. What a wonderful ring that is." Being a tramp and being very plain she went to the door and asked him what he wanted for that ring.

He says,

"Lady, I'm afraid to tell you the price of that ring. You might be offended."

She said, "No, any price at all that I can pay. That ring I must have."

"There's only one thing can take that ring," he says.

"What is that?" she asked.

He says, "The garment that is next to your person is the price of that ring."

So she sent away into the house and changed and gave him the garment that she wore.

He went away then because he knew that on that night one of the brothers was to be married to that girl, but they still didn't know which could tell the best story. He dressed himself up then as a gentleman and he made a great appearance. He had the date of the wedding, and that day he wanted to be in that house.

He arrived at that same house and rang the bell and there came to the door the father of the girl. He says,

"Pardon me, but this being a country place and no hotel, is there anywhere that I could be put up for the night?"

He says, "We are very much taken up tonight as my daughter is to be married, but just wait till I see my wife." Being a gentlemanly looking man they said,

"If you don't mind a wedding being here we can put you up."

He saw that he had things coming all right so he said he didn't want to be an encumbrance and he could go to the next house. But being very nice about it, they insisted on him coming in.

The time was about ready for the wedding, so the brothers came in and told the story of their adventures and it didn't amount to very much, the first fellow. The next fellow told his story, but she in the meantime had her eye on him because there was something familiar about him that attracted her attention. She didn't care for either of the stories so she went over to him and said,

"What about you? Are you a married man?"

He says, "No, I'm not. I might have been but it wasn't meant for me to be married." So she told him the mystery of her marriage and that they were to tell a story to decide which one it would be, but that neither of the stories had been very satisfactory. She asked him if he would like to be married and if he wished to tell a story he could be the man.

So he tell about going away for seven years and coming back, and the first day he was there he went a-gunning in a place he was very familiar with and he had very good luck. He saw game, a very pretty fawn, and he fired the gun and he just merely wounded her. The second time was the same, only he made a deeper wound. The third day he went a-gunning and he saw the same fawn and he says, "I fired and the shot took effect." He says, "I've got her. If you don't believe me here is her skin." So he undone his grip and threw out the garment she had worn next her skin.

So she knew him from the story and those two were married right away. They embraced one another in true love and were married that night.

[Motif H327. Suitor test: cleverness and learning]

HELEN CREIGHTON: Then we were treated to delicious fish chowder, biscuits and tea made by their neighbour, also a fisherman. Everybody seemed pleased to have the old men living there and what with Mr. McGrath's folk tales, or "fable stories" as he called them, and Mr. Johnston's tall tales, the local residents spent many pleasant hours. But when my artist friend arrived the next day to sketch Mr. McGrath, she saw that he had shaved and put on a white shirt and tie. This invariably happens when informants know your plans ahead of time. His story of "The Devil as Card Player" is different from others I have found, but interesting.

19. The Devil as Card Player
AS TOLD BY NORMAN MCGRATH, PORT WADE, N.S.

THERE WAS AN OLD MAN named Captain Gosse who settled in Maine, and he went captain of ships in his earlier days. He rented a house and lived there all alone and, although he was very sociable, he didn't want any person in his house. He was a great card player, and at night people could look through his window and see a hand of cards and him playing with the cards, but no other man; only a hand of cards.

One night when they were watching through the window they heard him betting. He had bet all the money he had at that time in his house, so it seemed as though this object they couldn't see would want to knock off. Captain Gosse had just got a vessel by the name of *The Lively Nan*, and had shipped three men as crew.

"Well," he says now, "I'll bet my vessel, myself and my crew."

So he went aboard and sailed, him with three other men, and one day they took a very bad breeze and thick stormy weather. A man on the lookout reported a ship going to colly *(collide)*, and called all hands on deck. The three men and the captain went on deck, and the other ship kept coming till it hit them and, when it did, their ship was dismasted and it made a real wreck of her. The men fighting for their lives grabbed everything afloat to save themselves, and finally they got onto a spar. There was three of them with the captain, but when they counted up, there was five of them on the spar. They drifted on that spar till the sea threw them ashore, and when they got ashore the three men were on the spar, but Captain Gosse and the other man weren't there.

Looking around the beach they found the old greasy pack of cards strewed over the beach. Captain Gosse and the vessel were gone, and the man he had played cards with had won his bet. That man was the devil.

[Motif M210. Bargain with devil, M219.2.1. Devil appears in great storm, takes away soul of person contracted to him, and N4. Devil as gambler]

HELEN: We ended our visits with a party. I bought seven pounds of lobsters for $2.80. The Andrew Merkle family, journalists who lived nearby, joined us and contributed sandwiches and sponge cake. These with our hard-boiled eggs and coffee supplemented by more hot biscuits made by the men's generous neighbour and all served on the wharf, made a feast fit for a king.

Two very nice men, happy in their declining years, friendly and courteous, soft-spoken and always willing to share, qualities I have often found among fishermen.

On a personal note, fisherman and pilot Joe Casey, now an M.P.P., took a few of us fishing one day and I caught four pollock, one measuring thirty-six and one-half inches. I was declared highliner. Life at Victoria Beach was very pleasant.

Louis and Evangeline Pictou

FROM HELEN'S DIARY: Then a disappointment to visit prospective informants and find them just going away. Then it turns to your advantage as it did with the Micmac Indians Louis and Evangeline Pictou. I had time to tell them the purpose of my visit and they had time to think about it. They were camping in a tent at the side of the Hollow Mountain Road. It was pleasant to sit under the trees. They were well-prepared and talked continuously.

20. The Turtle

AS TOLD BY LOUIS PICTOU, LOWER GRANVILLE, N.S.

WE'LL HAVE TO BEGIN at the centre of the story. The duck and the loons, they're all mixed up in it.

These girls, the duck family, didn't like this loon. It was a big-feeling fellow. He would go out and jump in the water you would be drinking, and a-hollering and try to make a big show and they didn't take to him. But the duck they call wood duck is a pretty bird. The drake has all the pretty coloured feathers you can mention, and the girls took to him. Every time this loon would get a chance, he'd jump in the water and dive and come up and holler and put on a big show, but the girls hated him.

Then he had dogs. All wild animals ran his dogs.

This night a great big bear came around there, and some of them kinda got scared and they said,

"What's that?" He said, "Oh, that's my dog, a bear." Next night a rabbit would come, and he'd always say, "Oh, don't be scared of that. That's my dog. He'd chase them away."

The girls' uncle was a turtle, and he was no good and he lay around in the way, and if they were cooking they'd have to step over him, and if they told him to move he was just a nuisance. At last the girls made up their minds they would have a little sport with him. One said,

"What are we going to do?" they whispered. The other said,

"We ought to chuck him in the lake." The second one said,

"No, we'll chuck him in the fire." But the turtle heard them and he said,

"Don't throw me in the lake, girls, whatever you do, don't throw me in the lake. You'll drown me. But fire, I don't mind that. But don't throw me in the lake; you'll drown me." He didn't want to be drownded, but of course that was where he wanted to go.

The girls didn't know what to do. They said,

"If we throw him in the fire we won't get rid of him. He's no good; he don't gather wood or nothing. He's only in the way." So they decided to throw him in the lake.

So the next day he got in the way more than ever, and they had to step over him, and at last they got mad at him. They said,

"Uncle Turtle, we're going to get rid of you. You're always in the way and you don't do nothing." He said,

"No, no, don't throw me in the lake. Put me in the fire."

So one day they caught him asleep. He wasn't asleep; he was just foxing. So they grabbed him and heaved him into the lake. There was just a splash. He went down and he never come up no more. They said,

"We fixed him. We got rid of him; he's drownded." They never seen no sights of the old fellow. But the old turtle goes way down under water to the outlet of this lake, and then he crawled out and lay around in the sun.

The girls laughed and were delighted, so when the wood duck come and the loon, they said,

"Where's the turtle?" They said,

"We done something awful. We drowned the old fellow. He wanted us to burn him in the fire, but we drowned him." The duck and the loon started laughing, and the girls wanted to know why. They said,

"What are you laughing at?" So when they stopped, they said,

"Uncle Turtle is the best swimmer we've got round here. I can dive and swim, but he's better than I am. You'll see him again." Sure enough, next day they see this big thing drifting along. They think,

"By golly, that looks like Uncle Turtle with his legs stretched out." He looked as if he was dead. So he floats along and gets out of the water and dries himself on the beach.

When the duck and the loon come again they said,

"You said Uncle Turtle could swim. He's drowned." They said, "We saw him drifting along past here."

But the duck said,

"You can't drown that old fellow and I bet he's round here now laughing at us," and sure enough, he was there listening to them, and bye and bye he laughed out at them. He said,

"You fellows thought you was pretty smart. You thought you drownded me, but you chucked me right in my old home and I'll live forever, in a way of speaking. You'll always be bothered with the turtles, because I'll have families, and there will always be turtles around here."

So when I heard that, I went down the lake.

[Type 1310 Drowning the Crayfish as Punishment]

HELEN CREIGHTON: Louis Pictou learned this legend from his grandmother. "She would tell part of the story one night and the next night say, 'Well boys, we'll have to go on with the story. Where was it we left off?'—and we'd have to remember it." Note Louis' characteristic ending. This is apparently only a small part of a long tale.

Later Louis recalled this: "The story goes on and after a while they didn't like the loon because he was a big-feeling guy, so the duck married one of the girls. They had a wedding and they lived together and it went on and this old loon goes on too. He didn't exactly lose out. He found a girl after a while, and they all lived together in lakes and rivers and they all fared good after all. The story goes on."

21. The Rabbit and the Turtle (Snow White)

ALL THAT COULD BE RECALLED BY LOUIS PICTOU, LOWER GRANVILLE, NOVA SCOTIA

THERE WAS A STORY about the rabbit and the turtle, but I forget it. It is another one like "Snow White and the Seven Dwarfs," but it isn't called that.

It tells about where the deer and birds of all kinds and that witch are in the story, and put that girl to sleep. It was something the witch gave her. In it the prince was to come and say,

"Wake up, my sweetheart."

[Type 709 Snow White] *Collected August 1947.*

HELEN CREIGHTON: Evangeline and Louis Pictou were Micmac Indians who in the summer of 1947 were camping just off the Hollow Mountain Road near Lower Bramell's in Annapolis County. They were preparing materials for making baskets and told me the whole process. I mentioned legends and to my surprise Louis told me his grandmother used to tell the children stories and he had always loved them. They were a quiet hospitable couple, industrious, and need no coaxing to get them started. Loving the stories themselves they were glad to share them, of course they recalled memories and their happy childhood. It was probably an event to have someone interested in what to them were prized possessions. Between visits they had time to refresh their memories and if one forgot the other would fill in the missing part. It was pleasant on a summer day to sit under the pines and spruces.

22. Hunting Story: The Woman and the Devil
AS TOLD BY LOUIS PICTOU, LOWER GRANVILLE, N.S.

O NCE UPON A TIME there was an Indian village with about seventy-five or a hundred families. This was a long time ago. The place they called it in Indian is the name of a lake back of Bear River. In English it would mean "the place where you get beads." They trapped and fished and traded with each other and then in the fall of the year before hunting time, several would come out to the salt water for the winter. They got their salt at the Bay of Fundy, and then they'd go back and trap, and they'd trap around different places.

There was a young couple like Vange *(referring to Evange-line—Louis Pictou's wife)* and I—just the two of them. They left their place and started on their own and went trapping. They got everything ready and lined up the traps, and the woman was just as good as the man. First along they didn't have too good luck. The man would take his traps and be gone all day, and the woman just the same. They'd be gone all day and come back with mink and otter and wild cat, so they went on like that, not making too big a progress at it.

At last this woman got thinking some evil thoughts and they claim she got in with the devil and she sinned this man. This man *(the devil)* told her that if she'd believe in him she could get all the game she wanted. Then the trouble started. She'd come home nights with all the fur she could carry—beaver, otter—and the man didn't get very much so at last he wondered why she was getting so much more than him. So he asked her. She said it was just her luck, but he kinda thought it was more than luck. It went on but she wouldn't tell him.

They got through and went back, and he got to telling the chief, and he told him,

"If that's the way she's been acting there's something more than luck. It ain't good." The old fella got kinda scared about it. He took her to have a talk with this head fella, the chief, but it didn't do any good and it went on.

Next fall they went back again and started in trapping and they no sooner got their traps out than the same thing happened. The last day they were getting ready to get through. He says,

"We only got a few more days, then we got to quit." He talked and talked to her and coaxed her to tell him what made her have so much good luck.

At last one day it was dark and kinda rough and he told her not to go, but she went, and that's the last he ever seen of her. She got lost and never returned, so he returned to the village and he told them. So they got to work and got up a party and they went back to the place and they hunted over the lakes and the hills and they never found her, and from that day they couldn't imagine what happened to her. So at that point I had to leave.

That was before the French came, and all the people thought that the devil had taken her. Often in trapping you go for weeks without anything, and he got scared because she got something every day.

[Motif M210. Bargain with devil] *Collected July 1947.*

23. Lightning

AS TOLD BY LOUIS PICTOU, LOWER GRANVILLE, N.S.

THERE IS A STORY TOLD of an Indian who was quite a brave. One time a storm was coming up, so this Indian took a harpoon and crawled up on top of one of the teepees. He said he wasn't scared of thunder, and if it came he was going to punch it to pieces with the harpoon.

The storm got savager and savager, and he kept on up there with the harpoon. The harpoon was made of steel, and finally the lightning struck it and tore the teepee all to pieces. He was thrown fifty feet and knocked unconscious. Some of the people got hurt, and the buttermilk turned and tasted like sulphur.

[Motif Q552.1.1. Lightning strikes monk who despises humility] *Collected July 1947.*

24. The Boy Who Defeated the Mohawks

AS TOLD BY LOUIS PICTOU, LOWER GRANVILLE, N.S.

THE MOHAWKS USED TO COME to gather medicine here, and they interfered with the Indians. They were here and picked up a lot of stuff and they used to steal Micmac food like eels, moose and deer meat. This went on and they got brazen. The Micmacs would go hunting and leave home.

This time the Mohawks came to a village and killed a couple of women and children. When the men came, the Mohawks were leaving, and they captured one for a prisoner. They didn't know what to do with him so they tied him up, this Mohawk, and built a fire to burn him but not to kill him—just to make him talk. They made him talk and he told where they lived and what village, so they got all the braves gathered up and held a meeting and there must have been thirty of them. They got rigged in fighting materials, with tomahawks, bows and arrows and war-paint and got ready to fight it out.

There was one young fellow who was sort of simple. He was no good to do any work; he was hardly fit to get water. He told his father.

"Father, can I go with you? If I go I can gather wood and keep camp and keep the fires going at night and keep the water gathered." The old fellow said,

"No, they'd kill you in no time." But he coaxed and the chief said,

"Let him go," so they went.

Sure enough, he'd help to get water and wood and keep the fires going and they took the prisoner along and were to camp two or three miles from this village and then raid it at night. They got to this place and made a camp and got rigged up for war and that night they started to this place. It was a much bigger place than they thought, and they were five to one. They commenced to get beaten pretty badly, but they killed a lot of the Mohawks.

They were fighting, and at last this boy they thought would be killed turned out to be the strong man. In those days there was a lot of witchcraft among them and here he was one and they didn't know it. So he took over when they were getting beaten and he killed and destroyed that village and was a sort of Superman. Once he started, the others didn't have to do anything, and he cleaned the village out and there wasn't one man left there.

When they got back he got the praise for being the best fighter, and they held war dances and made him their second chief, a great honour. He got to be chief, and the other Indians from other places didn't bother them again. There was nothing he couldn't do after that, although he returned to normal life. So when I got to be old I left them.

THE BOY WHO DEFEATED THE MOHAWKS *73*

HELEN : The last sentence seems to be a typical ending.

There were several visits, always fruitful. Unfortunately, I had no recording equipment that year, so all they told me had to be taken down by hand. Micmac material from older sources were recorded later. Eventually, everything was put on tape for the Nova Scotia Museum. There are six hours of Micmac recordings.

25. Jim Charles: Micmac Indian

AS TOLD BY LOUIS PICTOU, LOWER GRANVILLE, N.S.

THEY MADE BUTTONS out of Jim Charles' gold, and grandmother made bullets. *(The Indians all seem to pronounce his name as though it were Charlos, with an accent on the second syllable.)* Jim Charles brought his gold to Annapolis himself. He had a gold mine and he brought nuggets from the size of a pin head to a pea. How he found them, it was a sort of a dry summer. Water was scarce and he was hunting and he wanted a drink and he went to a brook. He had to follow it down to a pool—sort of a little falls. While he was drinking he sees this stuff in the water, and he reached down and got some of this stuff and picked it up and, after he looked around, he saw it on the shores. He used to go there and take the gold to Halifax. After a while the white folks got wise to it and got after him.

"Now," they said, "Mr. Charles, they claim you found a mine out there to Kedge Lakes. How much will you take for that mine?"

He didn't want to sell, but three or four of them went with him to Kedge Lakes and he got off the canoe and got on shore and he warned them,

"I'm going, and I'll be back in an hour's time, but I don't

want anyone to follow." So he went, and he come back sure enough, and he brought these people the gold. They had liquor and they tried to get him drunk, but he was wise to that, and they tried to coax him to show where he got that stuff and he wouldn't. That mine was never found by an Indian or a white man.

They claim he killed a man, and then the rest of the Indians claim he didn't. The Indians claim he wouldn't have done a thing like that. People round Lequille said he was a real nice man; not treacherous.

[Motif N596. Discovery of rich mine] *Collected July 1947.*

26. More about Jim Charles

EDITORS' NOTE: This story is probably *not* told by the Pictous. Helen identifies the teller of this story only as "Irish." She recorded it in North Port Mouton, Queen's County, June 1947. Perhaps, after collecting this story a month earlier, Helen asked the Pictous if they had heard of Jim Charles, which led to their version of the legend.

JIM CHARLES' WIFE used to drive to town with gold, and would go to the States with it. He was a very treacherous Indian. He made baskets. After his first wife died he carried another Indian squaw named Multi, and when he had to go out hunting, he would tie his wife so she couldn't get away.

Jim shot at two Burrills. He thought they were trapping on his ground, and he shot three men altogether; two Burrills and their brother-in-law, Stoddard. Bullets were found in the body.

Jim Charles wore a pair of small gold earrings that weighed one hundred and sixty pounds. His first wife dressed well. They had a horse and carriage, and lots of gold, and they used to go through the woods. There is a brook that leads to his tenting ground. Jim would wander off, but he would never show any-body his mine, and his gold came out freely. My wife had a chunk of Jim Charles' gold.

(Three men were drowned from a canoe, and Jim Charles is supposed to have shot one of them.) Before the canoe shooting, he shot a man named Hamilton. Jim Charles had a brother-in-law named Bradford, a fine Indian, but scared to death of Jim Charles. Everybody was scared of him.

[Motifs N570. Guardian of treasure, and S110.5. Murderer kills all who come to certain spot]

HELEN CREIGHTON: It was generally considered bad policy to pay for material. Yet when I called on Louis and Evangeline Pictou, an Indi-an couple, my inner voice told me to break the rule. This was easy money for Louis because he could relate stories learned from his grandmother and continue basket-making at the same time. Sitting beneath spruce and pine, he and his wife talked easily, and among other things Evangeline told me was that her father was a witch and had the evil eye. I mentioned this to a newspaper reporter who wrote it up as I learned on a return trip to Dartmouth. Immediately I went back, fearing they would think I had abused their hospitality and per-haps Evangeline would suffer, for she had said, "If my father says you'll die, you will die." As I turned into their camping ground they raised their hands in greeting and I said, "I see we're still friends."

"Why wouldn't we be?" So I told them and Evangeline said her father would be proud to be called a witch in the paper, and she would be too, to know she had that power. Louis was soon off on an-other tale but I could see they were thinking this over. Finally she said, "I know what we'll say if they mention it. We'll say, 'Of course we told her that stuff; she gave us money.'"

—from Helen Creighton's *A Life in Folklore*

Some of the Storytellers...

Helen Creighton writing a story told by Norman McGrath; Norman McGrath and Horace Johnston; bottom left, Richard Hartlan; right, Enos Hartlan.

Acadian Women
of West Pubnico

Left: Mme./Mrs. Henri (Hermance) Pothier; above, Mme./Mrs. Sephora Amirault; below, Mme./Mrs. Laura McNeil and children playing, 1947.

The ghost house on
the Hartlan estate;
Rory MacKinnon; Mrs.
Lillian Crewe Walsh;
Helen Creighton with
John Obe Smith.

Louis and Evangeline Pictou;
Dr. Helen Creighton;
Wilmot MacDonald with his grandson.

PART FOUR

Acadian Women of Pubnico...

Acadian Tales
and Mrs. Laura McNeil

HELEN CREIGHTON: "It's just a point of land," a West Pubnico resident told me, his face glowing with pride. The dirt road they had always lived with had been paved, and all the villages with the name of Pubnico (in Yarmouth County) along Nova Scotia's southwestern shore were holding their heads a little higher. Their government had deemed them worthy of this great expenditure.

This was long after my first visit in 1947 when I had been advised that of all the Acadian settlements in this end of the province, Pubnico was the oldest. It had been founded in 1651 and except for a few years of exile had been occupied by the same families ever since. That meant some of their songs and tales would be 300 years old, at least, having come when the settlement was founded.

If there is folklore in a community there is usually one outstanding person who knows where to find it. Here it was Mrs. Laura McNeil (née Laura Irène Pothier) a schoolteacher, probably in her fifties. Slender in build and delicate in health she could accomplish the impossible when someone came along who appreciated her beloved songs and folk tales. Above all else, she wanted to preserve them so they would be known and enjoyed far beyond their limited community. Although other residents knew some songs and portions of tales, she was the only one who could put them all together.

Before my arrival she had written down a number of their tales and had shown them to M. Desire D'Eon, editor of their weekly newspaper, *Le Petit Courrier.* He was so fascinated that he asked her permission to publish them, but in his enthusiasm he made editorial changes, adding bits here and there and giving names to characters who should have been simply "the little boy" or "the little girl." When I pointed out that this would ruin them for scholastic purposes he volunteered to publish them all over again.

This meant that Mrs. McNeil must edit them and remember which parts were the original and which were added. She spent many hours which included discussions with older women. The best informed was her mother Mme. Henri Pothier (Hermance). They were gradually pieced together, and it was with no small feeling of pride that they were passed on to me.

When I returned in 1948 equipped with a Presto recording machine provided by the Library of Congress, Washington, my expenses were paid by Canada's National Museum, Ottawa. The machine was heavy and so were the blank discs packed in strong wooden boxes. A sapphire needle fitted into the recording arm and had to be watched carefully lest the thread cut by the needle tangle and ruin the sound. The microphone fitted on a tripod and I had to hold it. Otherwise the storyteller would forget about it and perhaps put it on her lap or wave it about. Unlike tapes which would soon replace disc recording, these records were not to be played over more than was absolutely necessary, if at all, because the Library of Congress would put them on a master record. The women knew their stories well, so there was little need to repeat. Having been brought up comfortably but frugally, they knew that precious space must not be wasted.

The following week was one of the most fruitful and enjoyable I've ever had in this work. Songs from one singer, customs, home remedies and tales from others kept my machine in so much use that in no time I had made 29 records. The women were intelligent and by then as anxious as Mrs. McNeil to preserve their heritage. Their homes were comfortable and had the serenity of congenial family life. Many a cup of tea and many a cookie were provided for our refreshment. Sessions went on for three or four hours and there were few early nights.

My diary reports a quiet dignity, a quick humour, and a great kindness among these elderly women. Can you picture them sitting in a circle close to the microphone and singing with all their hearts, or listening intently while one related her favourite song or story?

Mesdames Louis and Sephora preferred to sing together when recording, although they had never done so before. Sometimes Mme. Pothier would join them. It was hard to keep her quiet as she kept turning pages in a book and usually spoke the moment the item was recorded. But I liked their spontaneous comments and kept the machine running to show how deeply involved they were. They would jump from one subject to another until all of a sudden they would tire. And no wonder, after three hours of concentration.

Where were the men? In your experience, hadn't men been your best informants? Indeed they had, but when I was in Pubnico most of the men were at sea fishing. However, one would expect to get tales from women who would have told them to their children. By the time my blank discs had been filled I was so satisfied with my harvest that I didn't enquire further. How much I missed I will never know.

Recordings were made in French and translations typed by Mrs. McNeil and M. Desire D'Eon. She made occasional changes when something came to memory that had been forgotten in the recording. This would account for any difference between the tape and the translation.

27. The Wolf, the Fox, and the Barrel of Honey (Le loup, le r'nard, et le baril d'miel)

AS WRITTEN BY LAURA MCNEIL, WEST PUBNICO, N.S.

ONCE UPON A TIME a wolf and a fox lived together. In the autumn it was their custom to save a full barrel of honey for the winter, for when cold weather came it was hard to find food outside. They had a good cellar, and it was there that they placed their honey every year.

One autumn after their honey had been put in the cellar, and this was a few weeks before it was time to eat it, the fox began to be hungry for this good food, and he couldn't resist his hunger. One day he even dared to ask the wolf to open the barrel of honey, but the wolf refused. The days continued and the fox was always hungry for the honey. He was so hungry he decided to get it by a trick as he had no other means, so one day during dinner he said to the wolf,

"I have been asked to be godfather at a baptism which will take place this afternoon."

"Ah, yes," answered the wolf, "that is very interesting. I wish you good luck." The fox got ready without letting anything out. He went up and went along the road, and when he was back out of sight of the wolf he ran through the fields and came back to hide in the little wood near the house. The wolf came out after that and disappeared in the woods. The fox knew that he had all afternoon to himself now, so he soon reached the cellar and opened the barrel of honey.

How delicious it seemed. He started immediately to eat it and wasn't satisfied until he had eaten about a quarter of the barrel. Wiping his face, and carefully putting the cover on the barrel, he returned to hide in the little woods.

A few minutes later the wolf arrived at the house, and soon after, the fox came back the same way he had taken at noon. He found the wolf getting the supper ready.

"That certainly lasted a long time," said the wolf, saluting the fox. "What is the godchild's name?"

"Ah, yes," answered the fox. "We have had a great feast. I have named the godson Well-Begun." The wolf found the name quite strange, but as it was none of his business he said nothing.

A few days later the fox felt hungry again, and since he had succeeded so well the first time, he didn't hesitate any more to plan another trick. Making the same excuse to the wolf, he took the same way and arrived at the cellar. This time he ate half of the barrel and, covering the barrel, he washed himself again and returned to hide in the woods. He saw the wolf arrive and started running through the fields by the same road. He went in and found the wolf busy in the kitchen.

"Well," said the wolf, "what have you called the god-child today?"

"This time I have named him Well-Advanced," answered the fox.

"Hum," said the wolf, and didn't say any more.

The days passed but the fox couldn't forget the honey. He knew very well that he would have to pay for all this, but for the present nothing was so important to him as to satisfy his hunger. So for a third time he told his companion that he had to help at a christening. The wolf shrugged his shoulders and said,

"You are very popular this summer. Aren't you beginning to be tired?"

"Yes," answered the fox. "It is not very pleasant, but how can I refuse?"

This time the fox was even hungrier that before, and he didn't stop till he had licked the bottom of the barrel. When the fox arrived home the wolf asked him again,

"Well, what name have you given your god-child today?"

"What have I named him? I have named him Lick Bottom," answered the fox.

"They're very strange names that you give your god-children," said the wolf a little harshly.

One day at breakfast a few weeks after the fox's last visit to the barrel of honey, the wolf said,

"It's getting cold, so tomorrow we will go and see if our honey is good." The fox didn't answer at once. His head was low and he felt very uncomfortable and looking towards the wolf, he said,

"My friend, the wolf, I think you are in too great a hurry. Wouldn't it be better to wait a few weeks before going?"

"Maybe it would," said the wolf without thinking of anything being wrong, and the conversation ended.

Weeks passed, and one day the wolf asked the fox again if it were not time to see the honey.

"I understand very well that the winter is near," answered

the fox, "but the season might be long and I think it would be better to wait a few weeks."

"What has changed so much?" said the wolf to himself. "The other years he was always the first to torment for the honey, and now he wants to make it later than ever."

But the fox was beginning to be very worried. He knew he could fool the wolf for some time, but there would come a day when the wolf would discover the empty barrel, and then what would happen? These few weeks of waiting seemed long for the poor fox. Every day he expected the wolf to mention the honey again, but it was the last day of the year before he mentioned it. During supper of that same day he seemed determined and said,

"Tomorrow is a feast and we must have some honey. It's a good day to open the barrel and see what is in it." But the fox who couldn't think of any more excuses, just said,

"Couldn't you wait until the sixth?"

"No, no, we have waited long enough, and tomorrow we'll have honey for dinner." The fox, seeing it was useless to go on, kept quiet.

The next day when he went down to the cellar behind the wolf, the fox had his tail very low. Without suspecting anything, the wolf went to get a hammer. He took the cover off, but there was no honey left. The wolf understood what had happened, and he jumped on the fox and said,

"Miserable one! Now I understand the names of your godchildren. You are going to suffer for this villainous trick you have played on me," and he almost strangled the fox.

"Oh my good wolf, my good wolf," cried the fox in return, who was trembling all over, "do not kill me. Do not kill me, I beg you. It is true that I have played a trick on you; that I have taken your share of the honey, but if you let me live, I will let you have the best eels in the world that you will like as well as your honey."

The wolf's anger ceased. He took pity on the fox and he started to be hungry for the eels and asked the fox where he could get some.

"Where are those eels?"

"Over there in the red brook," answered the fox. "These are the nicest eels in the world. We will take a big basket, and I promise you that we will fill it in a few minutes."

"Let us go," said the wolf to the fox. "This time I forgive you, and if we can get enough eels for winter this will replace a little of the loss of the honey."

The fox went and got a basket and put a piece of string in his pocket. He took the wolf to the brook, and it was frozen solid. Then he cut a hole in the ice.

"Now," said the fox, "turn your back to the brook and I will tie the basket to your tail and will stick it in the water. I will go on the other side, and when your basket is filled with eels I will tell you to haul it up. You will give a good jerk because it will be heavy."

The wolf thought it was a funny way to fish but his hunger kept him from speaking. When the basket was well fastened to his tail, the fox plunged it in the water and then heard the ice freezing anew. It was very cold and the wolf was shivering.

"Isn't the basket full yet?" he asked.

"Not yet," answered the fox, "but they are certainly nice eels and they are climbing in the basket now." The wolf was cold and his patience was beginning to give out.

All the time the ice was getting thicker. The fox cried out to the wolf,

"You can haul up now. Give a strong pull for the basket is full."

You must understand that the fox thought the wolf would not be able to come out, but the wolf by his impatience and cold gave a violent pull and fell headfirst and a little farther, and at the same time felt a terrible pain that went all through him. He couldn't understand at first what had happened, but he turned around and saw his tail in the ice.

Ah, if the fox could have escaped at that moment, but in a jiffy the wolf was on him.

"This time you're finished," he cried, getting on his hind

legs, and crying so hard the forest resounded with his howls.

"I assure you," replied the fox, "that the eels really are in your basket. I didn't realize that the ice was so strong, and beg you my friend, brother wolf, spare my life. I know some fairies that are doing nice work, and if you want, we will see them and get them to make you a tail of hemp."

At first the wolf didn't want to listen to the fox, but the fox got the best of him when he said that the new tail would be even better than the first one, so they both set out. The fox knocked at the door.

"Who is there?" said a little voice.

"It is your friend the fox who is bringing you a visitor and some work to do." The door opened, and when the fairies saw the wolf they were afraid, but the fox made them understand that he was to have a new tail made, and that the wolf wouldn't hurt them. The fairies got to work at once, and in less than an hour they had made the nicest tail of hemp in the world. The wolf was happy, and on returning home was very careful when he walked so he wouldn't soil it. The fox pretended to be glad, but at the same time he felt very uncomfortable. He knew that in spite of his new tail the wolf would still feel hungry for the honey, and more and more he saw that if he couldn't please the wolf he would lose his life. All at once a thought came to his mind and he said, turning towards the wolf,

"My friend the wolf, do you know what we are going to do now?"

"Aren't we going to the cabin?" answered the wolf.

"No, not just now. It is yet too early in the evening. We are going through the forest where I think we will find some nice dry bracken, and we will stop and make a bonfire. It will be a celebration for your new tail." This made the wolf vain, so he agreed right away. They went to the forest and in a few minutes the fox had gathered a big pile of branches. He lighted them, and you could hear the crackle as they burned.

"Don't you think this nice?" asked the fox of the wolf sitting near him.

"It's the nicest thing I've ever seen," answered the wolf, "I don't know how I'll be able to repay you for all you've done for me."

The fox didn't answer. He watched the fire and was waiting until it grew brighter still to try another trick. When the branches were all in flames the fox said to the wolf,

"It's very nice to see the branches burning, but we need something better than that. We will try which of us can jump the most times over the fire without touching it," and before the wolf had time to answer, the fox had jumped over the fire and was on the other side.

"It's your turn now," he said. The wolf got up and approached the fire but he didn't dare jump.

"Go ahead and jump, my brother the wolf," said the fox. He poked fun at him, and for the second time he himself jumped over the fire. The wolf was ashamed of himself. He backed a few steps and started to jump, but he stopped as he had done the first time and the fox said again,

"Jump, my friend the wolf. What are you afraid of?"

The wolf was humiliated to see the fox beat him like this and he got angry. Forgetting his tail of hemp he jumped, and when he did his tail caught fire. He understood the fox's trick and ran to catch him, but the fox had run away. The fox had hoped that the wolf would burn to death, but he was mistaken because the wolf didn't fall in the fire and as he started running his tail burned without giving him any pain. The wolf finally got the fox and went to strangle him like the first time, saying,

"Ah, at last I've got you. I have spared your life twice, but now it is finished. You won't catch me again with your tricks. If you have anything to tell me say it now because you have but a few minutes to live."

"How cruel you are," said the fox weeping and lamenting. "you know very well, my brother the wolf, that I haven't done this purposely, and to show you how sincere I am and how much I love you, I want you to come with me in the forest, and I will show you how to build a large cabin where we will live happily for

THE WOLF, THE FOX, AND THE BARREL... *87*

the rest of our days," and again the wolf gave in to the fox. The vision of the nice cabin in the woods made him forget his anger.

"I forgive you this time," he said to the fox," but remember, this is the last trick you will play on me."

"What I am doing for you this time," said the fox, "is to make up for all the harm I have done you, but I swear to you, my brother the wolf, that I didn't ever intend to do any wrong. It's only by bad luck that these things have happened, and I am very sorry," and they started walking together to the forest. As usual, the wolf was walking ahead. The fox himself didn't know too well what to think. Would other tricks succeed? If the wolf escaped this time it would surely be his end.

That night the wolf and the fox slept in an old cabin in the forest. Early the next morning the wolf woke up.

"Let's begin," he said to the fox. "It is day. Let us start our new cabin." The fox jumped up, making believe that he was in a great hurry to undertake his work. They both took an axe and went towards a little hill further on to cut some trees.

"Cut only the ones that are nice and straight," said the fox.

The wolf did as the fox had told him, but he hadn't chopped his first tree when he heard the fox cry. He hurried towards the fox to find him pulling with all his might on the axe that was caught on the trunk of an old stump. The stump was high, and the fox had almost split it to the bottom.

"I thought you were stronger than that," said the wolf making fun of the fox. He got hold of the trunk to split it open but the fox was watching his chance. Before the wolf had time to realize what he was doing, the fox took his axe out quickly and the two parts of the trunk closed on the wolf's paw and at the same time he uttered a cry that made the forest tremble.

"Come, come, do come and do help me to get out," he cried to the fox who started to run away. When he had run a mile he could still hear the wolf's howls, but he kept on running, and he was sure that now his friend would never reach him. The wolf died in his trap, and the next spring some woodcutters found his carcass hung on the same old trunk on the hill. The birds of the forest had devoured him, but as far as the fox, nobody ever knew what had happened to him.

[Types 2 The Tail-Fisher, 2C Bear Persuaded to Jump Over Fire, 15 The Theft of Butter (Honey) by Playing Godfather, and 38 Claw in Split Tree]

28. John of the Bear (John de l'ours)

AS TOLD BY SIPHRONE D'ENTREMONT, WEST PUBNICO, N.S.

ONCE THERE WAS A LITTLE BOY, and because he was so very strong, they called him Jean d'l'ours. One day at school he hit a little boy, so when he came home at night the mother said,

"Well, when your father hears of this I don't know what he will say," and the little boy got frightened and went and hid behind a big box upstairs. When the father came home the mother told him what Jean d'l'ours had done at school and the father asked where he was. The mother told him he was upstairs. The father went upstairs and found him, and the little boy pushed the box over his father and hurt him. Then the father and mother said to Jean d'l'ours,

"You can't stay here any more." Jean d'l'ours said,

"I'll go and travel around the world." He took an iron cane and started. After he had walked some distance he saw a man who was twisting oak trees. This man was called Tord Chane (Oak Twister). Jean d'l'ours said,

"Leave that alone and come with me on my tour around the world." *(The narrator thinks there should be some conversation here, but she has forgotten what it is.)*

They keep on going, and after a while they find a man who was holding a mountain on his shoulders. His name was Corps de Montagne (Body of Mountain). Jean d'l'ours said,

"What are you doing there?" and Corps de Montagne said,

"I've got to hold this mountain. If I let it go it will crush the town." Jean d'l'ours said,

"Oh, that doesn't matter. Leave that alone and come with us on our tour around the world."

Now there were three—Jean d'l'ours, Tord Chane and Corps de Montagne.

Then they kept on going and they met a man who was carrying the millstone. His name was Meule de Moulin. Jean d'l'ours said,

"Come with us and make a tour of the world."

Now there were Jean d'l'ours, Tord Chane, Corps de Montagne and Meule de Moulin. They walked and walked and by and by they came to a house. They got into the house and they said,

"There seems to be nobody around and we'll stay here now." They said among themselves that they would cut wood and keep on living there. Meule de Moulin would stay to make the dinner and the others would go out to cut the wood, and when the dinner would be ready, Meule do Moulin would ring a little bell. They started out to cut the wood.

Meule de Moulin began to make a little soup. He went to put some pepper in the soup and a little black man *(or black hand)* came out. Meule de Moulin went to take the little man *(or hand)* out, and the little man threw down Meule de Moulin on the floor. When the other three men thought it was time for the bell they decided they would come home and see what had happened. They found Meule do Moulin on the floor *(or in the bushel basket)*. Jean d'l'ours said,

"What's the matter? What happened?" Meule de Moulin said,

"I have a sore back and couldn't make the dinner." He wouldn't tell them.

The next day Corps de Montagne said he'd stay and make the dinner and just as he was putting pepper in the soup the little black man came and threw him down. The three who were in the wood thought it was dinner time and that they'd come home anyway and see what happened. All this time Meule de Moulin suspected but he wouldn't tell the others. When they got to the house they found him on the floor. They asked him what had happened. He said he wasn't feeling well and he couldn't keep on with the dinner.

The next day Tord Chane said he'd stay. Jean d'l'ours, Meule de Moulin and Corps de Montagne went off to the woods. Tord Chane started to make the soup and just as he was putting pepper in it the little man struck him down. All that time Meule de Moulin and Corps de Montagne suspected what had happened and when the bell didn't ring they came back and they found Tord Chane on the floor. Jean d'l'ours asked what had happened and he said he wasn't feeling well and couldn't finish the dinner.

The next day Jean d'l'ours said he would stay and see what had happened and if he couldn't finish the dinner, and the other three went off to the wood and they all knew what would happen but they didn't speak of it among themselves. They wondered what he would do.

Jean d'l'ours started to make the soup and as he was putting the pepper in the little black man appeared. The little black man went to strike Jean d'l'ours, but Jean d'l'ours was quicker. He grabbed the little black man out of the soup and crushed him all to pieces and put him in the bushel basket. Then the three other men who were in the wood heard the bell ring and they were surprised and looked at one another and, when they came in, Jean d'l'ours greeted them at the door and he said,

"I'm surprised that none of you could master the little man. Look at that," and he showed them the bushel basket. Then he said,

"We must explore more what is in this place."

They came to a hole and they said,

"We must go down and see what we can find," and they descended and it was very steep and they kept on walking and they met an old woman a hundred years old. She was so old that the moss was growing through her teeth. They asked her why she was there and she said,

"I can't tell you that." They said,

"You must tell us." She said,

"I'll tell you this. You go a little beyond and you'll find the king's three daughters inside." They asked the girls why they were there and the three king's daughters were so glad to see these men they said,

"We have been imprisoned by the big giant seven years. We have no way to come out and now that you have found us, you must take us out of here."

Well, it was so steep the men didn't know how to get out, so they went to see the old woman who had moss on her teeth and they asked her how to get out of that dungeon.

"Well," she said, "get yourselves each an eagle and take enough mutton flesh that every time the eagles go quack, you can give them some mutton." So they all got their mutton and their eagles and they were all able to get up to the surface except Meule de Moulin. When he got halfway up he didn't have any mutton left and when the eagle said quack he didn't give him anything, so the eagle slid right down again, and he went back to the old woman and asked what he should do now that the eagle wouldn't take him up. So she told him to take more mutton so he did and it took the eagle three days and three nights to take him up to the surface.

During that time Jean d'l'ours, Tord Chane and Corps de Montagne had married the three king's daughters, and when Meule de Moulin started walking to find his companions he met them walking towards him with their three brides. Meule de Moulin was left behind and had to stay alone.

(Where the others were going the narrator did not know, so the story ends here. It is supposed that the men took the king's daughters with them on the backs of the eagles when they made their way up from the hole.)

[Types 301A Quest for a Vanished Princess, and 301B The Strong Man and His Companions] *Collected August 4, 1948.*

HELEN CREIGHTON: The ending of "John of the Bear," as recalled by Mrs. Augusta d'Entremont, is as follows:

"They said to Meule de Moulin,

"'We were only three, and there were only three girls so we married them.' So they went home with their three brides, and Meule de Moulin went home alone.

"The brides were so happy with their men after being in the dungeon that they lived happily forever after."

29. The Big White Horse
AS TOLD BY LAURA MCNEIL, WEST PUBNICO, NOVA SCOTIA

THERE WAS A WOMAN who had three little girls, and she sent one of the girls to pick up chips in the garden. There was a big white horse in the garden, and the mother told her to be careful because the big white horse might take her away. As it was very early, she didn't think there would be any danger, but just as she was returning to the house she was seized by the big white horse who was hidden very near, and she was carried away by him to the forest. The poor girl cried but it was in vain. The big white horse wouldn't listen to any cries or supplications. He ran so fast that in a few moments he was in the great forest.

After having run different crooked pathways, the white horse arrived at a great castle half hidden in the great trees. He put her down and had the great door opened for himself.

"Enter," said the big white horse to the girl. "You will now be my housekeeper. I will give you the liberty of going everywhere but one room. Follow me and I will show you."

He took her along the passages, and after showing her two long stairs they both stopped in front of a door.

"Here is a door that I forbid you to enter. If you disobey me I will kill you. Here are the keys of the house. I am going off now and I will return tonight. If you have gone into the room I will know."

Everything was so quiet she could hear the echoes of her sighs which filled her breast. She began to think of how her mother would grieve at her disappearance.

"She will know that white horse has taken me away," but she was a brave girl and she took her courage. She started to look at the keys that the horse had given her. They were of all forms and sizes. Not knowing too well where to begin, she opened a door. There was nothing strange in the first room. One after another she opened them all and put them in order until she came to the one the big white horse had forbidden her to enter.

At first she didn't stop, for she remembered the words of the white horse, but curiosity overcame her and she retraced her steps and with the keys in her hand she remained for some time in front of the door asking herself what there could be in that room that was so precious.

"After all," she said to herself, "there shouldn't be any danger just to look. The big white horse will never know it." Thinking thus she took the key and turned it very slowly so that the door would open just a little bit, but to her great surprise she had no sooner turned the key than the door opened wide and she found herself facing a spectacle which paralysed her with fear.

All round the walls women with their heads cut off were hung and in the middle of the room she could see a great tub to receive the blood that fell from the dead bodies, and the floor was all covered with heads.

In front of this horrible scene she remained motionless for some time. When she got her senses back she noticed that she had let the key fall in the blood. She picked it up quickly and started to wipe the blood with her handkerchief, but it was in vain. The blood wouldn't come off. She understood then why all the girls and the women had been killed, and she knew that she herself could but expect the same fate.

Trembling she turned towards the door and came out of the horrible chamber. Having locked the door again she went down to await the arrival of the big white horse. Towards night he entered and found her seated near the fire, her face pale and her eyes fixed on him so that her look immediately told him what had happened. But he asked simply,

"Well, my girl, did you have a nice time today?"

"Yes," she answered in a feeble voice that one could hardly hear.

"Have you unlocked the door of the forbidden chamber?" asked the big white horse.

"No," she replied.

"Show me the keys."

She was now more dead than alive, and with trembling hand she gave the keys to the big white horse.

"Ah, my villain," he cried, "you have disobeyed me and I will kill you as I have promised," and he seized her and carried her upstairs to the chamber of horror. He cut her head off and hung her body in line with the other victims.

And far away in the little village in the cottage the poor widow was lonely. She knew it was very likely the big white horse had taken her daughter away and that meant there would be no hope of ever seeing her again.

All day long the poor sick lady sobbed and wept and could not be consoled. The next morning there were no chips again to light the fire, so the mother called her second daughter to her side and said to her,

"My dear, you must go out to get some wood, but be careful. Run fast and look on all sides so that the big white horse won't catch you." She took the basket and ran as fast as she could to the pile of wood. Having filled it she ran back towards the house and was almost there when all at once the big white horse appeared again and caught her. As had happened to her sister, she was carried away to the castle where she received the same orders.

When the big white horse was gone she opened all the rooms and when she arrived at the forbidden one curiosity overcame her to open the door. The same thing happened to her as to her sister. The key fell in the blood and the blood wouldn't come off. That night the big white horse arrived and, seeing what had happened, he killed her in one blow and put her aside with her sister.

The poor widow was more grieved than before. She had only the one daughter left. Night was long for the poor sick lady. The next morning the third daughter got up early and as there was no wood again, the mother saw her take the basket to go out.

"My dear," she said sobbing, "what will I do if the big white horse catches you? Hurry, and be careful not to be surprised by him."

"Do not fear," she replied, "I will return in a minute."

She went out. She looked everywhere and couldn't see anything of the horse, so she filled her basket quickly, and when she got up she still didn't see anything. She ran towards the house, happy to think that the big white horse had not caught her. But alas, just as she was putting her foot on the doorstep the white horse appeared suddenly and took her very quickly away.

Before the young girl had time to think what had happened, they were both at the castle in the great forest. The big white horse showed her the rooms that she should manage, without forgetting the one she shouldn't open.

"If you unlock that door," he said in a grave voice, "I will know it when I come back tonight, and I will kill you." He gave her the keys and went out. She uttered a sigh and for some time remained as if paralyzed.

"Poor mother," she thought, "how she will grieve alone at the house," and while she thought of her mother, another thought came suddenly to her mind.

"My sisters are surely in that room that I am not supposed to open." This thought was like an inspiration from heaven and gave her courage. She began her work immediately, hurrying to put everything in order in the different rooms, and she arrived at last at the one that was forbidden. Thinking of nothing else but to deliver her sisters, she unlocked the door of the room and went in. Before the frightful spectacle she felt a moment of horror, but she had more presence of mind than her sisters, and didn't let the key fall on the floor. She looked all around the walls, and at once her eyes fixed themselves on the two dead bodies of her sisters. Gathering herself together she walked slowly towards them and, with a great effort, she picked her first sister's head up and put it on her shoulders, and immediately she came to life again. Seeing her other sister she uttered a great cry of joy, but she made a gesture with her hand and stopped her and said in a low voice,

"I'm going to return you to our dear mother. How happy she will be to see you again."

They both left the room, being careful not to put anything out of place, and she closed the door and locked it and, making her sister follow her, she went to the barn where she found some old canvas in a corner.

"You see this canvas?" she said to her sister. "I'm going to wrap you in that, and when the big white horse arrives I will ask him to take this package of straw to my mother. Be careful not to move, for then he will suspect our ruse."

She wrapped her sister up and then returned to the house. Towards night the big white horse came back. She went on with her work, not paying any attention to his presence, and the big white horse thought that she hadn't disobeyed him. This pleased him very much. Coming nearer he asked her,

"Well, my girl, how did you pass the day?"

She turned around and answered simply, "Very well, sir, very well."

"Have you opened the room I have forbidden you to open?" continued the big white horse.

"Oh no," she answered.

"Show me the keys," said the big white horse with a careless air.

She gave him the keys, and he was content to see that they were not stained with blood.

"Good," said the big white horse, "you are an obedient girl. From now on you will continue to be my housekeeper with the same care as you have done today."

"I will do it, sir," she said, "but I have a favour to ask in return. I have wrapped a package of straw that I have found in the barn. Would you like to take it to my mother when you go out tomorrow morning?"

"With pleasure," said the big white horse.

The next day the big white horse went to the barn and found the package that she had prepared. He put it on his back, and going near the widow's house he left it at her door and continued his way. The poor lady who was alone, hearing the noise, got up in spite of her weakness and came to the door to see what was there. She noticed the package, and without suspecting anything, she began to open it. Seeing her eldest daughter she uttered a great cry and fainted. Half strangled, but now unbound, her daughter jumped up, caught her mother in her arms, revived her and carried her to her bed. When both of them got over their surprise she told her mother all that had happened at the castle of the big white horse.

"In a few days," she added, "my sisters will be here, because the big white horse doesn't suspect what is being done." Such news consoled her poor mother, and shortly afterwards she fell asleep. Her daughter began to arrange the house and put things in order.

At the same time at the castle of the big white horse the youngest daughter was hurrying to put everything in order in the many rooms there. Arriving at the forbidden door this time she hastened to open it and went immediately to her second sister to bring her to life.

"Come," she said, "let's get out of here as fast as we can." With great precaution they both left the room, the youngest daughter closing the door and locking it.

"Follow me," she said again in a low voice, "and let us not make any noise." They arrived at the barn and she wrapped her sister in another old canvas that she found there.

"Tomorrow morning," she said to her sister, "I will ask the big white horse to carry this package of straw home. Be sure not to move so that he will not know that I am deceiving him. Say to Mother that I will return home before too long."

She returned to the house then and presently heard the big white horse. When he arrived he asked her what had happened during the day, took the keys, and was satisfied to see that everything was going his way. This time he thought,

"I have a housekeeper that is worthwhile."

"I have again found a little bit of straw in the barn," she said, "that I have arranged in a package. Would you carry it to my mother when you go out in the morning?"

"With pleasure," said the big white horse.

The next morning the big white horse went to the barn, took the package on his back and left it at the door of the poor widow. As soon as he was out of sight the eldest sister brought the package into the house, hurried to untie the canvas, and her second sister fell into her arms and they were all very happy together. After a few seconds she revived her and they went in the house to their mother together. Again they had a great rejoicing.

At the castle of the big white horse the youngest daughter had her work done early and she made her preparations for the next day. When the big white horse arrived she told him that she had picked up the rest of the straw and made a last package and asked him if he would leave it at her mother's the next morning.

The big white horse was beginning to get tired of her errands, but as she seemed to be doing her work well, he didn't want to displease her, and he consented again to carry the package to her mother.

The next morning she got up very early. She had prepared a dummy dressed in her clothes. She took out of the cupboard the woman she had prepared the day before, dressed her with a clean dress, and placed her on a chair near the table. Then she put the churn on the table and tied the arm of the woman to the handle as if she were churning butter. That done she went to the barn and wrapped herself in the canvas.

The big white horse got up and went out without passing through the kitchen. He took the package at the barn and started galloping. Passing near the widow's house he got rid of what he thought was a package of straw and continued on his way. The two older sisters were waiting patiently, and as soon as the big white horse had disappeared they ran out to the doorstep and carried her into the house.

What joy to the family to see themselves united again, after such a cruel separation.

Towards night the big white horse returned to the castle. He saw the third daughter who was seated motionless near the churn.

"Churn the butter," he said.

She didn't move.

"Churn the butter," he cried a little louder. She still didn't move.

"Churn me the butter," he cried a littler louder. She still didn't move.

"Churn me the butter," he cried out in a terrible voice. At the same time he gave her a violent kick and said,

"Puff!" The woman and the chair and the churn fell down from one side of the room to the other.

Seeing what it was the big white horse suspected the ruse. The girl was not in sight. He ran to the forbidden room and then he understood what had happened. He became violently angry, and kicked the floor so hard that he went right through, and since then nobody has ever seen the big white horse again.

[Type 311 Rescue by the Sister] *Collected September 1947.*

HELEN CREIGHTON: The same motif occurs in the Acadian tale of "Bluebeard." Here is all of that tale that could be recalled by Mrs. Laura McNeil and Mrs. Stanislas Pothier, West Pubnico, told in Acadian French:

"In the story of Bluebeard, when the girl opened the door of the forbidden room she dropped the key in a pool of blood and it was here that all the dead bodies were. She was unable to wash the blood away. When Bluebeard came in he said,

"'Have you been in that room?' and she said,

"'No,' so he said,

"'Show me the key,' and then he knew she had been there."

30. The Great Black Beast
AS TOLD BY LAURA MCNEIL, WEST PUBNICO, NOVA SCOTIA

ONCE UPON A TIME a little boy was going to school, and he always took his dinner with him. He was thin and looked sickly, so the teacher asked him what the matter was. He said that he brought his dinner with him everyday, but a big black beast always came and took it from him, so the schoolmaster said to the little boy,

"You take a bottle of holy water, and if the beast comes, jump on her back. If she troubles you further, throw a little bit of holy water on her and say to the beast, 'Take me wherever you undertake to take me.'"

The next morning the little boy started for school with his dinner in his hand, and he was very careful not to forget his bottle of holy water. When he arrived at a certain road in the woods he saw the great big black beast coming, but this time he wasn't afraid. As she had the habit of doing, the beast came again to take the basket, but the little boy took the bottle of holy water and the beast didn't dare touch him. At the same moment he jumped on the beast's back and commanded her to carry him home. The beast started to throw him down, but the little boy cried,

"Big beast, black beast, carry me where you are supposed to bring me or else I'll kill you." The beast was obliged to obey, and took the road that led to her home.

To get to her home they had to go through the wood where it was cold and dark, and sometimes the little boy would ask himself if the beast wasn't going to lose him, and often when they were going through the dark parts the beast would stop and look at the little boy with big black eyes as if she wished to throw him off her back and run away. But each time the little boy would take his bottle of holy water and repeat,

"Big black beast, carry me where you are supposed to or I will kill you."

The voyagers crossed the forest and arrived at a great prairie on the other side where there was a little hill. The little boy could distinguish something like a village.

"It is here I live," said the big black beast. As they drew nearer, the little boy could see that the house was growing bigger and bigger, and when they got up to it he saw that it was a castle. They entered. Everything was quiet, and as it was night, the black beast told him the room in which he should sleep. The little boy went to bed immediately, and fell asleep.

The next morning the little boy got up with the first rays of the sun, and when he came out, the beast was already there waiting for him.

"I'm going away all day," she said, "and I'm leaving you in charge of the house. I'll give you the keys. You can go from upstairs to downstairs. You can go everywhere but one room where I forbid you to go. If on my return I discover that you have unlocked that chamber I will kill you."

The little boy promised the beast that he wouldn't go in that room, and as soon as she left, he started to open the different chambers. The further he went, the more magnificent were the furniture, the paintings, and the decorations.

As the house was very big, and there were so many chambers, it was towards afternoon that he arrived at the forbidden room. He remained for some time looking at the door and asking himself if he should go in, and what could there be inside? He put his eye to the keyhole, but he couldn't see anything. His curiosity tormented him so much that he decided to unlock the door and open it a little. Alas, he had hardly opened the door when he found himself facing a beautiful garden in the middle of which flowed a little silver brook. There were flowers of all colours and the perfume of the flowers filled the air while the murmur of the silver brook added to the tranquillity of the place. The little boy had never seen such a superb scene. At last his astonishment passed, and when he came to his senses he advanced towards the silver brook. Bending over, he plunged his index finger into the brook, and he wasn't surprised to find it covered with a nice layer of silver.

"That will come out easily," he said, "and nobody will ever know." But it was in vain that he scrubbed and scrubbed with his handkerchief, for his finger remained stained with the silver, and he was afraid that the beast would see he had disobeyed. What would he do? Maybe it would come out with soap and water. He left the room quickly, locked the door and went to the kitchen. He took soap and water, but it was all useless, and he was very embarrassed. He could think of nothing but to wrap his finger and tell the beast that he had cut it a little.

"Well," said the beast when she returned, "what have you done all day?" The little boy had his hands behind his back and even if he were trembling with fear, he answered calmly,

"Oh, I had a good time. Your house is very pretty."

"Have you looked at the forbidden room?" continued the beast.

"Oh no, oh no, here are the keys," and he stretched out his left hand to give her the keys. So the beast said,

"Show me your other hand." The little boy thought himself lost now, but he showed her the other hand and the beast asked,

"What is the matter with your finger? Have you hurt yourself?" He said,

"I hurt my finger." The beast suspected then what had happened.

"Take off your piece of rag and let me see if the cut is very serious." The little boy knew that he must obey, and he showed her his finger covered with silver.

"Ah," cried the beast," you have gone in my room. I'm going to kill you," and, saying that, she got up on her hind legs. But as she was going to pounce upon him to strangle him, he thought of the bottle of holy water. He took it out and sprinkled the beast well, and she disappeared immediately. The little boy thanked God for saving him, and he went back to sleep for the night.

The next day when he got up the beast was again at the door waiting for him with the keys, and she gave him the same orders, with a special one not to unlock the forbidden door. Then she went out for the day.

The little boy began to go around the house again and he went over all the same beauties of the preceding day. In the evening he arrived at the forbidden door. He walked slowly in front of it saying that he would not unlock it this time, but he hadn't gone more than five steps when he came back to look in the keyhole. He couldn't see anything, but he thought he could easily keep his hands behind his back and not touch the silver river this time, and he opened the door.

The door opened wide, and he saw a beautiful garden with a gold river flowing through the midst of the flowers. The spectacle was even more lovely than the day before. When the little boy arrived at the golden river he crossed his hands behind his back so he wouldn't touch it, but he couldn't help bending very low to look more closely at this mysterious brook. Unfortunately he put his face down too far and his hair touched the river. He got up quickly and tried to wipe his hair, but the gold wouldn't come off. What would he do? Maybe he would cut his hair.

He went to the kitchen and tried to cut his hair with scissors, but it wouldn't cut. It was in vain. What could he think of after that? An idea came to him and he put his cap on his head. He put it on very carefully so that not one hair would show.

When night came the beast arrived home and said,

"What did you do today?" and the little boy said,

"I have followed your instructions," and he handed the keys to him.

"Good," said the beast, "but why are you wearing your cap on your head?"

"Because I have a headache," the little boy replied, "and I feel better with my head covered."

"Oh well," said the beast, "take off your cap and we will see what we can do to make you feel better." The little boy obeyed, and the golden hair fell on his forehead. The beast cried out,

"Oh, my villain, you have gone in my room. I am going to kill you," and she wanted to strangle him. But the little boy took the bottle of holy water and the beast ran away. The little boy went to bed then and slept.

The next day the beast did the same thing. She went away and gave the keys to the little boy who came again to that same room, and again he didn't want to go in but he couldn't resist it. He opened the door.

"What new surprise shall I find today?" He meant to look without touching, and not even to cross the doorstep, but he found himself in a field of grain and he saw a little pony there.

"Ah," cried the pony, "here you are at last. I've been waiting seven years for you to deliver me. Go and get a stone, a comb, and a razor, and we will run away before the beast arrives." The little boy went off and got the three articles the pony had asked for, and then came back to the field.

"Get on my back," said the pony, "we have no time to lose." He did this, and they galloped across the fields and took a road where they could see everything in front of them and behind. The little boy was happy and thought that this adventure would finish well. When they had travelled for quite a while the pony said,

"Look behind, and tell me if you don't see a shadow coming." The little boy looked and saw the shadow of the beast mounted on an ox and coming at a great speed towards them. The pony told him to throw the stone on the ground, and when he obeyed there arose a great hill of stones. When the beast and the ox came to that hill they weren't able to climb it and had to make a detour. This gave the pony and the little boy a chance to go ahead until they could no longer see the beast and the ox. After a while the pony said to him,

"Look behind and tell me if you don't see a shadow coming." He looked and again saw the beast and the ox coming towards them very fast. The pony said,

"Drop the comb," and the comb became a hill of combs between the pony and the beast, and for the second time the beast and the ox were obliged to make a detour because the ox couldn't walk on the combs. When they took the road again the beast and the ox were no longer in sight, but before too long they had caught up with them again.

"Look behind and tell me what you see," the pony said to the little boy.

"I see the beast coming," so the pony said,

"Drop your razor." The razor became a hill of razors, and the beast and the ox were obliged to make another detour.

By this time the pony and the little boy were far away from the beast, but the pony was getting tired, but didn't say anything about it. After a little while the pony said again,

"Look behind and tell me what you see." The little boy turned around and saw the beast coming again.

"Don't be afraid," said the pony, "if we can reach the river that you see there in front of us before she catches us, we'll be safe." The little boy couldn't understand why the beast and the ox couldn't cross the river as well as they could, but he didn't say anything. He looked again and said,

"The beast is catching up. In fact she is only a few steps behind us." Fortunately the brook was only a few steps from them too. The pony went faster and was just about to jump when the big black beast put her paw on the little boy's back. But she was too late, for the pony jumped over just in time. The little boy felt as though he were stunned, and he fainted, and when he came to his senses everything was strange. There was no sign of the beast or the ox or the pony, but only a little girl beside him.

"Where am I?" he asked, "and where is the pony that saved my life?"

"The little pony is me," replied the little girl. "When I was tiny somebody stole me from my parents and I was bewitched by this black beast who was stealing your dinner. But she will never be able to catch us again, for we are in the Holy Land, and that is why she was unable to cross the river.

"Now we shall go to my parents, and you will stay with us for the rest of your days." And here ended the story of the little boy and his adventure with the big black beast.

[Type 314 The Youth Transformed to a Horse; related to Type 311 Rescue by the Sister, and 313, 314 The Magic Flight] *Collected September 1947.*

Mrs. McNeil stressed the fact that the beast is always feminine. The opening is slightly different from that in the published story in *Le Petit Courrier*, and in the traditional tale the little boy is not called by name.

31. The Three Little Girls Lost in the Woods

AS TOLD BY LAURA MCNEIL, WEST PUBNICO, NOVA SCOTIA

ONCE UPON A TIME there were three little girls. The eldest was called Belle d'Amour, the second Belle de Jour, and the youngest La Petite Finette. Their mother was dead, and they lived with their father who loved them tenderly. All three of them were good workers and they loved to do the housework. Never had a more happy home been seen.

But after a certain time the father began to think it would be better for him to get married again. He didn't have any trouble finding another wife for many girls of the village wished to marry him, and one day he came home with his new wife. The little girls found her pretty and sweet, and that day was a day of feasting for everybody.

For some time everything went well in the house, and the little girls showed much love for their second mother. But little by little their stepmother became jealous of the love their father gave to his daughters. She began to lose her tenderness for them, and in the end her jealousy became so strong that she couldn't endure them anymore around her. Not daring to kill them, she thought she would make them disappear. She spoke about it to their father, but surely he couldn't permit such a thing to happen. She spoke about it many times, and it caused him so much grief that he couldn't consent to it.

One fine day the stepmother made up her mind. She would persuade the father that it would be better for them to get rid of the little girls. She would put them to bed early and would tell them to get a good rest, for on the morrow there would be a holiday, and they would all spend the day in the woods. When the little girls were asleep she would tell the father what she was going to do. He would be obliged to consent, and everything would go as she wanted it.

During that day the mother was sweeter than before, and the father thought that she had abandoned her bad plans, but secretly she prepared their clothes and the lunch for the next day. While doing her work she sang and seemed happy; so happy that nobody suspected her ideas in the least.

When night came the mother said to the little girls,

"My little girls, I have good news for you. Tomorrow we are going to have a feast. We will go to the woods for the whole day. Come, go to bed early and get a good rest for tomorrow you will have to get up early."

The little girls went to bed. Belle de Jour and La Petite Finette were very happy and went to sleep right away, but Belle d'Amour who was wise suspected something and stayed awake. When the mother thought the little girls were asleep she said to her husband,

"Tomorrow we will go to the woods and lose our little girls. We will start early in the morning, and we will walk until we will be very far in the great wood, and the little ones will be tired. We will tell them to lie down and to sleep while we go to cut a few branches nearby to make a fire for dinner. When they are sleeping we will return to the house. When they wake up they won't be able to find their way to come back, and they will be obliged to stay in the woods. We will be much happier with only you and I in the house."

The poor father was very unhappy to hear of such a plan, but he couldn't say anything. He saw that his wife was determined and that she would give him no chance to refuse. Belle d'Amour had heard all about it. This made her grieve sadly, and she couldn't think that such a thing could happen as for them to be lost in the great wood, and that she and her sisters would never see their dear father again. Maybe they would be eaten by the wild beasts. No, she couldn't believe that her stepmother could really do such a dreadful thing, but what could they do?

"Here," she thought, "I must go to see my godmother. She will find some way to save us."

She waited until her father and mother were asleep. Softly she got up and dressed herself, and without making any noise she went out of the house. She ran fast and arrived at her godmother's house out of breath. There were no lights because the night was late and the godmother was in bed and was sleeping deeply. Belle d'Amour knocked at the door of her godmother's room and cried,

"Get up, my Godmother, and open the door for me." The godmother wakened up suddenly and she couldn't think what had disturbed her during the night like that, and she didn't recognize Belle d'Amour's voice. She asked,

"Who's there?"

"It is I," answered Belle d'Amour, "your godchild. Open quickly."

The godmother hurried because she thought that Belle d'Amour must be in misery to have come so late at night. She opened the door and Belle d'Amour fell into her arms.

"What is the matter, my dear Belle d'Amour?" said the godmother. "You look alarmed."

"Oh, Godmother," answered Belle d'Amour, "if you knew what our stepmother is going to do," and she told her godmother all that she had heard. "What are we going to do? We will not see our father any more, nor you, my dear Godmother. Maybe we will be eaten by the wolves and bears." Poor Belle d'Amour started to weep, and her godmother had a hard time to console her.

"Calm yourself, my dear child," she said, "I'm going to tell you what to do. Tomorrow morning before you start, you will hide a big ball of wool under your coat. When the others start on their way, you will stay behind, and while you are walking you will unwind the ball of wool and hang it on the little trees until you reach the spot where you will be left. When you want to return, follow the road indicated by the string of wool."

"Oh, you are wise," said Belle d'Amour, "I will do as you tell me." She thanked her godmother, kissed her and went home. She didn't make any noise, and nobody heard her return or go to bed. She fell asleep suddenly, for her outing had tired her.

Very early the next morning the stepmother woke the little girls to get up.

"Get up," she said. "It is going to be a fine day and we must leave as early as we can so we will reach the great wood before noon." Belle de Jour and La Petite Finette were very happy and dressed themselves, but Belle d'Amour didn't speak. She was feeling sad after her experience of the night before.

When all the family had gathered in the kitchen, the stepmother took a cheerful air as well as Belle de Jour and La Petite Finette. They didn't suspect what was waiting for them. For them it was a holiday. They helped their stepmother prepare the lunch baskets for their dinner in the great wood, saying,

"Oh, it's going to be good, those little cakes and biscuits and dainties. When we have walked far we will be hungry."

The stepmother talked with them and did everything she could to pretend it was a holiday, but the father and Belle d'Amour just walked the floor slowly and sadly. The father had his heart full of sorrow and he was thinking it would probably be the last day that he would spend near his children.

"Dear little girls," he thought, "what are they going to do in the midst of the great woods? Maybe they will be eaten by the wild beasts." This thought tore his heart. Belle d'Amour was seeing very well that her father was afflicted, and she gave him consoling looks, but she was careful not to let her stepmother know how sad she was. Secretly she took her stepmother's ball of grey wool and put it aside in order to take it at the last minute without letting the others know.

At last everything was ready. Belle de Jour and La Petite Finette were on pins and needles to start. The father and mother went on in front carrying the basket of food. Belle de Jour and La Petite Finette started running and jumping, sometimes in front of their parents and sometimes behind. Belle d'Amour had offered to lock the windows and doors of the house to enable her to take the ball of wool and to hide it well under her coat, and she walked a little behind the others. It was a fine morning. The sun started to rise, and it was a pleasure to walk with the air so pure and fresh.

Belle de Jour and La Petite Finette continued to jump and exclaimed about this and that, and their stepmother joined them in their talk saying to herself that it would be for the last time. The father walked silently, his head hung low. Belle d'Amour walked behind, unwinding her wool and hanging the string in the little trees as she went along. The others didn't notice what she was doing. They walked and walked very far in the woods until the little girls were very tired. The sun was high and it was warm. The stepmother knew that the little girls were tired enough to sleep and that they wouldn't be able to find their way alone to return home.

"Well, my dear little girls," said the stepmother, "it is very warm and you are tired. Lie down here in the shade of the great trees and sleep. Your father and I will go and cut a few branches over there, and when you awaken we will eat." The little girls were very pleased to lie down, and in a few moments they fell into a deep sleep.

"Come," said the stepmother to the father, "let's go home now. The little girls will sleep all afternoon, and when they wake up they won't know where they are, and they won't be able to come home. We will be happy, both of us in the house." The father gave a last look to his dear little girls that he thought he was seeing for the last time. Slowly, and with a terrible grief, he followed the stepmother along the way as far as home. The stepmother was pleased. Everything was quiet in the house and she thought she got rid of the little girls forever.

The little girls were so tired that they slept until night. When they woke up they looked around and they didn't understand at first where they were. The moon was up, and by its rays they could see the great trees that surrounded them. They rubbed their eyes looking from one to the other and saying,

"What has happened? Where are we? It is night." Little by little they remembered they had come to the wood with their father and mother, and that they had laid down to rest waiting for dinner. La Petite Finette began to be frightened.

"Where are Father and Mother? Why have they left us here until night? Oh, we are lost in the woods and we'll never be able to go home. What are we to do? The wild beasts will eat us. We are lost," and she and Belle de Jour began to weep.

Belle d'Amour who was now wide awake remembered what had happened, and the string of wool she had hung from tree to tree.

"Do not weep, La Petite Finette," she said. "I know how to find the way home again. Follow me."

They got up and, as it was moonlight, Belle d'Amour didn't have any trouble to find the last tree on which she had hung the string of wool.

"There," she said, "is my string of wool. Come, we will be able to follow the way until we reach home."

Belle de Jour and La Petite Finette were very much surprised at what Belle d'Amour was telling them, but they didn't ask any questions because they were so afraid of the great wood and they wanted to return home as soon as they could. They followed Belle d'Amour without fear. It was a great joy for the three little girls when they finally saw their father's house. They went in without making any noise, not knowing what their stepmother would say. Their father and mother were having their supper, so they hid behind the door. They were eating a pie which seemed very good, and the little girls looked at the table, through the opening of the door. How hungry they were, for they hadn't eaten since they left that morning. All at once the stepmother said to their father,

"If our little girls had as good a pie as this they certainly would eat it." La Petite Finette couldn't stand it, and said in a clear little voice,

"Yes, Mother." *(One of the highlights of hearing this story told in her childhood was the way Mrs. McNeil's mother always said this in the voice of a very small child, high-pitched and quite breathless.)*

The father and stepmother jumped up. The little girls came from behind the door and ran to kiss their father who was overjoyed to see his little ones back safe and sound. The stepmother was very angry to see them, but she didn't dare say what she thought before their father. On the contrary, she seemed pleased to see them and said,

"Why did you stay in the woods so long? Your father and I were not able to find you and we were very much grieved to come home without you. You have been naughty to go away from us. Don't ever do that again."

Belle de Jour and La Petite Finette were very happy at what their mother had said, and hurried to bed. In a short time they were asleep, but Belle d'Amour wasn't so happy. She suspected again that her mother had something disagreeable for the following day and she couldn't go to sleep. When the little ones had been asleep for a while and the mother thought they would be unable to hear her, she said to the father,

"Tomorrow we will try again to lose our little girls in the wood, and this time we will go far enough to assure ourselves that they won't be able to return."

The father knew it was useless to contradict his wife. He didn't say anything but, as the first time, it was a great sorrow to him. However, he didn't give up hope, for he remembered that his little girls had returned safe and sound once and he consoled himself with the thought that it might be the same the next day.

Belle d'Amour, like the first time, heard what the stepmother said. This time she didn't lose hope either. After the mother and father were in bed she got up and dressed quietly and went out of the house without anybody hearing her, and she ran to her godmother's. The godmother was sleeping, but she heard Belle d'Amour's voice and got up to open the door.

"What is it again?" asked the godmother and Belle d'Amour, out of breath, told what her stepmother wanted to do.

"Do not fear, my dear child," said the godmother. "Tomorrow morning before leaving you will fill your pockets with ashes. When you leave, you will walk behind and drop the ashes as you go along until you are in the great woods. It will be easy to follow the path of ashes when you want to come home again."

Belle d'Amour thanked her godmother, kissed her, and ran home. She entered and went to bed quietly.

Early the next morning the stepmother woke the little girls up. This time Belle d'Amour looked almost as happy as her sisters because she knew they wouldn't get lost in the wood. All three hurried to dress and came down to the kitchen where they had a good breakfast. The mother was gay and smiling with her little girls, but the father was eating silently. After breakfast the little girls helped their mother to arrange the baskets of food.

Belle d'Amour and La Petite Finette were making themselves important and passed flattering remarks on the nice baskets and the delicious cakes. Without being seen, Belle d'Amour filled her pockets with ashes, and when everything was ready, they started. Belle d'Amour, as before, offered to close the house which gave her the chance to stay behind to sprinkle her ashes for a path.

It was a fine morning again, even finer than before. A great big sun was reflecting his sweet rays and the birds by their singing seemed to wish them all a happy day. Belle de Jour and La Petite Finette jumped up and down waiting for their parents. The father didn't say anything, but the mother talked and laughed with them. Belle d'Amour walked behind sprinkling the ashes.

They walked farther than the first time. The little girls were very tired, and the mother thought it was time for them to rest. Being so far, she didn't think they would ever find their way back again.

"Lie down," she said, "and rest a little while your father and I cut a few branches while waiting for dinner."

The little girls were pleased to lie down because they could hardly stand up. When they were asleep the stepmother said to their father,

"Come on. Let's go home now. The little girls will never find their way this time." The father followed silently and they returned home towards afternoon. When the little girls woke the moon was up. Little by little they began to understand things, and La Petite Finette began to weep saying,

"Oh, we are lost in the woods. What are we going to do? Our parents are lost and we will be eaten by the beasts this time."

"Don't weep," said Belle d'Amour, "I know how to find the way back. Come on and follow me." She found the last handful of ashes that she had dropped, and Belle de Jour and La Petite Finette followed her all the way home.

When they got back to the house they were tired. Going in silently they saw their father and their stepmother having their breakfast and they hid behind the door. The father and mother were eating pie and it seemed very good. All at once the mother, who thought the little girls were very far away, said to the father,

"If our little girls had a pie to eat as good as this they certainly would eat it," and La Petite Finette said again in a tiny little voice,

"Yes, Mother."

It was the same scene as the first time. The little girls had supper and everything went very well.

Before long the little girls forgot their experience in the wood, but the stepmother was not ready yet to abandon her plans to separate them from her. When she thought the time had come to try again she chose a day to arrange her work, and that night she sent the little girls to bed very early and told them the same thing about the feast. This time she said to her husband,

"We will make sure that they are lost." The father felt it was the end and that he would never see them after the next day, and he didn't say anything.

But Belle d'Amour had heard. There was but one thing for her to do, and that was to consult her godmother. After her mother and father were in bed she got up and dressed and went out of the house without being noticed. She ran fast, fast to her godmother's house, and cried at the window to open the door.

"But my dear child," answered the godmother. "What's the matter?"

Belle d'Amour told her for the third time of her stepmother's plans. "And this time," continued Belle d'Amour, "I'm afraid there is nothing that can save us. What are we to do?"

"There's nothing to fear," said the godmother. "Tomorrow morning before leaving you will fill your pockets with peas and you will stay behind and drop them all along the way and it will be easy to find your way back. Be careful not to let anyone see you," and Belle d'Amour returned home.

Next morning the stepmother called the little girls and they hurried to dress and came to the kitchen for breakfast. Their mother was gay, and Belle de Jour and La Petite Finette were happy also, but their father was very sad and Belle d'Amour, who understood her father's grief, tried to console him with her tender sweet looks.

Breakfast over they started out. Belle d'Amour locked the windows and doors and stayed behind to drop the peas. From everywhere you could hear the little birds in the woods. Belle d'Amour noticed them, but she didn't realize that while she was dropping the peas, the little birds were picking them up and eating them. The little birds were singing,

> Sow, sow, sow, I pick them up.
> Sow, sow, sow, I pick them up.

Belle d'Amour didn't understand that language. They continued to walk and walk until the stepmother thought there would be no way for the little girls to find their way home. They were now in the Great Forest. It was warm and the little girls fell asleep. The father and mother left them there and returned home. It was a great sorrow to the father but he could say nothing.

When the little girls woke up it was night and La Petite Finette started to weep again, but Belle d'Amour told her not to weep.

"Follow me. I can find the way home again."

Belle de Jour and La Petite Finette followed their oldest sister through the woods but alas, Belle d'Amour looked in vain for the peas. The little birds had eaten them all up. They turned from right to left and left to right and looked everywhere, but the more they walked, the more lost they were. This time Finette started to weep loudly. Belle d'Amour calmed her anew, telling her not to weep aloud.

"We will find our way," she said. They noticed a great tree, and Belle d' Amour said,

"Do you see this great tree? We are going to climb on top to see the surrounding country. From the top of the tree we should be able to see the lights from the wood."

The tree had grown during the day from the bean that had been dropped with the peas, and that the birds hadn't been able to swallow. Belle d'Amour climbed to the highest branch and she saw a little light.

"Take courage. I see a nice little house and it is shining just like a silver light. We will go in that direction and we will find lodgings for the night."

The little girls started among the trees, and it wasn't long before they noticed a light from a little house, and they were astonished to see that this little house was built with pins. This interested them very much. An old lady opened the door and, seeing the little girls, she cried,

"Go away, go away, you can't come in."

"Let us in," cried the little girls. "We are lost in the wood and we can't find our way home and we'd like to stay here."

"No no," said the old lady. "My husband is a giant, and if he finds you here he will eat you up."

"We will hide ourselves and he won't find us," said the little girls.

The old lady took pity on them and let them in and they felt at home, but the old lady was ill at ease and, showing them a cupboard, she said,

"Hide in that. When you hear the earth trembling you will know that my husband is coming. When he enters there will be a terrible noise, and when he talks his voice will be frightful. Be careful not to move."

The little girls went in the cupboard, and it wasn't long before they heard a sound like an earthquake and they knew the giant was coming. They began to be afraid.

The giant entered. He had a big nose, and all at once he began to sniff.

"What is it that smells like fresh meat?"

"Fresh meat?" asked the old lady, making believe she was astonished. "There's no fresh meat here. A shepherd boy passed by here with his sheep. It is probably that you smell."

"No, no," cried the giant. "There is fresh meat in this house. Tell me where it is."

The poor lady knew it was useless to try to mislead him.

"Well," she said, "if you promise not to kill them I will tell you what it is."

"I promise you," cried the giant. "Tell me quickly."

"Three little girls who were lost in the woods have asked me to take them in."

"Where are they?" asked the giant.

"They're in the cupboard," replied the old lady. The giant opened the cupboard door. The little girls thought that he would kill them and eat them.

"Come out," said the giant to Belle d'Amour who was the first. She came out, hardly able to stand up through fear.

"What is your name?" asked the giant.

"Belle d'Amour," she replied in a little trembling voice.

"And what can you do?"

"Sweep the floor," she replied.

The giant descended then to Belle de Jour.

"Come forward, you."

Belle de Jour came out trembling, and advanced towards the giant.

"What's your name?"

"Belle de Jour," she replied softly.

"And what can you do?"

"I can make bread," she replied.

The giant turned then towards La Petite Finette. Seeing that she was almost speechless with fear, he tried to calm his voice.

"Come, my little one, and tell me your name."

"It's La Petite Finette," she said, "and I can heat the oven ."

"Good," said the giant. "Now get to work, all of you, and you, Petite Finette, you are going to show me how to heat the oven."

Petite Finette answered,

"I put a piece of butter on the tongue and you stretch out your tongue in the oven. When the butter is melted, I know that the oven is hot enough to put the bread in."

"I will do that," said the giant. "Put a piece of butter on my tongue," and she did it. Then she had him lean his head in the oven with all her might and closed the door. The giant began to holler but he couldn't get out, and soon you could hear him roasting. The old lady began to lament.

"What have you done? What have you done?" she cried. "He's going to roast to death, my dear husband. You are very cruel, my little girls."

"Don't think about it," said the little girls. "We will make a bonnet to put on your hair, and you will go out and walk in the surrounding woods."

Little by little the old lady consoled herself, and the little girls made a bonnet of lace and ribbon and put it on her head. She looked in the mirror and liked it very much.

"Now," said the three little girls, "we will take a walk," and, talking to themselves softly, they said, "We will kill her dead too, and we will stay in the house of pins." They took her behind the house where a boy was cutting wood.

"Here's our luck," said the little girls. "We will have her head cut off."

When they arrived near the chopping block on which the boy was chopping the wood, Belle d'Amour said to the old lady,

"Bend your head on the block for just a moment. Your bonnet is a little lop-sided and I'd like to put it straight for you." The poor old lady didn't suspect anything, and leaned her head on the block. Belle d'Amour made a sign and the boy with one blow of the axe cut the head off the old woman. The three little girls and the little boy resided for the rest of their lives in the house of pins. They found many treasures and riches, and lived happily for ever after.

[Type 327 The Children and the Ogre; related to Type 327A Hansel and Gretel]

HELEN: In the first typing of this tale the youngest little girl was named La Petite Finette. When sent to the National Museum for re-typing, I was advised the La should be omitted throughout. This may have been one of the additions M. D'Eon put in the tale published in *Le Petit Courrier*.

32. The Golden Beard (La barbe d'or)

AS TOLD BY SIPHRONE D'ENTREMONT, WEST PUBNICO, N.S.

ONCE UPON A TIME there was a little boy, and all the people were telling the king that this little boy would marry one of his daughters, and the king wouldn't hear that at all. He said to the little boy one day,

"If you could go to the man with the golden beard and bring me three hairs from his beard," for the king thought the little boy couldn't do that and he would get killed and he would get clear of the little boy. This Golden Beard was a madman.

This little boy started to go to the Golden Beard. He met a man near an apple tree. The man said to the boy,

"How is it that this apple tree used to grow apples and now there's not an apple on it?" The little boy said to the man,

"I will tell you when I will come back," and he started walking and he met a man sitting near a well. The man said,

"How is it that this well always used to be full of water and now it is dry?" The little boy said,

"I will tell you when I will come back," and he started walking. He met a man near a brook and the man said,

"How is it that this brook used to be full of water and now there is not a bit in it?" and the little boy said to this man,

"I will tell you when I come back," and he started walking again and he arrived at the house where the Golden Beard lived. He knocked at the door but the Golden Beard wasn't home. His wife was there. She said,

"What do you want?" She said, "The Golden Beard killed every little boy that came here and he will kill you if you stay." The little boy told all that had happened to the Golden Beard's wife, and that the king had sent him to get three hairs from the beard. She said,

"I will try to get them for you. You will hide under the bed and I will try to get them for you."

When the Golden Beard came home he said, "I smell meat." She said,

"It's only some sheep that's been around the house," so the Golden Beard didn't ask any more questions.

They were waiting until he would be asleep, and when he was asleep his wife took one of the hairs from his beard and threw it under the bed to the little boy. So the little boy took it and he was listening. The Golden Beard awoke and he said,

"What are you doing?"

"Oh," she said, "I was dreaming. I was dreaming that there was a little boy that was passing by a brook and a man was near the brook and asking him why the brook used to be full of water and now there's not a bit of water in it." The Golden Beard said,

"There's a stick under the brook moving all the time and holding it back. If they take the stick out it will be full of water all the time." So the Golden Beard went to sleep again and while he was sleeping his wife took another hair from his golden beard and threw it under the bed to the little boy and the Golden Beard awoke again.

"What are you doing? What are you doing?"

"Oh," she said, "I was dreaming."

"What were you dreaming?"

"Well," she said, "I was dreaming there was a little boy that was passing near a well and there was a man sitting there and he asked the little boy what was the reason that the well used to be full of water and now there was no water in it." The Golden Beard said,

"Well, a frog is under the well and if they take the frog out, the well will be filled with water," and the Golden Beard got to sleep again. While he was sleeping his wife took another hair and he awoke again.

"What are you doing? What are you doing?"

"Oh, I was dreaming.

"Oh, I was dreaming there was a little boy who passed near an apple tree and there was a man sitting there and he asked the reason why the apple tree used to be full of apples, and now there was not an apple on it." The Golden Beard said,

"There's a toad under the tree. If they take the toad out the apple tree will be full of apples." The little boy had listened to all the Golden Beard was saying to tell the men and then he waited until the Golden Beard went to sleep again to get out of the house. When the Golden Beard went to sleep again his wife said to the little boy,

"You must go out." So he got out of the house with the three hairs from the golden beard, and he started to walk.

He met this man near a brook and this man said,

"Can you tell me now?" He said, "Yes, there's a stick that goes

round and if you take that stick out the brook will be full of water."
So they took the stick out and the brook was all filled with water.
Then he started to walk again and met the man near the well.

"Well, how is it this well used to be full of water and now
there's not a bit of water in it?" The little boy said to the man,

"There's a frog under the well and if you take that frog out
the well will be full of water." They took the frog out and the
well filled up again. He started to walk again and he met the man
near the apple tree.

"Now can you tell me why this apple tree used to be filled
with apples and now there's not an apple on it?" He said,

"There's a toad under the apple tree and if you take the
toad away the tree will be full of apples." So they took the toad
out and the apple tree was filled up with apples. The little boy
started to walk again and reached the king's palace. He knocked
at the door and the king went to the door and the little boy said,

"I've got the three golden hairs," and he gave them to the
king. The king was so surprised thinking he was so smart he said,

"You will marry my daughter when you will be old
enough," and so when he came old enough he married the king's
daughter and they lived with the king and had a happy life the
rest of their lives.

[Type 461 Three Hairs from the Devil's Beard] *Collected August 4, 1948.*

33. The Ship that Sailed as well on Land as on the Sea

AS WRITTEN BY LAURA MCNEIL, WEST PUBNICO, N.S.

ONCE UPON A TIME there was a king who promised his
daughter, the princess, in marriage to the one who could
build a ship that would sail as well on the land as on the sea.

Many young men wanted to try such an adventure, but there was never anyone who could succeed.

In a certain village in that country there lived together three brothers, and the youngest was called Jean. The two older brothers found Jean a little foolish, and always gave him the hardest work in the household to do. But Jean didn't mind, and was always loved by everyone.

One morning the oldest brother announced to the others that he was trying to build the famous ship that the king wanted. He took his dinner in a bag, and his axe, and started. On the way he met an old woman. She was a witch, but he didn't know it.

"Good-day, my friend," said she, "wherever are you going this fine morning?"

"I am going to build a ship for the king that will sail as well on land as on the sea."

"And what do you carry in your bag?" she asked.

"My dinner," he said, a little annoyed.

"Do you want to give me a piece of bread and some wine?" continued the old woman. "I'm hungry."

"Do you think I have nothing to do but to feed the passers-by?" he said, and he refused.

"Very well," said the witch, "as soon as you will cut a tree two more will grow in their place, and you will never be able to build your ship," and she disappeared. He was stunned by the words and the sudden disappearance of the old woman, but, feeling brave, and not wanting to be conquered by such superstitious ideas, he continued on his way. Arrived at the wood he put his bag down and began to cut a tree. He struck a few strokes and the tree fell down but, to his great surprise, he saw two more spring up on the same stump.

"Do my eyes mistake me?" He closed his eyes for an instant, but when he opened them again the two trees were there. He felled the second time and two more sprung up again at the stump.

"What does that mean?" He began to understand that the witch's wish was becoming true, and he grew angry. More through anger than anything else he began to cut trees, and in a short time he found himself surrounded by trees because for every tree he cut, two grew in its place. He was then obliged to stop his work and go home.

His brothers were surprised to see him coming so soon and asked him how the ship was getting on, and he told them he had taken a tremendous headache.

The next morning the second brother announced that he was going to build the ship for the king since his eldest brother didn't want to do it. He got his dinner ready and started for the wood. On his way he met the same witch and had the same conversation as his elder brother. He also refused to give her bread and she made him the same wish. He did not pay attention to her and went on his way. Arrived in the woods he cut the first tree and to his surprise two more sprang at the stump. He thought he was dreaming, but after he had cut many more with the same results, he understood that this was the witch's wish, and no doubt he was being punished because he had refused to give her bread. He understood, too, why his elder brother had not succeeded. He returned home and told his brothers he felt sick and would not be able to continue the work on the ship. The elder brother suspected what had happened, but neither of them wanted to admit anything.

The next morning the two older brothers noticed that Jean was more occupied than usual.

"What are you doing?" they asked.

"Me?" answered Jean, "I'm preparing some bread for my dinner."

"You are preparing some bread for your dinner?" said the two older brothers who both understood that Jean was going away for the whole day. "But where are you going?"

"Oh well, I thought that I would begin to cut some wood to build the ship that would sail as well on the land as the sea," answered Jean. "It should be I who is going to marry the princess."

"You who is going to build the ship that will sail as well on land as on the sea? You who will marry the princess?" cried the two older brothers in astonishment. "Have you lost your senses?" and they began to make fun of him.

Jean paid no attention to their mockery. He finished his preparations and left the house whistling. He hadn't walked far when he met the witch.

"Good morning, my little Jean," she said, "you look happy. Where are you going with your bag and your axe?"

"Good morning, my good lady," answered Jean. "I'm going to build a ship for the king that will sail as well on land as on the sea."

"What have you got in your bag?" she continued.

"A little bit of bread for my dinner," he replied.

"I haven't eaten this morning. Would you give me a piece of bread?"

"Yes," said Jean, and he opened his bag. "Eat all you want."

The witch took some bread and ate it. Then she gave the bag back to Jean and she also gave him a little stick, and said,

"Everything that you touch with this stick will turn into a part of the ship that will be able to sail as well on land as on the sea, and before evening you and your crew will be starting for the king's palace." Having said these words she disappeared.

Jean stood in astonishment and thought he must be coming out of a dream, but seeing his cane he thought the old lady must be a witch, and all her wishes would bring him good luck. He continued his way and reached the place where he had to cut his lumber for the ship. Remembering the witch's words he began to strike the trees with his stick and in a short while he had many piles of lumber. Then he started to strike the fallen trees and they turned into different parts of the ship, the keel, the bowsprit, the masts and so on. He struck again and the pieces went together. The ship was complete and all was ready for sailing.

Jean was certainly surprised at what had been done in such a short time. He wondered what his crew was but, as all the things had been going on as the witch predicted, he felt that all would end as it should. It was noon, and Jean seated himself on a stump and ate his dinner. He then went in the boat, this stick in his hand. With a little blow of the stick the ship started to move. However he couldn't stop asking himself why the crew hadn't appeared and, looking fixedly ahead, he noticed a black object. As the ship went along Jean saw that the object was turning into a man who looked as though he had been working. Arriving nearer, Jean was astonished to see that the man was licking the bottom of a barrel. Jean struck his stick and the ship stopped.

"Good-day, my friend," said Jean. "What are you doing there?"

The man lifted his head and thought he was seeing a ghost. But coming to his senses, the captain and the ship appeared real to him and he answered,

"For seven years I haven't drunk any wine, and I'm very thirsty, so thirsty that I am tasting the bottom of this barrel to quench my thirst."

"Put the bottom of the barrel aside and come with me. We will go to see the king," said Jean. "There will be plenty of wine there."

The man did as he was told and went with Jean. With a stroke of the stick the ship started to move, and this astonished the stranger. In a short time Jean noticed a man before him who was gnawing a bone. Again with a stroke of the magic stick the ship stopped.

"What are you doing there, my good man?" asked Jean.

The man opened his eyes wide, and after a few moments answered,

"For seven years I haven't eaten meat and I'm so hungry that I can taste it even in the bone."

"Throw that bone away," said Jean, "and come with us. We are going to see the king."

The man threw his bone down and went into the ship. He was astonished to see that it could move on land without any manpower and with nothing more than the help of the magic stick.

After a while Jean saw another man who was tying big millstones to his feet. Stopping the ship Jean asked what he was doing there. The man looked up with great surprise at the strange sight and said,

"I can run so fast that I can even beat the foxes and the wolves, and I'm tying these millstones on my feet to diminish the speed."

"Put these millstones aside," said Jean, "and come with me to see the king." The man untied his millstones and put them aside and went with Jean and his crew. Like the other men aboard, he was astonished to see the captain start the ship simply by using his magic stick.

Jean found his trip very interesting and laughed in his beard, thinking how angry his brothers would be if they could see him. Reminiscing, he noticed a man lying on the ground, his ear to the ground. The ship stopping, Jean asked,

"What are you doing lying down on the ground?" The man jumped up and said,

"My ear is so good that I can lie down on the ground and hear the grass grow."

"Would you not like to join my crew and go to see the king?" asked Jean. He jumped aboard and Jean used his wand and the ship started going again. This puzzled him quite a bit.

The fifth member of the crew was soon found, for a little farther along Jean noticed a man standing with a bow and arrow pointing in the air.

"Well, my brave man," said Jean, "what are you going to kill?" The man turned around in surprise and answered,

"I'm sighting to kill a swallow that I see in the fog a hundred leagues away."

"Marvellous," cried Jean, "come with us to see the king."

The man went along with his bow and arrow, and was astonished to see the strange ship obey the magic stick and sail as well on land as on the sea.

At last they arrived at the king's palace. It was towards night. The king was walking in his garden when he heard an extraordinary noise. Looking towards the road he saw the well-appointed ship in front of the palace. For a moment he didn't understand what it was, but all at once he recalled the promise he had made and he was embarrassed, for he had never thought such a thing possible. Moreover, he was not ready to give his daughter in marriage to the first one to come. He had to think of another scheme quickly so he could save his daughter. Jean and his men were now there. They disembarked and saluted the king.

"Your majesty," began Jean, "I have succeeded as you see to build your ship that is going to sail as well on land as on sea, and I've come to ask the reward you have promised, and that is your daughter in marriage."

"Well," replied the king, "there are yet a few little things to do before you can claim my daughter. I have a cellar full of wine. If you and your men can drink all that wine during the night, tomorrow morning I will fulfil my promise," and he thought he had got rid of Jean because he didn't think it could be done.

A page boy took Jean and his men to the cellar, and Jean said to the one who loved the wine,

"Here's your chance to drink to your fill." Before morning the man had drunk all the wine. The king came to see how they had passed the night, and was confused to find all the hogsheads empty. However, he didn't want to give his princess without another try, so he said to Jean,

"If you can eat all my cattle that are in the field over there before tonight, you will have your reward." The page boy took Jean and his men to the field. The man who was so hungry for meat started to eat the cattle, and before night they had all disappeared. The king was more stupified than ever. He began to lose hope, but another thought came to his mind.

"Do you see that well over there?" he asked Jean. "I'm going to send the princess to get two pails of water. You will ask one of your men to go with her. When they get to the well she will put the man to sleep and she herself will come back. If the man can wake up and return to the castle with the two pails before the princess, I will give her to you for your wife."

Jean sent the one who could run very fast to go with the princess to the well. When they arrived she began to comb her companion's hair, and he went to sleep. After a while Jean said to the man who had a good ear,

"Lie down on the ground and listen if you can hear anything." The man lay down and said,

"I hear the man who is snoring and the princess who is coming."

"Take your bow and arrow," said Jan to the last man, "and wake the sleeping man up." The man let an arrow fly and it struck him slightly and woke him up. He filled the two pails with water as fast as he could, and he ran and reached the king before the princess. The king didn't have any more schemes to give, so Jean married the princess and these two lived happily together for many many years.

[Type 513B The Land and Water Ship]

34. The Talking Fiddle

AS TOLD BY MRS. LOUIS AMIRAULT, WEST PUBNICO, N.S.

A man who had committed murder felt so badly about it that he went to the woods and told the trees. One day the tree was cut down and the wood made into a fiddle, and when the fiddle was played it told the story.

[Type 780A The Cannibalistic Brothers] *Collected August 11, 1948.*

All that could be recalled by Mrs. Louis Amirault, translated from Acadian French. She said it was an Irish folk tale and had been learned from an Irishwoman.

35. The Old Mule

TRANSLATED FROM THE STORY AS WRITTEN IN ACADIAN
FRENCH BY LAURA MCNEIL, WEST PUBNICO, NOVA SCOTIA

ONCE UPON A TIME a little boy only had an old grey horse and he called it an old mule. He lived not far from where the king lived, and he used to go past the palace on the mule's back every day. One day he was going along the road when he noticed the most beautiful yellow feather in the world. He picked it up and put it on his hat.

After a few hours he went by the palace of the king. The little page noticed the feather in his hat and asked him for it but he refused. This made them very angry, so they told the king that the little boy had said that he could catch the bird that had lost the feather. They brought him in front of the king who said to him,

"My little boy, if you don't bring me the bird which has lost this feather I will kill you for sure."

The little boy didn't answer, but he went away with the mule and his heart was very heavy. Then he told the old mule what they had said.

"Fear nothing," said the old mule, "I know what to do. Put a little bit of wine in a pan and put it at the place where you have found the feather. The bird will return there to rest, and when he sees the wine he will drink it and fall asleep. Then you will be able to catch the bird and take it to the king."

The little boy did what the old mule told him, and found the yellow bird asleep near the pan. It was a bird of a rare beauty, and he had never seen such a pretty bird before. He took it to the king who was very well pleased.

One day he went near the palace again, and the little page saw him and wondered what they could do to hurt him this time.

"Let us tell the king that he says he can bring the castle of the queen near his castle." They agreed to this and ran and told the king what the little boy was supposed to have said. The queen's castle was situated on the other side of the river, and it was there that the queen lived. The king had taken all possible means to bring her back to him, but so far all had been in vain, and the king was grieved because he couldn't have the queen near him. So when he heard the news that the little boy could bring her castle near his he was very glad, so he called him in and told him the same things before, that he would kill him if he couldn't do it.

The little boy returned home and was very sad, and told the old mule what had happened.

"What shall I do?" he asked. He was very discouraged. But the old mule said,

"Get a crowd of negroes and feed them with cornmeal until they're very strong, and then they'll be able to transport the queen's castle to the king's." So he went and got the band of negroes and he fed them with cornmeal and then he brought the negroes to the edge of the river where a big boat was tied. They embarked in the boat and they crossed to a point near the queen's castle. The negroes got out then and they put the castle on their shoulders and carried it to the other side of the river, and, arriving there, they placed the castle near the king's.

The king was very glad, but when the queen noticed that they had moved her castle she locked the doors and threw the keys in the river and after that nobody could get in the castle.

The servants were still looking for trouble, so they told the king that the little boy had said he could find the keys the queen had thrown in the river, so the king said,

"Go and tell the little boy to bring me the keys or I will kill him." This time the servants thought he would be killed for sure, because they didn't think he would be able to find the keys.

So again the little boy told the old mule his story, and the old mule said,

"Don't worry. Go to the shore and you will find the shark there. Tell the shark to look for the keys." The little boy did as he was told and he found the shark on the sand. The shark said,

"Roll me in the water. I have been on dry land for such a long time that I want to go away." So the little boy rolled the shark in the water, asking him to bring the keys for the king. The shark disappeared and in a few moments came back with a fish which he landed on the shore. The little boy took the fish and split it open and found the keys which he took to the king. The king was very pleased with that.

The king went down immediately to the queen's palace and opened the doors and went in, but alas, he was never able to make the queen talk, and she still didn't want to live with the king. More discouraged than ever, he returned to his own castle.

When the servants heard what had happened, they told the king that the little boy had said he was able to make the queen live again with the king.

The little boy didn't know what to do this time, so he told his old mule about it. This time the old mule looked worried and didn't know what to answer. At last he turned to the little boy and said,

"There is but one way, and it grieves me to tell you. You must kill me."

"Kill you?" cried the little boy. "Oh no, don't say that. I wouldn't be able to live without you."

"Listen," replied the old mule. "You are young, and there are many things for you in life while my life is almost finished, and before long I will be of no further use." But the little boy said,

"After you are dead I will have no one to help me, and how will I ever make the queen live with the king?"

"Don't you understand, little boy? I have already told you what to do. You must kill me, and when I'm dead you must dress with my skin and enter the castle of the queen doing all kinds of gestures and tricks as if you are a beast. The queen will be so scared that she will want to go away and live with the king."

The little boy remained silent a long time but, seeing there was but one thing to do, he took a knife and killed the old mule.

Then he took the skin and did as the old mule had said. He entered the castle making violent cries of fear, and the queen was so afraid that she just fell into the king's arms. She saw the mistake she had made and, asking pardon of the king, she promised that she would never leave him.

From that day they lived together, and you could never see the king without the queen beside him. The little boy was rewarded. The king kept him in his palace where he remained the rest of his days happy and contented.

[Type 531 Ferdinand the True and Ferdinand the False; related to Type 559 Dungbeetle] *Collected September 1947.*

HELEN CREIGHTON: This is the correct version, the one written for the paper *Le Petit Courrier* having been added to by the editor (and called "La Veille Bourrique"). The boy was not given a name in the traditional Acadian story, but was simply known as the little boy. The story has no setting, and the little boy did not stop to see the king.

36. The Little Eel (La p'tit andj)
AS TOLD BY SIPHRONE D'ENTREMONT, WEST PUBNICO, N.S., AND TRANSLATED BY HER SISTER AUGUSTA D'ENTREMONT

ONCE UPON A TIME there was a man that went fishing with his little girl and they fished for eels. They put the eels on a little string and they started to go home, and they put the eels in a little pond and the man went home. He left his little girl playing with the eels in the pond. He told his wife that they have caught four eels, and when the little girl was playing one slipped from the string, so there were only three left.

She went home with three eels, and her mother said her father had told her he had caught four eels and she had only three. Her mother said,

"I am going on a visit, and you must make some soup with water and rocks." The little girl didn't know what to do at all, so she went to the pond to see the little eel that she had lost, and she asked the eel what she could do. She said,

"Eel, eel, save my life because I have saved yours. My mother has left me home to make some soup with water and rocks," and the little eel said,

"Go home and put some water in a pot and put some rocks, and you take a little wooden stick and you stir and say,

"'Soup, soup, make the good soup, make a good soup,'" and the little girl did what the eel told her and it came out a good soup.

When her mother came home she said,

"Did you make the soup?" She said,

"Yes," so the mother went to taste the soup and it was real good. She didn't know how the little girl did that. She wanted to punish her, but the soup was so good she didn't punish her. She said,

"I am going on a visit back again tomorrow. You must take all the ashes out of the stove with a table fork." So the woman started again on her visit, and the little girl didn't know what to do. She went back to the pond to see the little eel and she said,

"Eel, eel, save my life because I have saved yours," and the little eel said,

"What do you want?" and she said,

"My mother told me to take all the ashes from the stove with a table fork," and the little eel said,

"Go home and take a table fork and you will take all the ashes from the stove," and she did that and she cleaned the stove all right. So when her mother came home everything was cleaned up. She couldn't understand how the little girl had done that. She was going to punish her if she hadn't done that. She said,

"I am going to go back again tomorrow and you must bail the well with a fork." She was afraid she couldn't do that, so she went back to the pond and she said,

"Eel, eel, save my life because I have saved yours." The little eel came back and said,

"What do you want?" and she said,

"My mother wants me to bail the well with a fork." The eel said,

"Go home and bail the well with a fork," and she went home and she bailed the well with a fork. So when her mother came all the well was clean, so she didn't punish her. Then she said,

"I'm not going any more on a visit. I'm going to stay with you, and I'll be very good to you."

So the little girl didn't get any punishment.

[Type 554 The Grateful Animals; Motif B375.1. Fish returned to water: grateful] *Collected August 1949.*

37. The Little Thumb (Le petit poucet)

AS TOLD BY LAURA MCNEIL, WEST PUBNICO, NOVA SCOTIA

ONCE UPON A TIME there was a little boy that was no bigger than his father's thumb, and because he was so small they called him Little Thumb. One day his father was working in the field and his mother said to him,

"Little Thumb, you must go and take your father's dinner to him." Little Thumb went outside and came back and said,

"It is raining, Mother."

"Well then," she said, "I'll wrap you up in a cabbage leaf." She wrapped him up real well in a leaf and he started off. On his way he passed the big ox Brunit. The ox thought it was a cabbage, and he swallowed it in one bite.

At night the father came home and asked his wife why she hadn't sent his dinner. She replied that she had sent Little Thumb with it in the forenoon. The father said Little Thumb hadn't come and, since Little Thumb wasn't home by then, they began to be worried. They went out and began to call,

"Little Thumb, where are you? Little Thumb, where are you?"

Little Thumb could hear them and he replied,

"I am in the belly of the big ox Brunit, Mother. I am in the belly of the big ox Brunit, Mother," but his father and mother could not hear him.

Two or three days after that the ox went to the brook to drink. Little Thumb was wriggling so much inside his belly that it bothered him and he vomited Little Thumb into the water. Little Thumb came out of the water and climbed a tree. Then he saw some little girls playing and he called to them,

"Little girls, I see you. Little girls, I see you." The little girls could hear him but they couldn't see him. Then he came down the tree and went home.

Another day his mother was making a pudding. She had the batter all ready and she had to go into another room for something. While she was gone Little Thumb climbed into the bowl and fell into the batter. When his mother came back she poured the batter into a pan, not noticing that there was anything in it, and put it in the oven to bake. After a little while she opened the oven door to see how the pudding was coming along, and she saw something moving in it, and she got so frightened that she took the pudding out of the oven and threw it out the window. It all spread apart, and Little Thumb came out.

One day Little Thumb's mother was milking the cow and, as it was a very windy day, she tied Little Thumb to her apron string. They were near a gooseberry bush and the cow was nibbling around it. Little Thumb was running around at the end of his string and got too close to the cow's mouth. The cow didn't see him, and ate him up.

[Type 700 Tom Thumb] *Collected August 2, 1948.*

Mrs. McNeil's mother, Mrs. Henri Pothier, says it should not be a gooseberry bush, but a rose bush; that the mother tied him to a rose bush, and not to her apron string. There seems to be a bit of confusion about this point.

38. The Half Rooster (La motche d'coq)

AS TOLD BY SIPHRONE D'ENTREMONT, WEST PUBNICO, N.S.

ONCE UPON A TIME there were two little boys. They had one egg between the two. They said,

"What are we going to do?" One wanted the egg, and the other wanted the egg too.

"Well," they say, "we must cut the egg in two pieces so we'll take each half of the egg."

One of the little boys ate his half and the other put it to set. So the one that put it to set hatched a half a rooster with his half egg and that half a rooster said,

"I must go to Paris to get five cents that they are owing me," and he started.

He met a fox and the fox said,

"Where are you going?" The half rooster said,

"I am going to Paris to get the five cents that they are owing me." The fox said,

"I want to go with you." The half rooster said,

"Jump in my pant leg," and then they started, the fox and the half rooster.

Next they met a wolf and the wolf said,

"Where are you going?" The half rooster said,

"I am going to Paris to get the five cents that they are owing me." The wolf said,

"I want to go with you." The half rooster said,

"Jump in my pant leg," and then they started, the fox, the wolf, and the half rooster.

Next they met a river and the river said,

"Where are you going?" The half rooster said,

"I am going to Paris to get the five cents that they are owing me." The river said,

"I want to go with you." The half rooster said,

"Jump in my pant leg," so they started, the fox, the wolf, the river, and the half rooster to go to Paris to get that five cents.

When they came to Paris they came to a house and the people said,

"What do you want?" and the half rooster said,

"I want five cents." They say,

"What are we going to do with him tonight?" They say, "We must put him in the hen house so the goose and turkey and roosters and hens would kill that half rooster." So they put him in the hen house. So when they began to attack him he said to the fox,

"Come out of my leg and kill the animals that are in the hen house." The next morning they heard from the hen house,

"Cock-a-doodle-do." They say, "He is not dead. Where are we going to put him tonight?" All the hens and the turkeys and the geese were all dead, all but the half rooster. They say, "Tonight we will put him in the barn so the horses and the ox and the cows will kill him." So they put him in the barn the next night. The horses began to kick the half rooster and the cows and the ox to gore him with their horns and the half rooster said to the wolf,

"Come out of my leg and kill the animals that are in the barn." So the wolf came and killed all the horses and the cows and the oxen, everything that was in the barn. The next morning they heard the rooster crowing cock-a-doodle-do again.

"Well," they say, "he is not dead. What are we going to do with him tonight?" They say, "We must put him in the oven with a big fire so it would burn him." So they put him in the oven with a big fire.

Well, when he began to feel the heat he said to the river,

"Come out of my leg," and the river came and the door of the stove opened and the half rooster got out of the oven, and it drowned everyone that was in the house, that river, and the half rooster was there alive yet.

And the half rooster went back home with his five cents.

[Type 715 Demi-coq] *Recorded in Acadian French, August 4, 1948.*

39. Three Grains of Peppernell (Trois graines de peppernell)

AS TOLD BY MRS. SEPHORA AMIRAULT, WEST PUBNICO, N.S.

THERE WAS A MAN AND HIS WIFE and they had a little boy and a little girl. They went to the woods to get peppernell *(or pimprenell; peppernell is the way it was spelled in Pubnico)* seeds and they hunted all day and couldn't find any. So they decided they'd go home, and the little girl said she'd stay and look some more, and the *(brother)* said,

"If you stay, I'll stay also." Then the little girl found the three seeds of peppernell. *(They were hunting for three)*, and the little boy asked her to give them to him but she wouldn't, and then he threw her into the brook to drown.

And when he came home he had the three peppernell seeds and they asked him where the little girl was and he said she was coming behind. They waited all night for her and she didn't come, so the father went to look for her, and when he came to the brook he found the bones, and he took one and held it up to his mouth, and then the bones sang,

"Father, father, you are holding me to your mouth by hands that are so soft. My little brother had killed me on the higher bray *(nobody was quite sure whether this word should be "bray" or "grey")* marsh for three seeds of peppernell which I had found." *(Repeated.)*

Then he went home and told his wife and she said she was going to go. When she came to the brook she put the bones in her mouth and they sang the same song, only this time it began, "Mother, mother." They suspected something, so they asked the little boy to go with them and he wouldn't go, but at last they got him to go with them. When they got to the brook they made him pick up the bones and they sang,

"Murderer, murderer, you are holding me in your mouth by your hands that are so cruel. You had killed me in the pré *(marsh)* of higher bray for three seeds of peppernell that I had found." Then they took him and he was hanged.

[Type 780 The Singing Bone] *Told August 5, 1948.*

HELEN CREIGHTON: Mrs. Sephora Amirault thinks the bones were thrown in the sea and they hunted a long time. When the father found them, he picked one up and put it to his mouth, but whether to eat or not she does not know. Then the bones began to sing.

Mrs. McNeil said that as children they were horrified at this tale because the parents were eating the bones of their own child.

Mrs. Sephora Amirault was visiting a friend in Pubnico when we found her and in no time she was trying to recall a folk tale that she had once known well. Fortunately two other friends arrived and a great discussion followed, each one remembering a portion, but none the whole story. This was helpful to Mrs. McNeil who was now able to put it all together. She thought there were special properties in the three seeds, and she remembered that there was a song based on the folk tale. Mrs. Amirault recalled the part of the song that began with the daughter telling her father about her tragedy. The words in the prose version that we were so uncertain about appear in the song as "in the fields of Haiegré."

EDITORS' NOTE: Sephora Amirault sang the song for Helen:

> Mon père, mon père vous me tenez dans votre bouche
> Par vos mains qui sont si douces.
> Mon p'tit frère m'avait tuée dans le pré de Haiegré
> Pour trois grain' de pimprenelle
> Que j'avais trouvées, que j'avais trouvées.

> > My father, my father, you are holding me in your mouth
> > By your hands that are so gentle.
> > My little brother had killed me in the field of Haiegré
> > For three pimpernel seeds
> > That I had found, that I had found.

> Mon mère, mon mère vous me tenez dans votre bouche
> Par vos mains qui sont si douces.
> Mon p'tit frère m'avait tuée dans le pré de Haiegré

Pour trois grain' de pimprenelle
Que j'avais trouvées, que j'avais trouvées.

> My mother, my mother, you are holding me in your mouth
> By your hands that are so gentle.
> My little brother had killed me in the field of Haiegré
> For three pimpernel seeds
> That I had found, that I had found.

Bourreau, bourreau, tu me tiens dans ta bouche
Par tes mains qui sont farouches.
Tu m'avais tuée dans le pré de Haiegré
Pour trois grain' de pimprenelle
Que j'avais trouvées, que j'avais trouvées.

> Murderer, murderer, you are holding me in your mouth
> By your hands that are so violent.
> You have killed me in the field of Haiegré
> For three pimpernel seeds
> That I had found, that I had found.

—From Helen Creighton, *La Fleur du Rosier:*
Acadian Folk Songs/Chansons folkloriques d'Acadie.

40. John Simpleton

AS TOLD BY LAURA MCNEIL, WEST PUBNICO, NOVA SCOTIA

JOHN SIMPLETON'S MOTHER sent him to the store to get a three-legged iron pot. He started carrying it home but it got so heavy that he set it down on the road. He took a little stick and then got into the pot and started to beat it and he said,

"You've got three feet and I've only got two. You can carry me home," and he beat it until it broke all to pieces.

When he got home his mother asked him where the pot was so he replied, "The pot had three feet and I only had two and so I got into it and beat it until it broke." Then she said,

"Poor Simpleton, poor Simpleton (*Or, "Poor fool, you were*

born a fool and you will die a fool"), why didn't you put it in a load of hay that would be going along the road?" So he said,

"Another time I'll know better." So another time she sent him for some needles. He went to the store and he got the needles and there was a load of hay coming along so he stuck them in the hay. When he got home his mother asked him where the needles were and he said,

"I put them in the load of hay and then couldn't find them." She said,

"Poor Simpleton, poor Simpleton, why didn't you stick them on your sleeve?" So he said next time he'd know better.

Next she sent him to the store for butter, so he got it and he spread it all over his sleeve. *(In another version he took the butter to soften the cracks in the road, and he used all the butter up to mend the cracks.)* When he got back and his mother asked him where the butter was he said,

"I spread it all over my sleeve and it's gone." She said, "Poor Simpleton, poor Simpleton."

The next thing she sent him for was a pumpkin, and when he said he couldn't bring that home his mother said,

"Why didn't you roll it down the hill?" So when he was sent next for a churn he got into it and rolled himself down the hill inside the churn and thought he was going to be killed.

The girls were afraid of him and his mother said to get a girl he should make a wink of the eyes. So he went and he pulled out the eyes from sheep and threw them at the girls and scared them all away. After that they were going to have a wedding in their house for his brother John the Wise. His mother made a lot of pies and she put them on the cellar floor for the wedding. When the wedding came they wanted some wine and they sent John Simpleton to get it. He had on a pair of new shoes and he was very proud of them. His mother told him to go down the cellar and get the wine, but to keep his shoes clean. When he saw the pies he thought it would be better if he stepped on them instead of the floor, and of course his shoes were covered with the pies.

Later his mother was sick and John the Wise got the doctor.

The doctor said she would have to have her feet soaked in hot water. After he was gone, John the Wise got a tub and got his mother's shoes off and told John Simpleton to get some warm water. So John Simpleton came with boiling water and poured it over her feet and legs so that she died. John Wise said,

"What have you done? What have you done? You have killed our mother. Now we will have to run away because the law will take us. I'll take the money and you will pull the door to." John Simpleton pulled the door right off its hinges and started running with the door on his back. John (Simpleton) said,

"Well, you told me to pull the door and here it is."

They ran into the woods and they saw some suspicious looking robbers coming so they climbed a tree, John Simpleton still carrying the door on his back. The robbers came under the tree and started to eat their dinner. By and by the door got too heavy and when John the Wise saw that it was slipping he tried to keep it from falling. But John Simpleton let it fall from limb to limb and it fell on top of the man's head. He was eating and it cut his tongue. They were frightened then, and the man with the bitten tongue tried to say,

"I bit my tongue, I bit my tongue," but because his tongue was bitten he couldn't speak plainly and what they heard in the tree sounded like, "Let's go to Ireland." So after the robbers went away, the two brothers went to Ireland.

[Types 1006 Casting Eyes, 1013 Bathing or Warming Grandmother, 1291A Three-Legged Pot Sent to Walk Home, 1291B Filling Cracks with Butter, and 1653 The Robbers Under the Tree; Motifs J1805.1. Similar sounding words mistaken for each other, J2129.4. Fool sticks needle in hay wagon, K866. Fatal game: rolling down hill on barrel, and K335.1.1.1. Door falls on robbers from tree; related to Type 1696 "What Should I Have Said (Done)?"]

HELEN CREIGHTON: When the robber said he had bitten his tongue, the storyteller tried to speak as though her own tongue had been bitten, much to the delight of the children.

41. Uncle John and Aunt Betsy

AS TOLD BY AUGUSTA D'ENTREMONT, WEST PUBNICO, N.S.

ONCE UPON A TIME there was a boy who lived in the city, and he had an uncle and aunt living in the country, Uncle John and Aunt Betsy. So this boy was visiting them quite often in the country, and he was inviting them to go and visit him in the city.

"Oh," they say to this boy, "we can't go for we would be too nervous in the city. There's lots of houses that are burning, and there's fire very often, and we can't go," and the boy said,

"Oh you must come some time and visit me in the city. It's nice to live in a city," he was saying to them.

So one day this boy had a whole crowd invited for a party that night, and Uncle John and Aunt Betsy hadn't let him know they were going that day. The first thing the boy saw was Uncle John and Aunt Betsy coming with a trunk tied with rope and each one carrying an end. The boy was nice, and Uncle John and Aunt Betsy didn't know any style at all. So when they came to the house the boy said,

"You ought to have let me know before. I would have sent a team to get you."

"Well," he thought, "tonight what am I going to do?" He said when it came 'round to the evening,

"You can go to bed early tonight for I have invited a crowd to spend the evening with me. You are tired and you will go to bed early." They says yes, and they went upstairs and took the trunk with them and went to bed upstairs with the trunk. Later in the evening the crowd arrived and they said,

"We must have some music now and singing," and they started to play and sing. The song they sang was "Scotland's Burning." Next they hear upstairs, "Fire, fire, pour on water." They were still singing.

My, Uncle John and Aunt Betsy thought the house was on fire. They were so scared of the fire, and this is what they heard.

They were so frightened they hadn't time to dress themselves. They took the trunk and came halfway to the stairs with it. The boy heard them coming. He went to the stairs and he said,

"What are you doing?" They said,

"We heard the house was on fire. We heard, 'Fire, fire, pour on water.'" The boy said,

"Go to bed again; it's only the crowd who were singing. There's no fire around here. Go to bed and sleep." So they went to bed again.

The crowd enjoyed themselves fine all the evening. The next morning when they came downstairs, Uncle John and Aunt Betsy, they say,

"This is the first time we have been visiting in the city, and it will be the last time." The boy said,

"They were only singing." So they took their trunk between them and they went back to their home in the country.

[Motif J1849. Inappropriate action from misunderstanding—miscellaneous; related to Type 112 Country Mouse Visits Town Mouse] *Collected August 10, 1948.*

EDITORS' NOTE: "Scotland's Burning" is an old children's round. Here it is as collected by Helen Creighton from Mrs. Katherine Gallagher, Chebucto Head Lighthouse.

> Scotland's burning, Scotland's burning
> Look out, look out
> Fire, fire, fire, fire
> Pour on water, pour on water.

42. The Mouse with the Long Tail (Souris a grand t'cheu)

AS TOLD BY LAURA MCNEIL, WEST PUBNICO, NOVA SCOTIA

A CAT HIRED A MOUSE to spin her yarn and she said, "If you haven't finished by tonight I'll cut your long tail off." When night came the mouse who had spun all day hadn't finished, so the cat said,

"I'm going to cut your long tail." So she cut the tail and the mouse started to wail,

"Give me back my long tail, give me back my long tail, give me back my long tail," and the cat said,

"I shan't give you back your tail unless you give me some milk," so the mouse went to the cow and said,

"Cow, cow, cow, give me some milk so I can give it to the cat and the cat will give me back my tail," but the cow said,

"I won't give you any milk unless you get me some hay," so the mouse went to the barn and said,

"Barn, barn, barn, give me some hay so I can give it to the cow so the cow will give me milk to take to the cat so I can get my long tail back." The barn said,

"I won't give you any hay unless you unlock me," so the mouse went to the blacksmith to have a key made and she said,

"Blacksmith, blacksmith, blacksmith, give me a key so I can unlock the barn to get some hay to give the cow so the cow will give me milk to take to the cat so that the cat will give me back my long tail," and the blacksmith said,

"I won't give you a key unless you give me a feather *(quill)*," so the mouse went to the eagle and said,

"Eagle, eagle, eagle, give me a feather so that I can give it to the blacksmith so the blacksmith will make me a key so that I can unlock the barn so that the barn can give me hay for the cow so the cow will give me milk so I can give the milk to the cat and the cat will give me back my long tail," but the eagle said,

"I won't give you a feather until you give me a little pig," so the mouse went to the mother pig and she said,

"Sow, sow, sow, give me a little pig so I can give it to the eagle so that the eagle will give me a feather so that the blacksmith will give me a key so that I can unlock the barn so that the barn will give me hay so that the cow will give me milk for the cat and the cat will give me back my long tail," but the sow said,

"I won't give you a little pig unless you get me some potatoes," so the mouse went to the cellar and said,

"Cellar, cellar, cellar, give me some potatoes so I can give them to the sow so the sow will give me a little pig so I can give it to the eagle so the eagle will give me a feather for the blacksmith so the blacksmith will give me a key to unlock the barn and then the barn will give me hay for the cow and then the cow will give me milk for the cat and the cat will give me back my long tail," but the cellar said,

"I won't give you any potatoes unless you sweep me," so the mouse took a broom and swept the cellar. Then the cellar gave her potatoes. She gave the potatoes to the sow, the sow gave her a little pig and she gave the little pig to the eagle and the eagle gave her a feather and she gave the feather to the blacksmith and the blacksmith gave her a key and she unlocked the barn. The barn gave her some hay and she gave the hay to the cow. The cow gave her milk and she gave it to the cat. Then the cat gave her back her long tail.

[Type 2034 The Mouse Regains Its Tail]

HELEN CREIGHTON: Mrs. Laura McNeil was not sure whether it was a feather or a quill that the blacksmith asked for. It was from her father that she learned this tale, so it was not only from the women that these tales were handed down.

See "The Old Cat Spinning in the Oven" on page 45.

PART FIVE

Two Cape Breton
Storytellers...

Mrs. Lillian Crewe Walsh

HELEN CREIGHTON: Comical situations often turn up when one is collecting. So it was on my first visit to the home of Mrs. Walsh in Glace Bay. A native of Neil's Harbour near the eastern tip of Cape Breton Island, I was immediately taken with her accent. This, she said later, was her own dialect, a combination of her parents' Newfoundland speech and that of Neil (or Neil's) Harbour where she had grown up. This can be heard on reels 174A and B. I often kept people talking after recording their songs when their speech was particularly interesting.

My companion was Mrs. Ruth Metcalf, a widow whose husband had died of tuberculosis contracted in a Cape Breton mine. Rather than have her children grow up in this unhealthy atmosphere, she had moved to Ontario, had become a trained nurse, and had prospered. In her girlhood she had sat entranced when her seagoing father and his friends had sung and told tales in their Louisbourg and Gabarus homes. In the 'fifties when she heard me playing similar songs on CBC radio, she began a lengthy correspondence, culminating in a trip to her old surroundings. I was also planning a trip to Cape Breton at that time and thought what a help she could be to me in introducing me to her old friends while at the same time I could drive her to the places we both wished to visit. It was a good idea.

It happened that I had just received my first honourary degree and had decided it would help me professionally to use the title that went with it. But introducing me, Mrs. Walsh who was normally outgoing and friendly reacted by becoming shy and reserved. A few anecdotes and songs "worded off" were the most we got that day, and she insisted she couldn't sing.

There was so much about Mrs. Walsh's character that shone in her face that I felt she was more in awe of my companion than of me, Mrs. Metcalf having enjoyed such success in Ontario. I felt she was stalling and we agreed that I should return alone in the morning. She sang readily and was delighted to have her songs and tales recorded. It was not surprising to learn that she wrote homespun verses on subjects of topical interest. Like Mrs. Caroline Murphy in this volume, they were sprinkled with humour with never a hint of malice.

43. Dicky Melbourne

AS TOLD BY LILLIAN CREWE WALSH, GLACE BAY AND NEIL'S HARBOUR, NOVA SCOTIA

WHEN I WAS A LITTLE GIRL I used to like to listen to Jimmy Carroll telling stories, especially this one:

Once upon a time, not in my time nor in your time, there lived a little man named Dicky Melbourne. Dicky was a good worker and did all he could for his pretty wife whom he loved dearly. One day when Dicky went home she was in bed crying.

"My dear, what's the matter?" cried Dicky. "Are you sick?"

"Oh yes, my darling. Whatever will you do when I am gone? The doctor says only a bottle of water from Absolem will cure me. Oh dear, oh dear, what shall we do?"

"Do not cry," says Dicky. "I shall go to fair Absolem and get the water and you will be better. I shall get the water or die in the attempt. I would not live without you."

Now in fair Absolem were all manner of wild beasts, and it was certain death to venture in the forest where the famous waters were, but next morning at daylight Dicky kissed his wife who begged him to stay home, and taking a large bottle, set out on his journey. He had not gone far when he met an old friend, Paddy the pedlar.

"Hi there," he called to Dicky, "where be ye goin' so early?" Dicky told him.

"My wife is sick and only a bottle of water from fair Absolem will cure her. I'm going to fetch it."

"Now then," says Paddy, "get up and away. I shall put thee in the light of a few things. When you're at work the parson goes courtin' your wife. Yes, she does. This is a plot to get rid of thee."

"Oh no," cried Dicky, "my sweet wife loves me. 'Deed she do."

"Now, now," says Paddy, "you listen to me. You're my friend. We shall stay here. I'll drive the horse and wagon in the woods and we shall hide by the side of the road. If we see the parson comin' we shall know he is going towards your house. If he does, we shall make our plans and if I have told thee wrong, I shall go to fair Absolem for the water myself."

Sure enough, two hours later the parson went gayly by towards Dicky's house.

"Now then," said Paddy, "we shall wait until dark. Then I'll dip the old knapsack in the river and tie thee up in it, and I'll drive up to your place and we shall see what's goin' on. Yes we shall."

Dicky agreed and when they got to Dicky's place Paddy got out and knocked at the door.

"I saw your light, Mrs. Melbourne, and knowing how kind-hearted you are, I thought you might let me dry my knapsack by your fire. I had the misfortune, I did, to get it wet in the river."

"Come right in, Paddy. Come right in. We're just havin' a little celebration. We'll be glad to have ye. Have a glass of beer, now won't ye?"

Paddy put the knapsack down and sat beside it and Dicky couldn't see, but he could hear what was going on.

"Now," said Mrs. Melbourne, "I shall sing a little song.

Little Dicky Melbourne a long journey had gone,
To fetch me some water from fair Absolem,
God grant him long journey, may he never return,

> And it's aye for a drop of more ale,
> It's aye for a drop of more ale.

"Now, parson, you must sing something."

"Well," he said, "preaching is more to my fancy but I'll try to do my best." He cleared his throat. *(The story-teller cleared hers in imitation of the parson.)*

> Little Dicky Melbourne, how little do you think
> I'm eatin' your vittals and drinking your drink,
> And if God spares my love I shall marry your wife
> And it's aye for a drop of more ale,
> It's aye for a drop of more ale.

"Now, Paddy, come on, me lad," he said.

"No, I can't," Paddy said. "I'll have to be on my way." He moved the knapsack in front of him as if he was ready to leave.

"Oh no," said Mrs. Melbourne, "here's another glass of beer. You can't go before you sing us something for our good celebration. Just a little fun, you know." Paddy took the beer and taking the knife out of his pocket and cutting the string on the old knapsack he sang:

> Little Dicky Melbourne, since you are so near,
> Out of my knapsack I'll have you appear,
> And if anyone offends you I shall stand to your back
> And it's aye for a drop of more ale,
> And it's aye for a drop of more ale.

The parson ran one way and Mrs. Melbourne ran into the bedroom and Dicky said, "Don't be frightened, it's only little Dicky Melbourne himself. We shall have another drink around and I'll sing my little song:

> Now Mr. Parson I will have you to know
> It's out of my house I will have you to go,
> As for you Mrs. Melbourne, next market day
> I shall sell you for two pence and a bundle of hay
> And it's aye for a drop of more ale. "

[Type 1360C Old Hildebrand] *Recorded July 1957.*

HELEN: Mrs. Walsh said the verses should be sung but she couldn't remember the tune. She says the story must be 150 years old.

Rory MacKinnon

HELEN CREIGHTON: I knew Lloyd MacInnis through radio and television in Sydney and Halifax. He was so interested in my research that he and his family joined me in a visit to a haunted house in Loch Lomond. Years later when visiting Cape Breton he heard of a man who told a long story of his encounter with the devil so he drove further north to the village known as Sugar Loaf and was fascinated with what he heard. Mr. MacKinnon had told the story in the first person, and may have told it that way so often that he thought it actually had happened to him. Lloyd called me on his return. Would I also go to Sugar Loaf and see what I thought of it, because it sounded more to him like a folk tale than a personal experience.

It was July 1961 that I set out for Sugar Loaf with the daughter of one of my early folk singers as companion. After taking the wrong road we had to drive over eight miles with scarcely a house in sight. We stopped at a neighbour's house and she was very kind. She said that Rory was at a camping ground playing his pipes for tourists, but would soon be back. She arranged to have him there in the morning. She said his wife was away and he never took anybody in his house, but we could use the schoolhouse as Lloyd MacInnis had done.

We arrived at 10:15 and Mrs. Gwynn got the key for the schoolhouse. Then Rory arrived, a man approaching sixty with a friendly face and kindly look. I told him I wanted him to set me straight on a story he had told Lloyd. He murmured something about money, but Mrs. Gwynn must have stopped that for he did everything he was asked and had a fine time doing it. After the devil story I'd come for, he told several more including one of fairies and buttermilk I had never heard before. It is in my book *Bluenose Magic*.

Then he got his bagpipes out and played them all out of tune. Or was it my ears that were at fault? Hearing them back he thought they were fine. Mrs. Gwynn sat with us for most of it, and Mr. MacKinnon also sat quietly and listened.

When we were leaving I found that he knew "Big Claus and Little Claus," "The Sword of Brightness," "Jack and the Beanstalk," and so on. Unfortunately we couldn't wait to hear them. I left him with four packages of cigarettes, and a copy of my *Folklore of Lunenburg County*. He couldn't read, but someone could do that for him. He seemed well pleased, and so were we.

Fifteen years later when working on this book I felt we should know more about this interesting man, so I enlisted the help of Ronald Caplan, editor of *Cape Breton's Magazine*. It is a folk publication, and by now he must know everybody in the northern part of the island. A cassette was the result, with an interview with Rory's daughter Hannah MacKinnon of Dingwall, Cape Breton. (Hannah told about Rory's story, "The Porridge Contest":)

"It was a boy and he had a contract with a giant to see who could eat the most porridge. (I can always think of this story.) He went to the giant's house. (He told it to me so often, and to us kids). They were eating porridge and what the little boy did I don't know. (He had a name for it but I don't know the name.) He made a pouch and he put it under his clothes and he had it up here some way (probably against his chest) and instead of eating his porridge he was putting it down this pouch some way, and they were eating and eating and eating this porridge and so this giant would say to him,

"'Have you got enough?'

"He'd say, 'No,' so they continued eating the porridge and after a while the giant got so full that he couldn't eat no more and he bursted open. Well anyway he (the boy) outsmarted the giant. He had this pouch eh, that he made under his clothes where he put his porridge down."

Like all Rory's stories, Hannah insisted he made it up. This is understandable. My father and I used to sing a hymn together and for years I thought we had composed it. The expression "eh" in the story after the word pouch is frequently used in Cape Breton. His story of the porridge-eating contest is new to me.

Hannah told of the many times children gathered around him, either on the kitchen couch where they sprawled all over him, or on the floor. All of them probably, like Hannah, thought he made them up as he went along, and she couldn't believe it when Mr. Caplan could fill in parts she had forgotten which he had learned from my collection. Where had Rory learned his stories? Hannah didn't know and to her it was a mystery that an illiterate man could know so much. She told how he had made his own bagpipes using apple wood for the flute, and killing a sheep to make the bag, and this she kept repeating all through the interview. He told his stories for entertainment, to make people happy and people of all ages came to hear him. None but a good father and friend could merit such veneration, and no doubt all of his fifteen children felt the same.

44. Gift of the Fairies
AS TOLD BY RORY MACKINNON, SUGAR LOAF, N.S.

THEY'D GIVE YOU LUCK, you know. The fairies. They say that, time long ago, they'd give you luck.

There was one fellow. One time he was cutting a stick of wood, and there were hills among the woods, you know. You could see smoke at the hills long ago. And they knocked down a big tree *(and it)* struck on top of *(one of)* these big hills in the woods, you know. *(The hills were)* built of clay. They heard underneath the ground, "Oh dear, my head," he says, "my head is hurted."

Well now, the tree struck the hill, they said. "Oh dear," he says, "my head is hurted." After a little while, out came a fairy with a wooden dish full of buttermilk.

One fellow asked first—we were cutting wood—"I wished I had a drink of buttermilk," you know, in this place where they were cutting. After a while—there were two of them cutting—after a while, this fellow come out, this fairy says, "Do you want a drink? Here's the buttermilk you were talking about."

And the fellow (who) wished (he) had the buttermilk, he wouldn't drink it. But the other fellow drunk all he could of it.

And the fellow (who) didn't drink the buttermilk never had any luck afterwards. And the fellow drunk the buttermilk, he had luck all long as you live.

Question from Helen Creighton: Is that so?

He was happy in the world.

Another woman: Isn't that good?

And the fellow didn't want the buttermilk, he didn't drink it. He falled back.

[Type 503 The Gifts of the Little People; Motif F211. Fairyland under hollow knoll]

45. Rory's Dream of Hell

AS TOLD BY RORY MACKINNON, SUGAR LOAF, N.S.

WELL, ONE TIME LONG AGO, just about I 'spose twenty-eight years ago, maybe more, my brother died. His name was Donald. He was dead just a month. I seen him coming to me.

"Hello, Rory." I took a look, and the clothes that went on him—I put the clothes on him—and they was full of burnt spots. I said,

"Where you were this length of time?"

"Oh," he says, "I was in hell for one month, I got out. I'm free now. I'm in heaven now.

"Well," he says, "do you want to see hell?"

"Well," I says, "I don't know if I'm going to see hell or not." I says, "I don't want to go to hell, to see hell, I'd be burnt."

"No," he says, "you'd never find the heat, and you'd see lots of people from your own country there that is in hell."

"All right." I went with him, so we started walking, going here and there and after a little while we *(followed)* a big rough road. I see the sparks of fire, and the big mountain of fire, and a big fence around hell and every rod of iron was five feet deep. Well then, I went in, me and Donelly, and there was a big field of ice, an ocean of ice, and there were about a million women froze down in the ice. One was trying to work her head back and forth; her hair was froze to the ice. I went and cut her hair out of the ice.

"Thank God," she says, "I've got my head, worked back and forth," she says, "I'm here now," she says, "fifty years, frozen in the ice. That's the punishment given to me when I died," she says, "right to the ice."

All right, we passed through, and there was a big boiler, a lake, boiling up, and there was a devil with a pitchfork, and everybody who had died, he would stick the pitchfork in and drive him—the fellow who had died to go to hell, he would put him in the lake. Just clipping up their toes like that in the lake, and the noise when they come up from the lake. Poor people.

Here in another place, here was Big John Fraser. He was living then alright. But here he was. Would it be the sweat pouring off him? Open a kind of door. Every man was bad enough, he'd open the door for him, Big Johnny.

"I don't think I know—this is a queer place for you to be," I said. "I know a bad man you were when you were up at the Lower End Cove jumping around and cursing, and this is your spot in hell." I told him. Told him right to his face, right in hell.

"Well," he says, "I'm here," he says, "for a lifetime."

"I know you are," I says. Well that was good enough. I went over to another place. Here was Donald McEachern in another place, putting fire underneath a big heater, with a poke. Poking the fire out and in. I told him,

"Donelly, you've got a bad job."

"Well," he says, "it's my job for a lifetime."

"I told you that," I says, "when you come over for the old bucket that is the place you were going to land, was in hell." I told him. "You was bad when you was up there at the Lower End Cove."

Well then my mother was dead for four years. Donelly told me, "Come over and see your mother, where she's at." Well she was laying down alongside a big heater, like that, and she was sweating herself with the heat, and there was a little girl, I'd say she was about four years old. When I went into the place she was, the little girl stand up on her—stand up and started talking to me. And I asked my mother,

"What took you here?"

"Well," she says, "I'm here in Hades to serve seven year, and when I've served the seven year," she says, "I'll get my freedom to get out." And I went—"I'd do anything to get you out of here." I pitied her where she was laying down there. I went over to the big devil was on a big chain. A big iron floor and a big chain rubbed his leg, and every link was about four or five inches through and a big horn from his forehead sticking out like that, going up in the air.

I says, "Look, Mister, you let go of that—do you know the woman you got in there?"

"I know her very well," he said. "That's your mother."

"Can you let her out?"

"No," he says, "I'm keeping her here," he says, "for three more years and I'm letting her clear," he says. "She'll get her freedom." I woke up. I was sleeping in a bed at home. That's the end of the story.

Question: How long ago was it that you dreamt it?

Answer: Oh, it was about twenty-three or -four years.

[Motif F81. Descent to lower world of dead (Hell, Hades); compare with Dante's *Inferno*] *Collected August 1961.*

46. Rory Rids Himself of a Devil

AS TOLD BY RORY MACKINNON, SUGAR LOAF, N.S.

WELL NOW, MAINDAY WAKEY WAS FISHING up at the Lowland Cove, and I used to stay in a shack, you know, alone. I used to stay over at the lighthouse. I left Meat Cove about—oh about four o'clock. I went up to the Lowland Cove and I went down the shore and I got some wood and I put on a fire. I had an old Waterloo stove. Well, after supper I lay down in the bunk. Well after about, about nine o'clock there was a man came in. He was all burnt and all full of splashes, burnt spots, and I knew him. I said,

"Mister, what's taking you up here?"

"Oh," he said, "I'm coming here," he said, "I died ten years ago."

"I know you did," I says. "I know. I know you. And what's taking you here?"

He says, "It's the devil," he says, "now." I had the big water-filled stove, you know, and a big fire in it. He opened the damper and he put his head in the coals, then he started, you know, breathing the coals up in his nose and his mouth. I says,

"What's taking you there? You'll be burnt."

"No," he says, "this is too warm for me *(cool ?),*" he says. I says,

"You better get out; this is no place for you."

"You are not the man that can put me out," he says. "The next mortal."

I didn't know what to do then. In the shack I owned then, you know, there was no rafter, only beams. I climbed up the beams and got the gun. I had an old gun.

"Oh," he says, "that gun'll do you no good," he says, "not a bit. You needn't fire at me," he said, "it'll do you no good."

I said, "Get out."

"I'm not going out," he said. "I'm staying here."

I said, "I'll put you out after a little while," and I had an old

Bible up on the place at the left. I took the old Bible; I started to open it out, open it out, and I called God, his name, and I clapped the Bible together like that, and Mister, boy, went out and took the door with him. And that was the end, and I walked down to Dave Wakey's, and poor Dave said, "What took you down here?" And I said,

"If you seen what I seen boy, you wouldn't stay up there." And to this day I never stayed a night there any more, and that's the end of that story.

[Motif G303.16.2. Devil's power over one avoided by prayer] *Recorded August 1961.*

EDITORS' NOTE: The stories continued. Helen asked Rory, "You have a long story?" And Rory said, "Yeah, about Jack the Lantern. You ever heard tell about Jack the Lantern, Ellie?" And another woman there said, "No." And Rory told the story.

47. The Jack the Lantern

AS TOLD BY RORY MACKINNON, SUGAR LOAF, N.S.

LONG AGO. Well, there was one man once, you know he got married. Well he wasn't very good in the world anyway. And he wasn't all in the old New World, I suppose—it's about a thousand years back. Well, he said he wished the devil himself would come and give him some money, or something.

After a while, he seen a man walking up from the shore, up the road. "You wished for me," he say, he told Jack, "today?"

I says, "Yes." He said,

"And you go and look in your cash box behind your bed, and it's full of gold. And you've got to go with me at the end of the year," he said, "you've got to go."

I said, he would.

Well, that was good enough. He went, and one look in the cash box and here was lots of gold. Ah my! *(He's)* a-having a great time. Used to blacksmith, too, in his forge. He was just working the forge. Oh, he was getting along fine, and lots of money, and lots of everything to eat, and everything you want to live on.

But at the end of the year, Mr. Devil came. "You going with me today."

"Oh," he says, "I got to go home 'fore I'll go with you. See my wife and children."

"All right," he says, "come on."

—No, I'm a little astray with my story—

Oh, he came—ah just a little old man came to him to make a lot of work at the forge for him.

Helen Creighton: This was before the devil came back?

Before the devil came back. You know I made a bit of a mistake.

And he worked for him about a couple of days. Well he says, "Now look mister, what do you want? Three wishes or the money for the work?"

"I'll take the three wishes," he says. All right. Well he says, "When I'll tell a man straight to catch this hammer, and straight the handle—

> The hammer stick to the handle,
> And the handle stick to the block,
> And the block stick to the floor,
> And the floor sticks to the earth—
> And he couldn't move out of that."

"That's done for," he said, "that's good enough."

"Well, the next wish I want to do," he says, "when I get a man *(to)* sit down in my rocking chair at home, I can keep him there for—

> He will stick to the rocking chair,
> The rocking chair will stick to the floor,
> And the floor will stick to the earth,
> And here he couldn't move."

"That's right," he said.

"Well, the next wish I want," he says, "if I could get the devil to sit in a fifty-cent piece, I can carry him around for a lifetime in my pocket."

"That's done for you," he said.

I said, "All right."

Well, at the end of the year, Mr. Devil came. "You going with me today, Jack?"

"Yeah, I'm going with you today," he says, "but I got to go over to the forge." And *(he)* went to the forge. Well he told the old devil, "You beat out that piece of iron for me, 'til I get back from home." Well, that was all right. He start hammering. Well God! He give the hammer one blow with the iron,

> And didn't he stuck to the handle,
> And the handle stuck to the anvil,
> And the anvil stuck to the floor,
> And the floor stuck to the earth,
> And here he couldn't move.

And he was there, yes, for about a week hollering and screeching. And everybody was in the town was *that* scared, they would never come out of the doors of the house. When they'd had a little dark come up, they'd stay in the house—couldn't come out with the hollering and screeching.

Well, he come down where he was at. "Hello devil," he says.

"Hello," the devil says. "What do you took me, keeping me here?"

"Oh," he says, "I'm keeping you there. You got to give me another year before I let you clear."

"Sure," he says, "I'll give you another year. Let me out of here."

He says, "Go ahead."

He went out through the roof. Took half the roof with him. And they wanting—every day after that, they'd fix the hole, and when the night come, the morning *(the hole would be)* open, same as ever. Could never close the hole.

Oh, Mr. Old Jack was going around here and there, and another year come to an end. "Well," he *(the devil)* said, "Look"—at the end of the year, he came—"Well," he says, "look mister"—he was in his old store he had—"Come on with me today. You're not going to trick me today like you tricked me the other day."

"Ah no, I won't trick you at all," he said. "But," he says, "come on with me to home. I got to put on me clothes so I'll go with you."

"All right," he says, "I'll go with you."

He says, "Sit down on that chair."

> He sat down on the chair,
> He stuck to the chair,
> The chair stuck to the floor,
> And the floor stuck to the earth,
> And here he was, he couldn't move.
> Not a stir.

"You coming now?" he told the old devil.

"Not a smoke! I can't get out of here," he said, "I'm stuck!"

They all left the house—left him there screeching and hollering, and like his tongue was come out, oh, 'bout a foot from his mouth from hollering. No getting clear. But old Jack came in. "Well," he told him, Jack told him, "give me another year, I'll let you clear."

"All right," he says, "I'll give you another year."

"Go ahead," he said. He made one jump out through the loft and out through the roof he went. A nice house, and they closed the hole in the day, and the night would close in—would be open in the morning. Had to leave there.

Well, that was all right. Jack was getting old, you know, and running here and there, and having a good time. Drinking and having great fun. By God Almighty, look here! *(The devil)* came. "Well, you're not getting home today," he said, "you're going with me."

"I'll go with you," he said. They were going, walking down the road there in town, and there was a barroom.

"Well," he said, "I'd like to have a drink of rum. Getting thirsty."

"All right," he says.

"I got no money," he says. Jack told him, "They says all the time that the devil go in every kind of shape it is in the world. Will you go in a fifty-cent piece?" he told the devil.

"Yes," he said, "I'll go in a fifty-cent piece." He went in his fifty-cent piece.

(Jack) put it in his pocket, and he turned back for home. He was home for, ah yes, maybe fifty year. He would get to be an old man.

Well he says he want to—all his purse was getting heavier and getting big, and getting heavier and getting heavier. At last he couldn't hardly carry it. The devil was swelling up in his pocketbook.

He went, he got twelve or thirteen of the strongest men he could find. A big hammer apiece. They put them—he got them and he took them in the forge. And he went and he laid the pocketbook on top of the anvil and started hammering on it. They were hammering there, was about half a day. At last they cut a hole in the pocketbook. And the devil got out of the pocketbook. He jumped clear and he took the forge and everything in a big pond of water.

And no more he had of the devil.

Well anyway, he was getting old. He was always worrying his children. Always strayed away. And his wife died, and he was all alone. Well, he said to himself, he'd try to get to Hell, or else to Heaven. He started travelling. He was going, going there for a good many days, and at last he got to two branches of a road. One road was going east and the other was going west.

He took the road was going west, and it didn't go very far, anyway. He got at the gates of Heaven, anyway. Oh-oh—was an angel met him in the gate. "Don't come here," he said, "you're too bad to come in here. You can't get through over these gates. Go back where you came from. Won't let you in here." He drove him away.

Well, he said he'd go the other road. He went the other road. There he was going for a piece, the other branch going east. He went a few miles. They got it—a big, big wire fence. And he seen a man coming, limping. One elbow and one knee. "Argh, you whore's-son," he said, "don't come in here. Because," he says, "you remember the day you tricked me the three times? You pretty near killed me. At the last time, you hammered me all to pieces. You broke my leg, you broke my arm. But the idea I'll give you," he says, "I'll use a spark of fire. You're between Hell," he says, "and Heaven. And all over the world, every spark of fire you sees in the night, that's you. We'll call you Jack the Lantern."

And I never know more about it. That one, you can call a story!

[Type 330 The Smith Outwits the Devil]

48. Rory and the Shoes

AS TOLD BY RORY MACKINNON, SUGAR LOAF, N.S.

WELL, I WAS ONE TIME in Pleasant Bay, up about a good many years ago. I went to Cheticamp and we were storm-stayed there and I told my brother we would walk home. It was kinda late in the evening. While I was walkin' down, you know, the place they call Cape Rouge Island down a way, down at the lower place of Cheticamp, there was a man walked up from the beach, and was all full of kelp, seaweed and everything.

"Hello, Rory," he said.

"Hello," I told him. "How do you know me if I didn't know you?"

"Oh," he says, "I'm the devil," he says.

I said, "If you're the devil what's taking you here?"

"Well, I got a pair of shoes here, and now if you can wear them," he says, "until the end of the year, wear them out, I'll give you a fortune, but if you won't wear them out, it's the end of you."

"That's good enough. I'll take you. I'll take you."

"To hell," he says, "that's where I'm from."

"All right," I was a pretty smart man at that time, you know. I put those shoes on and I guess I was going faster before, but I was going faster now. I got down to Pleasant Bay. I was staying with my brother and my brother's wife asked me,

"Where you got them fancy shoes? Where you got them shoes?"

"I got them from the devil and I was supposed to wear them out at the end of the year. If I wouldn't wear the shoes out that would be the end of me."

"Well," she said, "you better burn them."

"No, I'm not going to burn them. I'm getting me a fortune from those shoes yet."

Well, I started jumpin' around here and there among the rocks and everything. Couldn't wear them out. The soles were getting thicker every day. "Well," I said, "that's going to be the end. The end of me this time. It's the end." There was a wrack *(wreck)* away at the upper end of Pleasant Bay, oh maybe two hundred years ago and a wrack come in. I took my wife and I went up along the bank and along the shore looking for ducks. Well, I see a little old man coming out of the woods, you know. He was about three or four feet tall. A long beard on him going down to the ground.

"Hello, Rory," he told me.

"Hello," I told him. I says, "Looka here, Mister, how did you know me and I don't know you?"

"Oh," he says, "many's the time I seen you over here. I was alongside of you but you couldn't see me, but you see me now. I've come here to do you a favour."

"What favour are you going to give me?"

"You look what's on your feet," he says. "The soles is getting thick. You got shoes there from the devil."

I says, "Yes, the soles they're getting thicker."

"Well, if you'll do what I tell you," he says, "I'll give you—you'll be a lucky man. You know what them shoes is made of? Human flesh. The more you walk in them, the thicker they'll get, but when you go home in the night," he says, "you go and fill them full of clay. Every night fill them full of clay." He says, "When a man will die," he says, "you'll go into clay and it'll pare away little by little. The flesh won't stand the clay."

That was all right. I went home and I filled the shoes full of clay. In the morning the sole was getting thin, and a week this time I only had the top of the shoes, all weared away.

The year was to an end. I was going down the road at Pleasant Bay, and, oh, there were about fifteen or twenty young fellows like myself, you know, jumping around and fooling and when the end of the year came I seen a streak of fire coming right out of the air. Here was old man Devil come right out of that.

"Rory, did you wear the shoes?"

I says, "Yes, I wore them out to the end."

"Mebbe you did."

I says, "I did. Here, look, there is your shoes all gone," I told him. "No more shoes. I wore them to nothing. Take them. I want my fortune now you told me when I'd give you the shoes."

"Well," he says, "all right," he says. "You wore the shoes. Here's your fortune," he says, "in the bag." I opened the bag and I hollared all the young fellers to come over and get some of the gold, you know. *(But)* do you know what I had in the bag? It was a whole bag of horse manure, and the old devil went one streak to hell. And that's the end of the story.

[Motifs G303.21.2. Devil's money becomes manure, M202.1. Promise to be fulfilled when iron shoes wear out, and M210. Bargain with devil] *Collected August 1961.*

Was it really the end of the story? Dr. Linda Degh from Hungary attended the Folklore Congress in Kiel, Germany, in 1959, the only delegate I could find there who had ever heard this story. She said it was much longer than the outline Lloyd MacInnis had given me and became more obscene as it progressed. Had Rory stopped because he thought the rest was too indelicate for my ears and Lloyd's, or was that all he ever knew? Why was it so widespread in Hungary and unknown in other countries? And how did it get to the village of Sugar Loaf and Rory MacKinnon? From a shipwrecked sailor perhaps? The little man described in the story was only one of many sailors wrecked along that shore. Rory described him as wearing big long fishing boots. That this was his ghost and he had been "drownded" there.

This next story was told by a taxi driver in Edmonton, Alberta, July 1962, while going from Summit Drive to the MacDonald Hotel. He had learned it in Hungary from his grandmother whom he described as a deeply religious woman who was always taking him to church from the time he was a small boy, and telling him stories. Noting his accent, and being aware of so many foreign accents in this city, I had asked where he had lived before coming to Canada and, finding that it was Hungary had mentioned that I had once taken down a folk tale ("Rory and the Devil's Shoes") that was not known to have been found in any country but Hungary and my province of Nova Scotia. At once he asked me to tell him the tale, and at its conclusion he said he knew one something like it, and the drive was just long enough for him to complete his story. Perhaps under less hurried circumstances it might have been longer.

49. The Devil and the Seeds
AS TOLD BY A TAXI DRIVER IN EDMONTON, ALBERTA

THERE WAS ONCE A MAN who was very poor, but one day he met the devil and made a bargain with him. This devil told him that he must make a choice, for he would either die that day or live for a year, but if he lived for a year he must be able by that time to answer the devil's question. He would come three times at the end of the year for his answer and if at the end of the third question he still couldn't give it, the devil would claim him for his own. The question had to do with a seed which he must plant, and when this plant grew he would have to tell its proper name.

The man accepted the bargain and planted the seed and it grew, but he had no idea what it was. As the year drew to a close he began to worry, but one day he met a wise old man who thought he might help him, but he said he would have to think about it. He told him that on the devil's first visit he should say it was too soon and he must go back and return the following day, so he did. But by the next day the wise old man still didn't have the answer. He therefore told the poor man to come to his house for the day. The devil wouldn't be able to find him there, and he would have to come back a third time. He did this, but on the third day the wise old man still didn't have an answer, but he knew a way to get it. He said to the poor man,

"Tomorrow you must cover yourself all over with honey and then empty the eiderdown from your bed so the feathers will stick to it. Then when the devil comes you must do a dance all around the plant, but don't touch it. The devil wants the seeds, and will be so afraid you'll kill the plant he'll tell you its name without thinking."

The poor man did as the wise old man advised and when the devil came he jumped all around the plant and the devil called out,

"Don't kill my tobacco plant." So the poor man had the name of the plant, and the devil paid over the money he had promised if he could answer his question.

[Type 812 The Devil's Riddle; related to Rumpelstilzchen-type tale, see Type 500 The Name of the Helper]

PART SIX

A Trip to Prince Edward Island...

Mr. and Mrs. Hector Richard

HELEN CREIGHTON: I had been collecting folklore in Nova Scotia
and New Brunswick for many years before I finally made my way to
Prince Edward Island. I had recorded songs in English and Gaelic in
the Charlottetown area, but in 1962 I thought the western counties
should be visited. Alberton had interesting singing games and comical
stories about local characters, and then one day I heard of a fair to
take place a few miles away. I hoped in this rural setting that I might
make some useful contacts. I had no sooner parked my car than a
small truck drove up and the pleasant-looking driver stepped out and
stood beside me. This seemed providential, so I immediately told her
why I was there. "My husband sings," she said, and the upshot of that
was that we drove at once to Tignish a few miles away and made an
appointment for the following Sunday afternoon. Mr. Richard was
equally personable and I anticipated our next meeting with pleasure.

The Richards' house was tiny and neat as a pin. Here they had
raised a large family and a happy household it must have been. Now
all had grown up and moved to homes of their own, but they often
dropped in for a visit. After my machine was set up and Mr. Richard
had sung a few songs and his wife had played a few tunes on the fiddle I rejoiced that everything was running so smoothly and that nobody had interrupted us, Sunday being a special day for country visiting. I might have know what would follow such a thought. Almost
immediately a car drove up with five young men who had been
drinking heavily. One was helped out of the car and into the house
where he sat on a sofa beside our host with his head resting on his
shoulder. What interested me was that no remark or apology was
made. I never knew whether this was a son of the house or a friend,

but immediately after this interruption singing was resumed. Unknown to Mr. Richard, the young man's snorts can be heard on the following recordings, although not recognizable as such unless you knew the circumstances. Was it a sense of loyalty that made them so protective? No fuss, just a dignified acceptance of the situation. The Island can be proud of them.

50. Before the Law: Story of a Mare

AS TOLD BY HECTOR RICHARD, TIGNISH, P.E.I.

ONCE UPON A TIME there was an old man and an old woman. They lived in the woods a long way from the village, and the fall of the year supplies were running low and they had to go to the village to get supplies and they had no horse, no way to go. The old woman said to the old man,

"You better go see the neighbour for his old mare," so he went and the old neighbour said,

"Yes, you can have my old mare." So the next day he took the old mare and he went to the village and he got the supplies. He got some grub, some flour, and some stuff, and he got some nails and supplies and he put everything into a bag and he put that onto the old mare's back. So he started home walkin' alongside the old mare. After a while he got tired and his feet was sore so he said,

"I think I get on the old mare's back," so he got on the old mare's back and he sat down on the bags and the old mare didn't seem to like that at first. By and by she started to walk a little faster. After a while she started to run, and by and by she started to gallop and jump and by and by she fall down and she break her neck.

Well, well, poor old mare she's dead. So he took his bag on

his back and he drug them home and he went to the neighbour and he told his neighbour.

"Well," the neighbour said, "you broke my old mare's neck. You'll have to pay for her." Poor old man. He went home and he told the old woman. The old woman said there was a pretty smart lawyer in the village there. "You should go and see him. I think he'll clear you." So the next day the old man went to town and he went to the lawyer's house, knocked on the door four times. "Mr. Lawyer home?" and by and by the woman come out.

"Mr. Law home?"

"No, Mr. Law's away."

"Too bad, too bad. I got a very nice thing to put on his hand."

"Yes? Well. Well sometimes," she said, "when Mr. Law's not home I take the thing on my hand myself."

"Well, if you want to take the thing on my hand I'll tell you. Now." Of course the woman she was in the door, the door was open a little bit and she was talkin' with the old man. He said,

"Now supposing you were an old mare." The old woman she pulled back and she started to shut the door.

"Don't move. Don't move. Supposing you were an old mare and I jump on *your* back.

"Oh," she shut the door then.

"Don't move. Don't move," and she opened the door a little bit. "I jump on *your* back and I scratch you with my bag. Oh, don't move," and she shut the door again. "I scratch you with my bag, and she began to run and jump and gallop and fall down and break *her* damn neck. What do you want to pay for that?"

[Type 1698G Misunderstood Words Lead to Comic Results; Motifs J1849. Inappropriate action from misunderstanding—miscellaneous, and J2450. Literal fool]

HELEN CREIGHTON: Mr. Richard takes off an older Frenchman who taught him the story years ago. This may be an Acadian tale.

There are many Acadians in this part of the Island. Since Mr.

and Mrs. Richard are of that stock, it is possible that his folk tale is of Acadian origin. All but one of his songs were sung in French, but for the popular "Evangeline" they sang together. The inclusion of the folk tale was their idea for they were anxious to contribute all they could remember.

When their supply was exhausted, Mrs. Richard slipped into the kitchen for a moment, and I could see that they had prepared for me to stay and share their evening meal. Simple good home cooking was very palatable in their spotlessly clean house. And what was their recompense? The satisfaction of having dispensed hospitality to a stranger.

51. The Scot and the Shepherdess
AS TOLD BY NORMAN MACLEOD, MURRAY RIVER, P.E.I.

WHEN I WAS A BOY and my mother finished her spinning she would tell me stories about fairies and sing songs. One story was about a man in Scotland who fell in love with a shepherdess and his father and mother put him in jail to see if they could cure him. There was class distinction in the old country and it was disgraceful to be low in class, and when this fellow fell in love with the shepherdess and went crazy after her the only thing his parent could do was to put him in jail. Her name was Beautiful Mary.

He was in a dungeon and he couldn't see the moon or the sun. She took the sun from the westward and the moon from the eastward, and he was afraid of losing his reason. He said to her,

"You took the eastern sky from me and the western sky?" He said when she would be walking that it took the heart out of him. He couldn't see anybody else.

[Motifs Q243.5. Punishment for consorting with one of lower class, and Q433.5. Imprisonment for attempted seduction] *Collected in August 1962.*

PART SEVEN

Around
New Brunswick...

Joseph McGrath

HELEN CREIGHTON: When Lord Beaverbrook suggested to Louise
Manny that she collect folk songs in his home town of Newcastle,
New Brunswick, he could not have made a better choice. Having run
her father's lumber business for many years, she was closely associated
with people in all walks of life. Therefore, when she asked me to act
as one of the judges at her first Folk Song Festival in 1958, she was
able to put me in touch with singers and storytellers I would never
have known otherwise. One of these was 88-year-old Joseph Mc-
Grath. He lived in a double house near the tracks with his married
son (and the son's) wife and baby, and in my diary I described them
as a happy family. They made us most welcome and the old man was
glad to talk.

I remember Mr. McGrath as a gentle, kindly man. His story of
Jean de Calais took twenty minutes to record but he said if he had told
it all it would take one and a half hours. In the middle of recording he
took a coughing spell and we were afraid we had asked too much of
him, but he took a swig of cough medicine and gallantly finished his
tale. They all listened intently while I played the whole story back.

It had been quiet while we recorded except for someone chopping wood outside, and a dripping tap in the house. The old man
made gestures while he told his tale and sat with his eyes either cast
down or tightly closed and he spoke in French, his mother's tongue.
His father was the only Irishman in a French parish. His son gave me
a brief summary in English, and that is what we have here. Basking
in the atmosphere of appreciation our visit had created, he volunteered to sing a love song for us to sing when we fell in love, and followed that with three ghost stories. Dr. Manny was so pleased with

the success of the afternoon that she slipped out and got ice cream cones for all. Whether he knew more long tales I never knew because he died before I was able to see him again.

52. Jean de Calais

AS TOLD BY JOSEPH MCGRATH, NEWCASTLE, N.B.

ON THE SEASIDE, in the North of Gaul, lived a rich man. He had a son called John. John had done well at school and, after a while, he surpassed his teachers. When he had finished his studies, his father asked what he wanted to do. He replied that he wanted to be a captain, to sail on the sea.

His father had a beautiful ship built, one of the most beautiful ships that was to be found in Europe, and he sent him to discover new land on the other side of the sea. After a few days on board ship, a wild storm came up and it took all his experience to save his ship and his crew. By and by the weather improved. When the weather had cleared, he was completely lost. He did not know where he was. When the weather cleared, he sent one of his men to the top of the mast to see if he could see islands, something, land. The sailor replied that he distinguished—he thought he could see land. "There," he said to the one who held the wheel, "follow that direction." As they came closer, the land loomed larger. When they arrived, it was Portugal. He moored his vessel at the quay, near the city of Portugal, right in front of the city of Portugal. He began to walk to see the construction of the city and the beautiful buildings. He arrived in a street where a man had died three days ago. The dogs licked the skin of his ears and face, everywhere.

Then came the king of Lisbon. He asked the king why, in a country where the laws appeared so wise, so just and the king so wise, there was no charitable institution to give burial to the poor. The king answered that he obeyed the laws and that, all those who died without paying their debts, were thrown to the dogs. After that, he said no more. When John was on his ship, he took some gold with him, he hired some men, then he paid the debt of the dead person, then he had him buried, he gave him burial all right.

He continued to walk in the city, then he returned to his ship. When he arrived at his ship, he found on the quay two young girls who were crying. He asked them the cause of their unhappiness. They did not tell him the reason, only that they were distressed. He invited them to come aboard and, without any further thought, he left. On the way, he found that one seemed to be a very refined young lady. The other one also was very refined. When they were halfway, he fell in love with the one—the first one of the two. He asked their names. She said:

"Allow me to keep that a secret to protect my life, suffice it to say that I am called Constance and my companion's name is Isabelle."

He promised he would not worry her anymore. Along the way, he asked how they had come to be in such distress. She said,

"I am a princess. I am Constance and my companion Isabelle is my cousin. I am the princess of Portugal. I was taken on a foreign ship. They took us to sea and kept us imprisoned. Then they arrived at this city where they wanted to buy some food before going further." He said, "I am going to hide you."

He hid them in a cabin on his ship and then he fell in love with Constance. When he arrived at his father's castle, in the North of Gaul, he went to the church where he married Constance, then he presented his new wife to his father. His father disapproved of the marriage, to marry a girl who had run away from a foreign ship, without knowing her character. He sent them away. They went first to a hotel, then he rented an apartment for him and his wife. She found the time long there.

His father had another ship built, much more beautiful than the first one. When the ship was ready to sail, he said:

"I am going to discover more land."

His wife stayed in the hotel. The old father thought that, if his son went out to sea, in the long absence he would forget the love he had for this girl. When the son was ready to go, she said:

"I have a favour to ask of you."

He said, "Yes?"

She said, "I want you to hire the best painter and have him paint my picture and that of my companion Isabelle on the poop of your ship. Then go straight to the castle of Lisbon. Then you will find out how much I love you and how much I'm going to do for you."

There, he made straight for Lisbon in Portugal. He turned his ship, the portrait facing the city. Everyone came to visit this lovely ship all trimmed in gold. They brought the news to the king that the most beautiful ship they had ever seen was in town. The king, listening to the wonderful tales, thought he should go to see the ship for himself. He went down to the ship and looked at the construction, but when he saw the two portraits on the poop, he recognized his princess. He called the captain, Jean de Calais, and said:

"Could you tell me how you met up with those two girls?"

He said, "I found those two girls when I was in the city for the first time. I ravished them from a foreign ship which had stolen them. That is two years ago and I married one of them."

He said, "Which one did you marry?"

"The lovelier one."

"What is her name?"

"Constance."

He said, "Do you love this Constance?"

He said, "Yes." He said, "Were I to lose all my riches, I would not want to lose my Constance."

"Well spoken. Do not be surprised, but this Constance whom you love so well, is a princess, my daughter, heir to this empire." He said, "Go and fetch her as quickly as possible."

This done, the king had a ship made ready to accompany the ship of Jean de Calais who was going to France to look for his wife. He put a man in charge who was called Don Juan *(pro-nounced in English)*. He was a follower of the king and had spoken of his love to Constance. And now he began to think up all sorts of plans to destroy Jean de Calais. He wanted to drown him or kill him so that he could have Constance for himself. A storm came, with waves and a wild sea. The wind blew hard, the waves nearly engulfed the ship. Jean de Calais used all his experience to save the vessel. All the time, Don Juan pretended to help him, but instead he pushed him, he fell—Jean de Calais fell. Jean de Calais was a good swimmer. He found enough flotsam of an old ship to save his life. He landed on an island which he called The Boot. There was not a soul on the island, only he. He walked, until he became afraid—he found his own footsteps. He looked everywhere, but there was no one. He was on that island for a year and a day. All the time he was dead tired. He began to be desperate: "I'll not see my dear Constance again, I'll not see my country again. I shall die on this island." At that moment he saw a man walking towards him. He stood up.

"Ah," he said, "I thought I was all alone, but no." He said, "You are a man who landed on this island the same way as I did."

"Ah!" he said, "you're all alone—you are still alone." He said, "Promise me half of what is most dear to you in the whole world and I'll get you off this island and I'll prevent the treachery of Don Juan."

Well, he did not know...he was...it was.... He promised.

"Good," he said, "lie down, sit down." He said, "Lie down, then sleep." He said, "When you wake up you will be in your own country."

He lay down. When he woke up, he was at the door of his father's castle. Don Juan was there, ready to marry the princess. He had taken the princess to Lisbon, and Don Juan was ready to marry the princess when Jean de Calais arrived. Jean de Calais recognized her and took her in his arms. And Don Juan.... He told them how he had been saved, brought from the desert island to the castle. Then the man came in.

He said, "Do you recognize him who saved you from the

desert island?" He said, "Promise me half of what you promised me."

Jean de Calais said: "Ask and you shall receive."

He said, "I want half of your son."

Jean de Calais took the three- or two-year old child by a leg and he took a long sword to cut the child in half.

He said, "Stop!" He said, "Do you remember the man—the body of a man in Lisbon whose flesh the dogs were eating?" He said, "You paid my debts, you had me buried, you had prayers said for me and when Don Juan threw you into the water, it was I who was the flotsam of the ship on which you drifted to the island. It was I who took care of you for a year and a day and," he said, "it was I who prevented the treachery of Don Juan and who led you into the arms of your wife and child...."

[Type 506 The Rescued Princess] *Recorded in August 1953.*

53. The Frog and the Ox

AS TOLD BY CHAS. ROBICHAUD, NEWCASTLE, N.B.

ONE DAY A FROG SAW AN OX which was walking in the meadow. He wanted to become just as big as the ox. He tried very hard to inflate his skin more and more and asked his companions if he began to approach the size of the ox. They said no. The frog tried again to make himself swell up more and more and he asked the other frogs if he were becoming similar in size to the ox. The frogs gave the same answer as the first time. The frog did not try anything else, he persisted. The last effort was such a violent one that he died on the spot.

[Type 277A The Frog Tries in Vain to Be as Big as the Ox]

William Ireland

HELEN CREIGHTON: It wasn't by chance that I went to the village of Elgin in southern New Brunswick, but by invitation. This was unusual in my experience, but Mr. Angelo Dornan had read of my research in a national magazine and wrote to say that he knew many songs and thought it would be a good idea if I recorded them. His stories were all related in folk songs. The village blacksmith was a friend and I expect Mr. Dornan's surprise was as great as mine when Mr. Ireland turned from songs to prose. He had "smithed" in Elgin and Saint John and had spent many winters in the lumber woods, a great place for the exchange of stories in the form of folk songs, and of tales.

Mr. Ireland was a big man, probably in his sixties. His family had come from Northern Ireland and, with the exception of one other blacksmith, they were farmers. No time had to be spent in getting him to sing. He was ready and waiting. (Although some love songs were in his repertoire, the subjects were more often tragic.) To sit opposite him when he sang one murder song after another was to make me wonder why such a gloomy subject was uppermost in his mind. There would be a softening of expression as he sang tenderly "The Braes of Belquether" later published in my book, *Folk Songs From Southern New Brunswick,* National Museum of Man, and on a flexidisc in the same volume. Many of his tunes were beautiful. Once a song or story was begun, he would look straight ahead.

Then one day he slapped his knee as he always did when beginning something new, caressed it while he spoke, and perhaps with a gleam in his eye and no other change of expression he began: "One day a man went in the woods and saw a friend hanging from a tree with a rope around his waist. He said, 'What are you doing up there with a rope around your waist?' The friend said, 'I'm trying to hang myself.' 'Then why don't you put the rope around your neck?' 'I tried that,' he said, 'but it kinda choked me.'" There was no loud guffaw from Mr. Ireland, just a quiet look of contentment that his joke had been well received.

Poor Mr. Ireland, it is good that he had these lighter moments to reflect upon. He had been a widower for some years and his roomy house lacked the touch of his kind wife's gentle hand. I would like to think our visit had left him with cheerful thoughts.

54. The Ox and the Mule
AS TOLD BY WILLIAM IRELAND, ELGIN, NEW BRUNSWICK

A FARMER HAD AN OX AND A MULE for a team. They used to work together. So one morning the ox said to the mule,

"I'm going to take the day off. When the old man comes out I'm going to be sick."

So when the old man came out to hitch them up the ox wouldn't get up, so the old fellow gave him a few kicks and then hitched up the mule. The poor mule had to plough by himself all day. That night when they came home the ox said to the mule,

"How did it go?" The mule said,

"Pretty hard. Hard work." So the ox said,

"Did the old man say anything about me?"

"Oh no. No, he didn't."

"Well, I'm going to take another day off. I'll be sick tomorrow too."

So the next morning the old man came out and the ox was lying down again and he went over and kicked him and tried to rouse him up and the ox wouldn't budge. So he took the mule out again and hitched him up and ploughed all day with just the mule. That night when they came home the ox asked the mule what kind of day he had and the mule said,

"Pretty hard work. A pretty hard day." So the ox said,

"Did the old man say anything about me?"

"No," he said, "but he didn't. But on the way home he had a long talk with the butcher." So the next day the ox was up and ready for work.

[Type 55 The Animals Build a Road (Dig Well); Motif Q321. Laziness punished] *Collected September 1955.*

55. Three Hunters and a Horse

AS TOLD BY WILLIAM IRELAND, ELGIN, NEW BRUNSWICK

THREE HUNTERS CAME to a farmer's place and stayed all night and started hunting in the morning. Two went ahead and the farmer called the third man back and said to him,

"You're going out to the field out there? There's an old white horse I want you to shoot."

He says, "O.K., I'll shoot him." So he caught up to his partners and thought he was going to have a little fun with them. As they passed the field where the white horse stood he said,

"It's a funny thing, you know. When I'm out hunting I get an urge to shoot something. I just get an urge to shoot it." He walked up to this field and he saw the white horse and up with his gun and dropped him.

The two partners said, "What did you do that for?"

"Well, when I see something I've just got to shoot it." The rest of the day the other fellows watched him pretty close. He wasn't left alone after that.

[Related to Motifs H584. Jokes about hunters, and K31. Shooting contest won by deception]

Wilmot MacDonald

EDITORS' NOTE: Helen Creighton did not leave an introduction to the stories she had collected from Wilmot MacDonald. She had a strong sense of respecting territory, and clearly felt that Wilmot was Louise Manny's "find," referring to him as "Louise Manny's informant." Although Manny had invited Helen to record Wilmot, there is no record of the session in Helen's diaries and we have found nothing in her papers, other than Wilmot's wonderful stories. As it happened, Helen published a book with Dr. Edward D. "Sandy" Ives called Eight Folktales from Miramichi, *a book of Wilmot MacDonald stories collected, individually, by Helen and Sandy. Here is Sandy Ives telling about the day he collected this story from Wilmot:*

SANDY IVES: Louise Manny had often written to me about Wilmot MacDonald, particularly of his singing of "Peter Emberly." Now, since I was in Newcastle for the first time (I somehow managed to arrive on Election Day!) she felt I should meet him, so she made arrangements for him to come to her house the next evening, June 11, 1957.

I was prepared for a small elderly man, but Wilmot was a big man and in the very prime of life. He was a bit subdued when we first met, but he was tired; he had been celebrating the election the night before and had put in a full day's work besides. But there we all were and he was supposed to sing for me. I started asking questions. Did he know this-and-that song? Did he know "Ben Deane"? He smiled. "That's a hard one," he said, "but I'll try her." And try her he did.

From the very first phrase, there was never any question about that voice's authority. It was a hard, piercing nasal that filled the room and carried all before it. And Wilmot's control of rhythm, his easy handling of subtle acceleration and retard would make a professional sick with envy. Obviously Joe Scott's great ballad was in excellent hands, or so it seemed to me, when suddenly Wilmot quit, shaking his head and laughing. "I just can't do it," he said. "No sir, it takes *rum* to sing a song like that!"

We were able to oblige with some White Star, and what that man did with the most of a tumbler of rum made my eyeballs snap. It turned the trick, though. He got back to "Ben Deane," finished it, and sang several more songs besides. After that he had another shot or two of rum (I joined him again), and we talked for a while. All was quite easy now, not because of the rum (though certainly it contributed) but because Wilmot was in charge, doing something for which he was not only well qualified but in which he was taking great delight. Soon Mrs. MacLean, Louise's housekeeper, asked for another song. Wilmot shook his head. Then it happened: "I'll tell you this story before I go home anyway. Now this is a giant story, you see. And it was a—a man had seven boys. Well, they grew up and...." On and on it went—the story of an unpromising young boy who married a king's daughter and then had to get the three gold hairs out of the giant's back.

56. Three Gold Hairs from the Giant's Back

AS TOLD BY WILMOT MACDONALD, NEWCASTLE, N.B.

WELL, THIS IS ANOTHER STORY about an old fella and he had three sons. So anyway one Sunday they was all sitting out along the verandah. So the old king was walking by and he said to the old man, he says, "Boys, you got three nice sons there."

"Yes," he says, "I have, and do you know," he says, "that I've got one son here is going to marry your daughter?"

He said, "Marry my daughter?"

"Yes," this old man said, "yes. Now he's leaving this afternoon, and I want you to make out—to write him a note telling him where he's going and what he has to do when he gets there, for he's going to marry your daughter."

Well the old king thought to himself, "I'll fix him." So he took out an envelope and a paper out of his pocket. So he just turned around and he wrote this on it, and he put on this note to "Behead this man as soon as he gets there," which means kill him. So he folded it and put it in the envelope and sealed it and give it to the young fellow.

And anyway the young fellow started. Well he never thought to open this letter or do anything like that, so he traveled all day, and night overtook him. He was traveling through a great long chunk of woods which was no houses on each side. So he come to an old wood road, and up that road there was a fire burning there and a man setting alongside of it, so it was some old kind of a tramp of some kind, that was hungry and cold and thought he'd put a fire on. So he sat there and he talked to this guy and the old tramp says to him, he says, "Where are you going?"

So he told him.

And he said, "Do you expect to get her?"

And he said, "Yes, I got the letter right here in my pocket stating that the king's going to give her up to me."

Well, that's all right. So the young fellow was tired after walking all day anyway, and he fell asleep, and when he was sleeping this old tramp went through his pockets. So he found this letter. So he opened the letter and he took the letter out and he seen what was on it, so he just took another piece of paper the same as it and wrote on it to marry this man whenever he gets there. So he folded this up, put it in the envelope, and wrote it so much like the old king that it was just the very exact same.

So the young fellow woke up and he said to him the next morning, "Well I'm awful sorry that we can't have nothing to eat, but we'll have to go."

So the tramp said, "All right, go on."

So anyway he got there that day and he went in and he made himself acquainted who he was and where he come from and he was talking to *(her mother)* and he handed her this letter. So the mother took this letter and she read it and she give *(it to)* her daughter and they looked at this young man and well, she said, "Mary, it's his handwriting and he must want you to get married."

So then they got ready and was away getting married when the old king come in. He said, "Where is that young fellow that come here?"

"Well," she said, "they're away getting married."

"I didn't put that on the letter, to marry!"

"Well," she said, "it's right on it."

"Well," he said, "if it is, he must have wrote it. I told them on the letter to kill him."

Well she went and got the letter and he looked at it. "Well it looks like my handwriting." So the old king wrote it again, and no matter how he wrote it, it was the same—*(no matter)* how bad he wrote it was the same anyway.

"Well," he said, "he ain't going to live with that girl. He'll do road work before he'll ever get that daughter." So when *(the young fella)* come home from being married *(the old king)* said, "Lookit, before you can sleep with that woman, or live with her, or I'll ever give you anything, you must go to this giant and get the three gold hairs out of his back. Bring them to me, and then you can have her."

So he started out for this old giant's outfit. So anyway he traveled that day and he went into a house to have his dinner. He told the guy where he was going and everything, and *(the guy)* says, "Do you ever expect for to get that?"

"Well," he said, "my life is no good anyway if I can't get her. My life is no good anyway. I married her and I can't live with her."

"Well now," he said, "if you do happen to get talking to *(the giant)* you ask him how it is that I got a tree out in my orchard that grows one kind of fruit on one side, a different kind of fruit on the other side." Well he said he would.

So anyway he traveled on and he went into a place to have his supper. He told him where he was going and everything when he was eating his supper.

"Well," *(the man)* said, "I hope you get them, but there never was a man that ever went to that old giant's house that ever come out."

"Well," he says, "I'm going to try her anyway."

"Well now," he says, "lookit. If you happen to get talking to him you ask him—" he says, "when I married my wife she was the prettiest woman that ever you seen in your life. Now she's so homely I can't live with her." Well he said he would. So he had two stories now to tell the giant.

Now the next place he come, he come to a river, like the Miramichi here, and there was no bridge, nor was there no ferry. You have to swim her out. So he sat there on the shore wondering, "How am I going to get across this river, and the giant's house is just on the other side?" So by and by there's a great ghost comes out of the water. So the ghost said to him, "Hop on."

He said, "You mean I gotta go over on your back?"

"Yes, I'm ferrying here." So he and the ghost, he swum him right over. So when they got to the other side he stopped and he asked him where he was going. He told him.

"Well now," he said, "you might get it, but if you do happen to get talking to him, ask him how it is that I got to ferry so many men across this river and get no thanks for it. Can't collect no money. Money's no good to me; I'm only a ghost."

Well, he said he would. So anyway he went up to the house and he knocked on the door and the giant's wife come, so he told her what he come for, for the three gold hairs, and he told her these three stories what those people told him.

"Well now, you know," she said, "my man eats boys like you, but you go in and you get under the bed and you curl up there and stay there, and I'll see what I can do tonight to help you out if you can't live with your wife."

"Well," he said, "all right." So anyway it wasn't long before the old giant come home, and he come in, and he got snuffing and smelling around, and he says, "Fee, fo, fi, fum, I smell the blood of an Englishman."

"No, you don't smell nothing like that at all," she says. "It's just this supper I got on cooking."

He said, "Maybe so."

So anyway she put the supper on the table and he sat down to eat it. Well, he eat a half a barrel of potatoes and about twenty pound of beef, and three or four loaves of bread, drunk nineteen cups of tea, and he rolled into bed. Well when he got into his bed this young fellow was pretty small in his boots then, so she done up the supper dishes and she thought she'd go to bed to see what she could do. So *(the giant)* he got sleeping anyway, snoring away, so she reached over and she jerked one of those hairs out of his back. So she just put it down behind the bed. The young fellow got it, put it in this little box.

And *(the giant)* he kinda woke him up. He says, "What's the matter with you tonight?"

"Oh giant," she says, "I can't sleep. I fell asleep and I dreamt that that man's got a fruit tree growing one kind of fruit on one side, a different kind on the other side."

"Well," he said, "if the darn fool would dig up that pot of gold that's under the tree, he'd grow fruit alike, and he'd have enough money to do him the rest of his life." So he got the answer of this story, which he got one hair.

Well she got *(the giant)* to sleep again and she jerks another one out. This time it made him pretty ugly. He turns around and he said, "What's the matter with you tonight?"

"Oh giant," she said, "I'm just dreaming about that fellow married that girl and she's so pretty. Now she's so homely he can't live with her."

He says, "If the darn fool wasn't so mean and stingy she'd be pretty enough." So he gets two hairs, two answers.

So the sad part is to come yet. Well she got him so nice and sound asleep again, and she pulled the third one. He jumped and he hit her a box, and she said, "Oh giant, don't kill me," she said. "I can't sleep. I'm twisting and turning and I'm dreaming about a man ferrying those men across the river and getting no thanks for it and can't collect no money."

He said, "If the darn fool—the next man he swims across the river—throw him off and drown him, and let him ferry in his place." So he got the three answers and the three hairs. Well he put those three hairs in the box, and when they got to sleep he got out that door, and good-morning boss when he struck hard footing! For he left her.

Well the first place he came was to the river. Now he couldn't tell the ghost this because he knew it was his death. He'd have to be the ferrier. So he sat down on the shore and he got talking to the ghost and he told him, "Lookit," he said, "I was so scared when he told me, that I forgot what he told me."

"Well," the ghost said, "never mind. Get on and I'll ferry you over."

So when he got back on his own side he sat back on the shore again and he said, "Lookit," he said. ""I'm going to set here and see can I think of what he told me." So the last of it he thought to himself, he made up a little plot now. He said, "Lookit, here's what he said. He told me to tell you the next man you have to ferry across this river going towards his house to bother him, to throw him off."

He said, "Thank you, that's just what I'll do."

So (the young fella) he got out of there. So he woke the other man up in the middle of the night and he got up and got him something to eat, and was so overjoyed, and he told him he got those three hairs, and he said, "Yes, I asked him and he told me."

"Well what did he say?" Well his wife was getting this lunch ready for him. "Well he told me to tell her if she wasn't so mean and stingy she'd be pretty enough." Well she got to heaving dishes and breaking windows and thrashing furniture in the house. The last of it she was so pretty they couldn't look at her. So she got his supper anyway and he got out of that.

It was just about breaking daylight the next morning when he lands at the man with the fruit tree. So he went in, had his breakfast with them, and (the man) asked him (about his tree).

"Well now," he said, "I'll tell you what he told me and you to do. He told me and you to go out and dig up the pot of gold was under that fruit tree and divide it, and each take shares of it, and you'd have enough money to do you the rest of your life." So out they went with picks and axes and they dug up this big iron pot of gold, which was a barrel of gold—so they each had a bag apiece. He had an old horse and express wagon there, this fella had, and he give the young fella this old horse and express wagon. "Never mind bringing it back," he said. "I don't need it no more. This is all the gold that me and me old woman wants."

So he takes this horse and express wagon with his bag of gold and he lands at the king's. Tied the horse at the gate and the old king come out and he takes his three gold hairs in and he give them *(to him)*. He says, "There they are."

Well the old king says to him, "What kind of a man is he?"

He says, "He's the nicest man that ever you met. He give me those three gold hairs out of his back which I could redeem your daughter." He said, "Come on out to the wagon. Here's a solid bag of gold *(he)* gimme. Gimme a horse and express wagon. Go ahead."

So the king said, "I wonder could I get any if I went."

He said, "Naturally. I'd be only too glad to drive you there."

So they takes the horse and wagon, and him and the old king drove just as tight as they could jump. He galloped the old horse all the way there. So they come right to the river. They never stopped for nothing till they got to the river. So the young fellow says, "You got to cross the river on the ghost's back."

So whenever the ghost got him off the halfway, he threw the king off and let him ferry in his place. So anyway I swung around and come back anyway, and I took the daughter and we went away and we built a house and we had this gold and we had a whale of a time.

[Types 461 Three Hairs from the Devil's Beard, and 930 The Prophecy; Motif K511. Uriah letter changed. Falsified letter of execution]

EDITORS' NOTE: Recorded by Helen Creighton at Louise Manny's home in Newcastle, New Brunswick, September 1960. The words in parentheses are from the version collected by Dr. Edward D. "Sandy" Ives, as published in *Eight Folktales from Miramichi.*

57. Christmas Story

AS TOLD BY WILMOT MACDONALD, NEWCASTLE, N.B.

O NE TIME THERE WAS A FELLA AND HIS WIFE and they lived in a little farm on the side of a road. So anyway, this day they was getting ready for Christmas—they didn't have no children, just him and her lived there all alone. So anyway Christmas Day he was out around the barn picking up the cattle and his wife was getting the dinner ready so he sees a fellow walking in the road. "Well now," he said to himself, "now God only knows how far that man has gone, or how far he's from home, or maybe he ain't got a friend." So he says to himself,

"I think I'll go out and I'll invite this man in." So he went out and he spoke to him and this fella spoke to him and he looked at him and he seen that there was something about this man that he didn't like, although he's a stranger and—"He's not doing nothing to me anyway, so I'll take him in, but if I had a knew he looked as bad-looking as what he did, I wouldn't a' come out. But I'll take him anyway." So he asked him how far he was.

"Oh," he said, he was a long ways from home. He said, "I tried to make home for Christmas but I didn't make her." Well he says,

"You better come in and have your Christmas dinner with me; it's all ready." So in they come; so he had a wash and they was watching him around the house anyway and he set in and they really had a good dinner. They give him a glass of wine, and, oh, he had a lovely time. So when he was leaving he said,

"Now lookit," he said, "a year from today I want you to

come and have your Christmas dinner with me."

"Well," he said, "I'll think it over. I don't know whether I'll be living next Christmas but," he says, "I'll think it over and if I can make her—" So he told him where it was and he said he'd be used all right. So anyway about three days before Christmas his wife said to him,

"John," she said, "do you mind last Christmas what you said you was going to do? Are you going to do that?"

"Well, Mary," he says, "I don't know." He says, "I don't want to go and leave you alone."

"Oh," she says, "I'll be all right." She said, "You can go." She said, "I'll be all right." So he went. So he landed right Christmas day at this old fella's house. So he met him in the door, he said to him, he said,

"Well," he said, "my man, I see you made her." He said, "Yes, right on time."

"Well," he said, "come right in and have your dinner." So he took him out into an old black shed and he set him down, and here was an old table there and not a thing on it at all, only some cabbage leaves and some turnip tops and potato peelings. He said, "Go right ahead and have your dinner." Well, my goodness, this fellow he looked at him. He said, "You'll either eat that or be killed." So he decided, "What in the name of goodness ever brought me to a place like this?" So he made out to himself,

"I s'pose I'll just have to make out that I'm eating some of this till I get out of here." So behold ye after he got *(done)*, he said, he come in, he says, "Are ye done?" He said, "Yes," he said, "that's a pretty nice Christmas dinner."

"Oh," he says, "it's all right; I don't care." Well he said, "Are you ready to go to bed?"

"No," he says, "I think I'll—"

"No," he says, "you'll have to stay all night." So he took him into a room and there was no winda in it and there was just the one door, and when they opened the door he just shoved him in and slammed the door. Now in this floor was just nails all sticking up through that floor about six inches apart that he couldn't sit down and he couldn't—all like just shoving his feet in through those spikes, and they was ground sharp. Well he thought to himself, "Well, what an awful thing I've got into now, to come in a place like this." See? So anyway he stood there about twenty minutes or a half an hour, and by and by the door opened. So there was a girl come in and she said,

"He ca'lates to kill you, but now he's gone, so come out and have your dinner." So the girl took him out and he had his dinner. "Now," she said, "you'll have to stay in there but," she said, "you don't go in there till he comes home and it'll only be a half an hour till he'll go to bed and I'll take you out of that again." So he done what she told him. She said, "Just do what I tell you now till I get you out of here." Well anyway, that night when the old fella put him in there after he decided that he'd eat those turnip tops for his supper again—it wasn't a very good feed—but anyway, she took him out and she put him in a bed and at five o'clock in the morning she come and she took him out and she put him in there, after she gives him his breakfast she put him in there. So anyway he come out and he opened the door and asked him what kind of a night did he put in. He said,

"What did I ever do," he said, "that's caused all this?" he says. "Why have you to kill me? I used you good." He says,

"There never was a man ever come here that ever left." See? "Well anyway," he says, "I'm going away today, and there's a barn over there and," he says, "it's full of hay, and," he says, "I want you to fork that hay out of the barn and," he says, "in the bottom of that mow on the floor there's a box, and in that box there's a ring in it, and you have that ring on your finger tonight when I come home or I'll kill you." Well, all right. When he went away he went out to fork this hay out. Well he figured, "It's got to be an awful pile of hay if I can't fork it out; I'm used to forking hay all me life." But when he threw out one forkful there was about ten come in his face, and the last of it the barn was so full that he couldn't move the fork, and the girl come in. She said,

"What did he say for you to do?" Well he told her. She said, "Give me the fork."

"God bless your soul," he says. "I'm a man, and if I can't fork it out, how can you fork it out?" and she said, "Never you mind; you give me the fork." So she took the fork from him and she just put a little bit of hay on the fork and she threw it out and she said,

"May the rest all follow." So that it all went out and left it clean, so he picked up the ring and put it on his—"Now," she said, "don't you give him that ring." She said, "He won't kill you. You put that ring on your finger, and you keep it, for," she said, "you might need it." So he put the ring on his finger. So, anyway, he come home, and he says to him, he says, "I see you got that ring on your finger." He said, "Yes." He said, "Give it to me." He said, "No," he says, "I'm going to keep it. I worked too hard for that ring." See? Well, he done the very same with him as what he done before. He thought he was starving him to death, but she was helping him out. So the next morning when he was going away, he said to him,

"Now you see that grey horse down in the field?" He said, "Yes." He said,

"Tonight you have that horse in the barn." He said,

"All right." So he went down about twelve or one o'clock to get the horse, so whenever he'd go up about four feet from the horse, the horse would jump and kick and he'd run clean to the other end of the field. Well then he'd walk to the other end of the field and the horse would do the very same and come back so that he couldn't catch the horse, so over come the girl. She said,

"What did he tell you to do?"

"To put this horse in the barn and," he says, "I can't get it done." She says,

"Give me the bridle." He says, "If I can't get the horse, how can you go?" She says, "But the horse is used to me." So she just went over and put the bridle on the horse and led it in the barn. So he come home and he said,

"I see you got the horse in the barn." He said,

"Yes. Oh," he said, "it's not too hard to catch. You know," he said, "I'm used to that," he said, "horses all me life," so he thought to himself, "I'll give him something he can't do."

Now down behind the house there was a little lake and it was full of water, and in the middle of this little lake, was about fifty feet off in the middle, there was a glass pole, and on that glass pole on the top of it, there was a bird's nest, and there was three eggs in the nest, and he told him to go down today and to have those three eggs when he come home. Now you couldn't climb that pole, and anyway, if you could, you couldn't get out to this pole because there was twelve feet of water in it. He was really cornered, so he was sitting down on the bank, and down the girl come. Well, she said,

"What did he tell you to do?" So he said. "Well," she said, "you couldn't bale it dry with a bucket." He said no. "Anyway you couldn't climb it if you went out." He said no. She said, "Give me the bucket," so he handed her the bucket. So she just dipped down in the lake and she took one bucket of water out of the lake and she threw it out on the land and she says, "May the rest all follow," so the lake was dry.

Now him and her walked out to the pole. "Now," she says, "how do you expect to climb the pole?" He says,

"I have no idea."

"Now," she said, "you go up to the woodshed, bring down the splitting block and an ax and," she said, "we'll get the eggs." Well, he went up and he got the big chopping block, and he got his ax, and down they come. "Well now," she said, "I'm going to tell you what to do, and then I can't speak. Now," she said, "for you to go up that pole I got ten fingers, five on each hand. You must chop them off, and as 'cording as you chop them off, put them on your hand and stick them on the pole and it'll make a foothold till you go up, and put the eggs, then take off the fingers when you come down, and stick them on where you took them off." "Well," he said, "all right, I'll lose me life before I'll— "

"No," she says, "it won't hurt. Now," she says, "you just do what I tell ye and you'll be all right." So he swung and he chopped them off, both hands. So as 'cording as he went up, he stuck them on, one on each side till he went up and he got his eggs, but the last finger that he put on, he forgot to take off, and he come down, and when he put them all on, this little finger was gone. No little finger to put on and they looked up, and here was this finger up at the top of the pole.

"Well now," she said, "we can't cut them off any more, but," she said, "we'll just tie this one up with a rag and let it go." See? So anyway, the old fella come home. "Now," she said, "lookit, just give him one egg. Tell him you broke the other two, for," she says, "you'll need them just as sure as the world. You'll need them eggs before you get out of here." Well all right. The old fella come home and he said, "Did you get them eggs?" He said, "Yes, I got them, but," he says, "I broke two of them and all I got is one."

"Well, let me see it." So he showed him the egg. "Yes," he said, "that was the egg. It was in that nest," so he said,

"How did you get it?"

"Well," he said, "I got it anyway," he said, "it wasn't too hard to get." See? So he went down to the little lake to see if he could see any evidence what, and he looked out and he seen the finger sticking on the top of the pole so he come in and he said to the daughter,

"You're the one that's helping him out." He said, "At sunrise in the morning youse is going to be both killed. Both of youse." So anyway, when he put him in on those spikes that night for to try to kill him anyway, she took him out, see, and the next morning when she put him in again she said,

"Here's a razor. You put this razor in your pocket and," she says, "keep it. You'll likely need it." So anyway, the next morning they was going to be killed. Around about six o'clock in the morning the door opened again and it was her. She says, "Come on." She says, "They're both asleep; right now is the time for to go, and we're both going." So they went out and they went in and they took his horse and the old woman's horse, which was nice driving horses, and they saddled them and they started.

Well when the old man got up, she was gone and he went to the barn and his nice little fancy team was gone. So they got their breakfast and they took two of those big woods horses, and they started to follow them. So anyway, that day twelve o'clock she looked back. She says, "John," she says, "they're coming, my dad and mom is coming." She said, "Give me that razor," so he handed her the razor. So she just opened it and she threw it off behind her horse and she said,

"May that turn into be the biggest mountain that ever was known in Canada, and on the top of it be as sharp as that razor." So around about three o'clock that afternoon they come right to the bottom of that big mountain and went right up, and when the mountain got so sharp on top they swung around and the old fellow got out and took a big rock and dulled the top of the mountain and they come over, and about five or six o'clock that evening they was coming up on them again. Well anyway he said,

"This time we've had it; they're coming."

"No no," she said. She said, "Give me that ring." So off with the ring, so she threw it off, back of her horse again. She said,

"May this turn into be the biggest lake," she says, "that's in Canada." So anyway, that caused that lake at the head of Black River, and they was caught soon there. That's where I lived, at that awful big lake there, you know, and that was it. Yah, so anyway, they was about just before dark they was coming. They come right to that lake and they swum right across that big lake and right up the other side and she looked back about eight o'clock that night and she says,

"They're coming and our horses is played out," she says, "and we got—we're just stuck," she said. "Let them come right up on us." They stopped anyway. She said, "We're not beat yet," she said. "They're not going to kill us yet." She says, "You take that egg and give me one. You've got two eggs there; that's what we brought them for. Now," she said, "I want you to fire that egg at the old man and kill him, for I'm going to kill me mother." See? But she said, "You cast the first egg; I don't even trust you." So the old man come up and his big sword was hanging from his side and he was just waving her back and forth, he was going to clip the head off the both of them and he made a big swing and drove the egg and it never hit the old man at all. It landed away over in the woods; never touched him. So she just tossed her egg and clipped the old woman in the side of the head and reached over and struck the old man on the shoulder and killed the both of them with one egg. She was an awful smart girl, that.

So anyway, behold ye we turn around and they started to travel. They took the four horses. They come into a town and they sold two horses, and then he told her (where he came from) and left his wife all alone.

"Well," she said, "there's no difference about that." She said, "We'll just go right home to your home." So they come to his home and they went in and he told the story what happened, and she said,

"I don't believe you. I believe you've had this girl out for about two weeks." He said,

"No," and lookit, when I left, he was living it up with two of them.

[Type 313 The Girl as Helper in the Hero's Flight] *Recorded September 1960.*

58. Bull Story

AS TOLD BY WILMOT MACDONALD, NEWCASTLE, N.B.

THIS GUY THAT I WAS GOING to tell you about, he was married and they had a little boy. But anyway, his mother took sick and she died. Well then he couldn't very well bring up that kid, for the kid was only about three or four years old, so he went to his uncle and he asked the uncle how much would he take a week and look after the baby, board it. So it was all in the family and it was only a small trifle that he wanted, and the old man said that he would bring all his clothes and when it got to school he would buy all his books and look after him, but he just wanted him for to board him and look after him. So he did.

But when this boy come to be about thirteen years old, the old uncle that he was staying with give him a little bull calf. So this calf growed up to be, oh, a great big animal. So it was around the barn; they had it there for breeding purposes and everything like that, and the young fellow was making quite a few dollars with it, but then, after the bull got so old they decided, oh the uncle said to him,

"We're going to sell the bull to the butcher." Well the young fellow didn't want that to happen, to get rid of his only little animal he had in the world, so he didn't want to part with that. Well, the uncle said,

"The bull is too big now, we got to get rid of it; we're going to sell it to the butcher." So anyway he thought pretty hard on this and he went out under an apple tree and he laid down and he fell asleep and he had a dream. So he dreamed that he went to the barn and he screwed off this horn off of the bull, and when he screwed off this horn off of the bull, the bull could talk. And there was everything in the bull's head that you would imagine. All kinds of clothes, and there was anything you wanted to eat in the bull's head, and the bull could talk. Well he woke up laughing to himself, which when he laid down he was crying about the bull being sold. So the bull could talk, so he went out an he give him a yank anyway. He said,

"I'm going to try her a yank." So when he tried her a yank she started to spin off and behold ye it was, everything was right. So he told the bull what was going to take place. Well the bull said,

"The only thing for you to do is when they're come, when the butcher comes for to buy me," he said, "you tell your uncle that when—the last time you're going to lead me out. You want to do the job, lead me out and," he says, "whenever my heels is clear of that barn door, you jump onto my back and that's the last they'll see of us."

Well he did so. The butcher come and the young fellow said to the old uncle, he said,

"Being as you're going to kill the bull, I want to lead him out for the last time." Well the uncle said, "All right." He was going to get this chunk of money and he just blabbered the young lad up that way. So anyway, away he went. So he just got clear of the barn, and when he jumped onto that bull's back he just roared to the old man. He said,

"Good morning, Boss," he says, "when we're straight hard putting." So they travelled all that day. So that night they come to a brook and they got off and the young fellow screwed the horn off of the bull and took this big tablecloth and spread it on the ground and he had anything you wanted to eat there, baked beans and everything. So he had a big feed of hot biscuit, and the bull after that he fed around and drunk water in the brook, and he fed along the side of the road, and the first thing this awful howling and roaring struck up in the woods. And anyway he said, the bull said to him, he says,

"I got to go to a bullfight tonight and," he says, "lookit, when I'm gone," he said, "if that brook runs clear of water all night, I'll be back in the morning, but if she runs muddy, you'll know I'm dead, and," he said, "you take my traces the next morning and you follow me and," he said, "when you come to me, and if I'm dead, you take a rib out of my right side, take a strip of skin from the bottom of my heart to the bottom of my tail and wear it as a belt, and no matter what you ask those things to do, for you, they'll do it."

So, the bull went. The young fellow laid down behind the fence and he slept there all night and he watched the brook and by and by the brook got all muddy and then it cleared up and it stayed clear all night. So the bull come back the next morning with just a little tear in his side from another bull's horn.

So he screwed his horn off anyway and spread the tablecloth out and they had their breakfast and had a big jattin' on to the bull's back and away again. So they travelled all the next day. So the next night they come to another brook and he had his supper. So this awful deathly roaring was in the woods again, so he told him the same story and what to do.

So when the bull was gone about an hour the brook got muddy and it stayed muddy the whole night. Well, he knew his friend was gone. So he took this track the next morning and he followed and he went into a big swamp where there was a big herd of wild animals, cattle and everything, and here was his bull dead. So he took his knife and he took this skin, what the bull told him to do, and this rib out of his right side. So he travelled anyway and he came into a town. So he went into a house anyway, and he got talking to a man and he had a great herd of horses, lovely horses. So this young fellow told him all about where he had come and what this old uncle had done to him and he didn't have too much money, and everything, so this old fellow said,

"Well, John, I can't do nothing for you," he says. "I can't keep you here but," he says, "I have a lot of horses and," he says, "I'll tell you what I'll do. I'll rig you all up and I'll give you a horse and a saddle and you start, and if you can get a job," he said, "keep this little horse and," he said, "when you ever get able, you send me so much money," which was only a mere trifle, about forty or fifty dollars for this outfit, and, he said, everything would be all right. Well, he said he would.

So he travelled and travelled with his horse day after day and day after day till he travelled to a place where there was a girl and she had done some bad crime and this old king was going to put her to death. So they took her down to the shore and they tied her, and there was a great fish that was going to come in from the sea for to kill her, eat her. So he found out about this girl. So anyway he said,

"I'm going to try to save her life."

"Well," this guy said, "if you can save her, you can have her for your wife." So he went down and he had a talk to the girl anyway and she asked him; she said she'd be only too glad. "I can get you," he said, "clear," he said, "if I can kill this fish. We don't know how big this fish is or anything like that, but we're going to try anyway." So he stood his horse there on the shore with the saddle and they took some pictures of him and her, and then there was another guy was kinda going with her see, but he couldn't save her life. So the old man thought an awful lot of this other fellow, see. But anyway, he sat down there talking to her and he said,

"When that fish is coming to you, you tell me when he's coming." So he sat there for a while, and by and by she says,

"That fish is coming; I can see it coming." So he up and he jumped on his horse and he waded out for to meet the fish which he couldn't wade out too far because he was down there at the head of Black River. The bog was awful deep, so anyway he waded out and the fish was coming, so when it come pretty handy to the shore he thought he'd try this rib. The bull told him what to say, those words, and he said,

"Rib rib about." Well, it just turned the fish over but it didn't kill him and he swum back down the river. So he came back in and she says,

"Did you kill him?"

"No, I only turned him."

"Well," she says, "I'm afraid."

"No," he says, "never mind." He says, "Never mind, we'll see what we can do next time he comes. You tell me when he's coming again." So he sat there and talked away to her and she said,

"He's coming again," so he went out again and he met his fish. So he was going to try this skin which he forgot, and he says,

"Rib rib about," again and he only turned the fish again and he swam back down the river. So anyway he come back in and he said,

"No," he said, "I didn't get him yet, but you tell me the next time he's coming; we're going to try him again this time and for all. This will be the final trip." So there were thousands to see this, all up on the bank now watching what this man was doing. So anyway he wasn't gone over three or four minutes till back he come. This time he's coming to get her for sure, so he went out and he just waited till he come up pretty handy and he took this skin from his side and he pulled her out a long whip like that and he said,

"Split him, belt." Well, it split that fish wide open, and when he come up he was ninety feet deep, seven hundred and fifty-five feet long, which was a nice trout. So anyway he come in and they took the pictures. Well then, down steps this other fella. Well, the girl is all right now. The fish is dead, and well, then they takes their pictures. They takes their pictures with this horse and the fella that saved her and the girl. Well, then this other, the old man her father, wanted this other fella and the horse and she said no. So they had quite a row about it, but anyway the young fellow said, he said he didn't mind saving the girl and he didn't care whether he had her for a wife, for he didn't have too much to keep her, anything like that, only just going through the country, but she said if she didn't get him she'd just as soon be dead anyway, see?

But anyway the girl was still tied with this awful chain. Well, he said to the other fella, he said, "If you can untie her and take her from this chain without hurting her," he says, "the only thing, you can have her for your wife." Well, then they run them all the crowd away; they couldn't do it. So he made them all get off of the whole shore and everything like that, and so he went out and he put his arms around her and he talked to her and he told her he was going to cut this chain from her legs with this belt. So he just roared to his belt for to, "Split him, belt chain," he said. Well, the links just flew off her, never hurt her at all, and him an her went up on the road and they went down in this place and that night about ten o'clock they was married, and I stayed around there and they had a couple of children when I left there. I stayed around there for a few years, you know, and I couldn't get hold of that belt though, or I'd done wonders with it. So there you go.

[Type 511A The Little Red Ox; Motifs H310. Suitor tests, and H331.15. Suitor contest: animal fight] *Recorded September 1960.* For John Obe Smith's telling of this tale, see page 28.

59. The Sword of Brightness

AS TOLD BY WILMOT MACDONALD, NEWCASTLE, N.B.

W ELL, ONE TIME THERE WAS AN OLD FELLA and
he had three sons and they grew up. The youngest boy was
twenty-one. Of course the other two was maybe twenty-eight
and the other fella thirty, and so on whatever. But the farm
wasn't divided. There was no one had any holt on the farm, so
the old man decided, he says, "Yez got to earn this farm. I'm going to give it to neither of yez, but youse must go," he says, "to
this *(old king and bring me back the Sword of Brightness)*."

There was an old king and he was very wealthy and he had
lots of money and he had three swords. But he had a sword of
silver, and *(the old man)* told them whatever son could bring back
this Sword of Brightness to him, which was three feet long, and
get it from the king, he'd get what the old man had. So they
started. The three of them started out.

Well, two fellas, the oldest two, they was kinda well-to-do
fellas and had been running around, and the youngest fella, he
hadn't been very popular anyway, and they said to him, "What's
the use of you coming? You can't come because you don't know
too much. You ain't got too much learning, and you'll never get
nothing from the old king."

Well the young son, the brother, said, "Well I'm going to
go. I'll stand just as good a chance as maybe you will." So they
traveled all day. In fact they didn't know where to go when they
started out *(or)* where this king was, but they just started out to
look for him.

So that night when night overtook them they come into a
town. Well, they were walking down the street and anyway there
was two hotels, one on each side of the street, and on the great
big sign on the hotel, on the door, it said, "Come in and be welcome; pay nothing." So the two oldest boys said, "That's the
place to stay; we ain't got to pay nothing." On the other side it
said, "Come in, be welcome; pay what you can." So the youngest

fella went in there. So when he went in, there was an old man sitting in a rocking chair, and the young fella spoke to him.

"Do you keep boarders here for the night?" he said.

"Yes."

"Well," he said, "it don't look much like a boarding house."

"Well," he said, "my help has all left me, but you're a young man. There's all kinds to eat here. Go ahead; go ahead and get her ready for me and you."

So the young fella he got the stove going and he makes a big feed for him and the old man and sat down and told him this transaction where he was going. "Well," *(the old man)* he says, "you have a good chance. You have a chance to do it providing you do what I'll advise you to do."

So they went to bed anyway, and next morning they got up and they got their breakfast and the young fella washed the dishes and swept up the floor and he said to the old man, "Well," he said, "how much do I owe you?"

"Oh no," he said, "you don't owe me nothing. You paid what you could. I'd have had a lonely night here all alone. I'm not able to get anything to eat, but you've paid what you could. But you ain't got to go yet. You're in lots of time. Take it easy. I want to tell you, you go out to the barn and there's a straw in the red cow's manger, a great big wheat straw. You bring that straw in here and give it to me. I want it."

So the young fellow went out and he looked in the cow's manger. Well naturally the biggest one was there and he just picked it up. Whatever the old man wanted it for he didn't know, so he took it in. So *(the old man)* he took the scissors and he clipped off eight inches of the straw. He says, "You put that straw in your pocket and it might come in handy."

So they stood and talked for a while and…the young fellow he said, "Well I better be going."

"Well now," he says, "listen. You're *(in)* lots of time," he says. "You go out to the barn and go in the hen's house and bring me an egg that the white hen laid last night," he says. "You might need that too."

So he brought the egg in and he give *(it to)* him, and the old fellow put it into a nice little box about the size of an egg and he give it to him. "Now," he said, "you might need that."

The young fella *(said)*, "I'll have to go. My brothers has gone."

(The old man) says, "It wouldn't make no difference about your brothers, where they're gone. They're not going no place anyway. So you're ready to go now? Well now listen. I'm going to tell you. Here's a little book. Now you put this book in your pocket and," he says, "when you're stuck and don't know what to do or where to go, open this book and it'll tell you what to do."

Well naturally when he got outside on the road and started to work he needed that book the worst in the world, because he just didn't know where to go. Well he opened the book and the book said, "Straddle your barley straw." Well naturally he didn't know how to straddle it, but he threw his leg over the barley straw, and when he did he was on a big grey horse's back going about forty mile an hour right in the road on the big horse, and he was sittin' there.

And first thing he come and he seen this place. And when the horse came up to it—before he got right handy to it—he opened the book and it said, "Put the barley straw in your pocket." So he put the barley straw in his pocket, and he was just walkin'.

Well, he come up to this place anyway, and here was six or seven soldiers all with guns, and they was around this building for fear anyone would steal *(these)* Swords of Brightness *(which)* was all hanging 'round the wall. And the book, he opened it again to read to see what he would do, and those soldiers never looked at him. They was leaning against the wall and they seemed to be all sound asleep, see? And it said to take the Sword of Brightness off the wall. "Don't put it in the gold scabbard, don't put it in the silver scabbard," he says to himself. "Oh I'll steal the silver scabbard."

So anyway when he picked up the silver scabbard these big chimes of bells just started rattling, and up come the soldiers and they was going to drive the bayonet in. A man got the old king and *(the young fella)* he told him there he come to see what he could do and he couldn't redeem his farm.

"Well now," the king said, "we're supposed to kill you. You're not supposed to get out of here but we'll give you one chance. The next tree from here on *(belongs)* to an old giant. He's got a tree with gold fruit on it, and if you can bring me back a gold fruit you can have the Sword of Brightness." So he figured that the old giant was going to kill him there, so it would just cause *(save?)* him the bother of not killing him, so he started for this tree.

Well, he opened his book and it said, "Straddle your barley straw." Well, he started, and he was going up a long mountain and he looked ahead and here was this giant silver tree. Oh, the fruit on it was just glittering for miles and miles, so when he come up he opened his book again and it said, "Put your barley straw in your pocket." Well, then he was down walking again.

So anyway he was down walking, and when he came up to the tree here was those two fiery dragons in the yard there just snorting steam right out of their nose. Lookit here, and he was scared to death, but he must get this fruit. So anyway whenever he touched the fruit on the tree those big giant bells they started to rattle again and oh they were going to murder him this time for sure. So he pleaded, and *(told them)* where he had come from and *(how)* he had got defeated on the other place where he couldn't get the Sword of Brightness and they sent him for this gold fruit from off the tree.

But they said, "There's only one way for you to get this fruit.... There's a girl up here on the mountain. She was chained there on the mountain. She was put up there. She come for the fruit too, and she was here yesterday, and we put her up there for to die, to starve to death, and you go up, and if you can get her off the mountain without her killing you now, you bring her back to us, and we'll give you the gold fruit." Well, he said he'd try it.

Well, he started up this mountain. So he traveled on his barley straw. Away he went again. So when he was coming up this long mountain he seen this place. He seen the crows and the ravens of all kinds flying over this girl and she was tied there *(to)* stay there to die. So he got off the horse. He put his barley straw in his pocket and he started to sneak up on her. Well then he thought to himself, "Now if I ever get there she's liable to—she'll likely scratch the eyes out of my head. She'll kill me anyway."

So he opened the book, and the book said to take the egg out of his pocket and break it and put the shell on his head and he could fly all over the mountain. So he said to himself he'd just break it and...see what happened anyway. So he turned into a little bird and he flew all over the mountain. And he flew down, and when he took this egg off his head again he was a man, and he pounced down and he grabbed her. Well he talked to her and he told her where he had come from and all like this, and boys, he got her untied and he took her back.

Well now, he started down the mountain, eh? So him and her got on the barley straw again, and they come with this big grey horse again just flying down off of the mountain, and they come to the fruit tree. So the old giant was so enjoyed about it and everything like that, he give him the gold fruit to take to the king.

So he straddled his barley straw, him and his girl again. He took the girl right with him, and he come to the fella with the Sword of Brightness. So he went in and he give him the gold fruit, and he told the old king where he had to go. He was so overjoyed he said, "Being as you wanted to steal the Sword of Brightness with the gold scabbard, we'll put it in the silver scabbard that mates it, and here's the lock, and here's the keys to lock it. No one can't get into this except you."

Well he put those keys in his pocket anyway, and him and the girl started on their barley straw again. Well he come back to about a mile from home, see, and they was awfully tired, so they got off their horse and they went over and they sat down on the side of the road. So he laid his head down on her lap and he fell asleep.

Along come the other two sons that never was no place, *(and they)* stole the girl from him, took the Sword of Brightness, and went home. So when the young fellow woke up, here he had nothing no more than *(when)* he started, see? Well all right. They tore that girl and they made her go. They gagged her and tied her and made her go. Well they had nothing and they told nothing.

So the old man, they walked right in *(to the old man)*, and took the girl in and they said they got the girl too, made up this great story to their father, and they wanted the farm...between them. And there was this Sword of Brightness. Well it was laying on the table. No one could get it out of the scabbard, see?

So when the young fellow wakes up he turns 'round and he starts home, and when he was coming by along the old man's property, she seen the young fellow coming, so the girl says, "There's the man that got me off the mountain."

"Oh no," this *(older)* fella said, "no."

She was telling the old man all the time, "Them boys was never on the mountain for me."

So when the young fella come, the old man says to them, "If you're the men that got this Sword of Brightness, why not take it out of the scabbard?"

And the young fella said, "They couldn't take it out of that, for I got the keys that unlock that. The king give it to me."

So he took the keys and he unlocked it and he pulled the Sword of Brightness right out of this scabbard, and he told all his transactions where he was and everything. So the other fellas, both sons, was put out and he got the farm, and when I left they had a family of three children.

[Type 550 Search for the Golden Bird] *Recorded September 1960.*

EDITORS' NOTE: The words in parentheses are taken from the version collected by Dr. Edward D. "Sandy" Ives, as published in *Eight Folktales from Miramichi.*

SANDY IVES: When Wilmot finished telling this story, he turned to my son and said, "Can you tell that story now, Steve?" Steve said no. "Well, now," said Wilmot, "I did after the man told it to me. I told it to the next fellow." He said he had heard the story only once, and that was back in the 'thirties on the spring drive on Jewett Brook. "There was a fella there—he was a sailor, a sailor on a boat. He said he sailed on a boat for about, he told me, eleven years. But maybe not, but it was a good story anyway.... Dan the Sailor we called him. Well that man would just sit there and he'd rattle and tell those stories. And when he told them, I got them."

—from *Eight Folktales from Miramichi*

60. John the Cobbler

AS TOLD BY WILMOT MACDONALD, NEWCASTLE, N.B.

THIS STORY IS TOLD ABOUT A MAN and he had one son. Well this son grew up and he give him a pretty good education and his father was a cobbler. You know what a cobbler is? So after the boy got his schooling—he went to about grade nine—so anyway he took him in his shop and he learned him to be a cobbler. Well the young fellow was a better cobbler than his father then. So anyway, he turned out to be pretty bad. He got to work drinking and playing cards and running around, so one day there was an old witch come to the house, so the old man asked the witch would she tell the boy's fortune. He said the boy wasn't very good now, which he was an awful good boy at one time, but he was pretty rough now. So she told his fortune, and she told him he was going to be in great trouble; he was going to be all in, down, and out. Then he was going to become awful rich. Oh, he was going to be about the wealthiest man in the world, and then he was going to be married, married very well off. But the last of it, after all that he had done, he was going to be hung. So the boy, he just didn't fear that. He just let that in one ear and out the other, so he just went on with his transaction, and by and by the old man—he got so bad the old man had to put him away from the place.

So he traveled and traveled on till he traveled into another town. So he was going by this shop and he seen this cobbling shop so he thought he'd go in. So he went in, and there was a fellow there fixing some boots and stuff there, so he asked this man did he live in the town. He said yes, he said he lived in a little place out about a mile, he said. "Out in the country is where I live, but me shop is here in town where I get my work." Well he said he had no job and he hadn't too much money, but he said he'd like to hang around.

"If you have anything for me to do, I'd like to hang around and," he said, "if you have anything for me to do, I'd like for you to get me a job."

Well the old fellow said to him, "Hang around for tonight and you can stay with me all night." Well that night him and the old man talked about how much business was in town and he said to the old fellow, he said,

"Why don't you hire another cobbler?"

Well he said he didn't have business enough.

"Well," he said, "why not hire me? I can do a lot of that kind of work," he said. "I used to work for my father. I can do a pretty good job."

"Well," he says, "I don't think you'd be any good if you're not a cobbler."

"Well," he says, "tomorrow morning I'm going to the shop with you and I'm going to show you what I can do with a pair of shoes or a pair of boots, whatever it might be," he said. "If I spoil them I'll pay for them." So he went down to the shop the next morning and they went to work, and he took this pair of shoes and he went to work and he fixed them. He says,

"How does that suit you?"

"My goodness," he said, "that's a beautiful job."

He said, "That's my trade; I'm a cobbler." Well the old man hired him and they went to work and business started rolling in and the shoes started rolling in and Mister Man, you talk about making some money. But according as they worked along day in and day out, and he got to know the old man, and the old man says, "You know," he says, "there's a king up here on the hill. He's got a house made out of rock," he said. "It's a cave, and in that cave there's nothing but just barrels of money and there's no way of getting into that."

And the young fellow says, "You know, if you'll come with me tonight and show me the place, I can get that money."

"Oh," the old man says, "I don't think we do." So they talked about it anyway and went on, and by and by the old man he consented that they would go anyway and have a look at it. So he took a couple of crowbars with him that night and a couple of bags to gather up the money, so anyway they went right around and they tried the first tier of rock. So just when they come back where they started on their second tier, there was a loose rock, and the young fellow he pried it out with the two crowbars and he jumped right in. So he jumped right in and he said to the old fella,

"You stay there," he says, "they don't want the two of us in there," so the young fellow jumped in and he bagged up what money they wanted in his bag, and went out and they put the rock in again and took the crowbars and they went back. So anyway he says to the old fellow,

"Now you know," he says, "we've just got to keep on working till this blows over but," he says, "we didn't make no show there and it's not likely there'll be anyone in there; they'll never know." So they was working the next day and the young fellow says,

"You know we didn't do right last night. If we'd a filled those bags we'd never have to work another day in our life."

"Oh," the old fellow says, "I think we should be satisfied with what we got."

"No," he said, "we're going back tonight and get one more haul of money and then we'll haul out of her after two or three months, we'll close up the old shop and haul out of her." Well, back they went.

Now the young fella knew right where to go. The king had been there, sent his men there that day and had seen the money was gone and knowed it was no use in going out looking for that, but we'll set a trap for the thief. So the young fellow was aware of this. He knew the game, and the poor old man didn't know what was going on. He thought it was all clear sailing, so the young fellow he just pried the rock out and he said to him, he said,

"I went in last night; you go in tonight." So when the old man went in there was a barrel of thick tar which was full, a puncheon full setting at the bottom of the hole, and the poor old man jumped into that, right to the waist. Well he commenced to scream. He said,

"Lookit, I'm caught into some thick stuff; I can't get out."

He says, "Never mind about that. Just reach around and get the gold," he says. "I'll get you out of that." So he knew it was useless. He wasn't going to get him out of that. So the old man he felt around all the barrels of money, and he gathered up and was passing out the money and the young fellow was putting it in the bags, so when he got what the young fellow could carry he just hauled this sword off his side and he took the old fellow by the hair and he clipped the head right off the old man and put it in the bag with the money, and left the rock out and took the two crowbars and went. Well the next morning—he went home and told the old man's woman.

"Now," he says. "I'll tell you what I have to do. Now the old man was getting old anyway and," he says, "lookit, if you don't squeal on me I've got enough money to give you that you could step out of this town and you'll never have to want for nothing. You've got all the money you want." So she thought it over. She thought the old fellow was getting old, something like Wilmot MacDonald. It wouldn't much force now anyway, so she just let it go. So the next day he went back to the shop. He said,

"Now we've just got to keep quiet. We've just got to let on that we're just cobbling away," so he was cobbling in the shop, and the king had the only two pigs in the world at that time, and whatever he sent them for, they could find it. So they sent them out to see could they find the old fellow's head, wherever this would be buried. So this Johnny he was cobbling away, and he looked out, and here the pigs is going through the orchard with the old fella's head, after they dug it up, so he grabbed the old gun and he went out and he shot the two pigs and took them in and he dressed them up. So the pigs never went home, and no head of the old man or nothing, so the king says,

"I'm going to get him. I'm going to get him." So there was a hundred houses in that town, so he sent soldiers to stay at each man's house all night, and whoever had pork fried, that was the man doing all this crooked work. So he was working away and the two soldiers come and they told their story, so he just let on he was married to the woman. He said,

"You go in there and my wife and I will take care of you." So anyway, when he went in for his supper, here she had them set down to a big plate of fresh pork. So he thought to himself,

"This is it. I've had it now." But anyway they had to stay all night, so after they got done eating he said,

"Well now, me and me wife is going out tonight," he said. "I'm going to show you your room and then you can go to it when you like." So he put them in this room, and there was no window in it or anything, so when the two lads went in he turned on the light, and when he come out he just locked the door. They'll stay there for the night till he'd think up a plan what he was gong to do. Well he went down anyway and he looked across the street and there was two fellas going into the next house and there's two going in there. Every man has got two soldiers for the night, so he sat down at the table and he started to write those bills out. So he wrote a hundred of those bills, and he put on those bills,

"Kill those two men in the morning." So he went around, and he hung them on every man's door that night.

So the next morning Johnny's two lads didn't get up very early 'cause they knew they had him, so right across the street he seen the two dead soldiers coming out the door, and other two dead soldiers, so he just went in and opened the door and he gaffled his two fellows and killed them with the sword and threw them out too. Well this was on every man's door, on Johnny's door and all, so he couldn't find out what on earth is going on, who's doing this. "All right anyway," he says, "I'll get him this time." He had a party, and the king announced this that he invited every man in town to come. Well there was a hundred men to go, and Johnny says to her, he says,

"Lookit, I got to go too, for if I don't go I'll be caught." Well he went anyway, so he thought to himself,

"Well now I'll go to that party and see what's going on there." So after they had their supper the king turned them out into a great big field-bed which was about a hundred feet, fifty by a hundred, and they was all beds on the floor, and the men all slept like feet to feet, on each side of this building.

"Now," he said to his daughter, "the only thing, I'm going to get this fellow. He might be young and he might be old and we don't know what he is, but you have to make a lot of him. You're going to go through this when they're all laying there, and you're going to have a quart of whiskey with you, and you're going to have cigarettes and stuff like this on this little end table down at the end of that which you're going to set there and you're going to start to drink whisky by yourself, setting there. Now whoever's bad enough for to do all this, is going to have gall enough to go right down and start to drink whisky with you, and," he says, "you must get him drunk and get him asleep so you can put a mark on him. So I want you to put a big blue X right on his forehead."

So Johnny was laying there among the rest of them and anyway she walks in with this big quart of liquor, and she walks right down through the hall, and they was all laying watching her, and they was all laying there and Johnny watched her going down, and she sat down at this table and she filled up her glass and smoked a cigarette and she started to drink. So he thought to himself,

"I can't stand this any longer. I must go down and have a drink with her anyway," so up he got and he goes down, and she insisted on him.

"Sit down. Sit down, dear man."

He said, "Give me a drink," he said. "The king has left me."

"Oh," she said, "the king won't be back till the morning. He don't come in here." She said, "I'm running this," and he said, "Who are you?"

"Oh, I'm his daughter."

"Oh, um, great." So he kept lacing the liquor into him and by and by he got drunk, so he kinda leaned over on the chair and he was sleeping away and so she took this pen and she put this mark on him. Well, she picks up her bottle and she goes out.

Now he woke up some time in the morning and his coat was half tore off him, his tie was all twisted everywhere like this so, behold ye, he thought he'd straighten around. The girl was gone and the liquor's all gone, so he got up anyway and he went over to the looking glass for to comb his hair and fix himself up, so he noticed this X on his forehead. Well, he spit on his fingers and he got rubbing this and he's going to rub this off, and the more he rubbed it, the prettier it got. Well he tried to tear it out of that; no sir, she was dyed right in his forehead so the mark was on to stay.

"Well now," he said, "I've had it now because she's put a mark on me when I was drunk. I didn't know anything about this. But," he said, "the only thing to do is to look around and see could I find the pencil she done it." So, as luck happened, she went away, she was a little groggy herself I suppose with the rest of the quart. When she left, she left the pencil. So he picked it up and he seen it was the same. So all those other men was sleeping on the floor, me along with the rest and she *(he)* turned around and she *(he)* put a big X on every one of their foreheads was laying there. Well he laid down again and oh, around about seven o'clock the old king come in. He told them all to stand one by one and walk out. Now she told him she put this mark on him and would get him. Well the first old man come out, he had this mark, and the next fella.

"Hold on," he said, so he said to his daughter, "Mary," he said, "did you set all these men drunk?" She said no. "Well they all got this mark, and they didn't know Johnny from the rest of them." Well they all went in and they set down to the table and they had their breakfast, and when they was eating their breakfast, just when they set down, eating away, the old king stood up by the table.

"Now boys," he said, "I'm going to tell you something you've done. This is the smartest man in the world does these tricks and," he say, "if he'll stand up as a man and say it was him," he said, "there'll be nothing harm him. You can have that daughter of mine for a wife. I'll build you a castle to stay in," he said, "that you'll never have to work another day in your life."

So Johnny he stands up. "Here I am."

"Well," he says, "if it's you, come up here." Well we had a big wedding that day anyway, and Johnny got married. So about a year after he'd built this nice castle for him, and he was setting around nothing to do, so he was setting this day with his head down. So his wife come in and asked him what was the matter. He said,

"Lookit, five years ago I had my fortune told by a witch, and," he said, "everything that she told me, which I didn't believe, come true right till today, and the last thing she told me, I was going to be hung."

"Well," she said, "that could never happen now. You ain't got to work; you ain't got to do nothing, just stay here with me."

"Well," he said, "it's been bothering me this last two weeks and I can't get rid of it."

"Well now," she says, "I'll tell you what we're going to do. We're going to go out in the back shop and," she said, "you'll get a chair and I'll put a rope up on a beam in the back shed, in the woodshed, and I'll make a knot, a hangman's knot, and I'll put your head in the loop, and then I'll take it out, and maybe you'll forget all about it."

"Well maybe," he said, "that will be all right." He'd try it anyway. Well she took him out there and she got him up on an old rickety bench of some kind and she put his head in, and just by that the doorbell rung. Well when she come out for me I had some milk for her, some groceries. Now anyway I give her this and the first thing we heard this awful crash. Well she run in anyway, and he got around there, which he had his hands tied behind his back, just made out that she was going to hang him, and when we went in, here his neck was broken and he was hung.

So I hung around there for a while and it got too spooky for me. I just had to haul out of her then and come home.

[Types 930 The Prophecy, 934A Predestined Death, and 950 Rhampsinitus; Motif N334.2. Hanging in game or jest accidentally proves fatal; related to Type 1525 The Master Thief] *Recorded September 1960.*

From *Eight Folktales from Miramichi*: "I learned [this story] on the drive on Burnt Hill," said Wilmot, "from Clarence Curtis and Wright [Curtis], both brothers.... That's a lot of old stuff to be running through your head now, ain't it?"

61. Out-Riddling the Judge

AS TOLD BY WILMOT MACDONALD, NEWCASTLE, N.B.

THIS RIDDLE WAS MADE ABOUT A GIRL. She was in jail and she was going to be hung. She was condemned to die, but the Monday before she was going to be hung they told her if she could make a riddle that all the judge and the jury couldn't figure out what it was, they would let her go free. Well she said—she had two hours to do it—but she said she couldn't hardly do it in jail. "You'll have to let me out; out to walk around."

So they let her out and the guard went with her, and she walked up around this great field that was around about maybe three acres around the edge of the woods. So she looked all around the edge of that field, and along the sides of the wood. The guard led her right clean around, which he didn't know what she was looking at, nor a thing. So she come right back around and she said, "You can go ahead and take me in. I have known the riddle right now."

So they took her out on the stage, on the stand. So she said this riddle. "Well," she said,

> As I walked out and in again
> From the dead the living came,
> Six there was and seven shall be,
> That will set the virgin free.

Now what was it?

Helen Creighton: Well, Mr. MacDonald, I know that riddle. I've heard it all over Nova Scotia, but Miss Manny doesn't know it. You tell her, will you?

Wilmot: Well now, Miss Manny, what was it? Eh? Well, this girl walked around this fence, and there had been a horse had died in the winter, which they took the remains to the woods. And in this horse's eye, the ball of the eye where the flesh was all gone, the bird had made a nest, and in that nest there was five little birds and one egg. If that egg come out there'd be six birds, but there was five in it then and the sixth one might come out. But they never guessed it, so they let her go free.

Helen: In Nova Scotia we say,

> Six there are and seven to be
> And that will set the prisoner free.

It's a very good riddle.

Wilmot: It is.

[Type 927 Out-Riddling the Judge]

EDITORS' NOTE: In a letter to Sandy Ives in 1962, Helen Creighton wrote that this riddle "is the most widespread of any told in the Maritime Provinces; it seems to turn up everywhere." It is one of the best-known riddles in English storytelling tradition, for that matter. The riddle itself is often found without the story.

62. The Haunted House

AS TOLD BY WILMOT MACDONALD, NEWCASTLE, N.B.

HELEN CREIGHTON: I usually stayed on for a few days after the (Miramichi Folk) Festival, and on one of these occasions Wilmot MacDonald and his wife arrived to visit Miss Manny. Logs were burning on the hearth, he had been acclaimed the best woods singer, and he was in the mood for storytelling. I set my tape recorder in motion and got a ghost yarn so well told that I used it over and over again to finish off a lecture, it was told with such obvious zest and enjoyment, and always with his receptive adult audience in mind. Another time he told the same tale to Sandy Ives not with the purpose of spinning a good yarn to make him laugh, but as he told it to two young boys to frighten them. It was an abbreviated version without the high spots achieved on my recording when every sentence was his own dramatic experience. Because storytellers and singers are so sensitive to their surroundings, it is often a good idea to go back and then, if the mood is right, to record them over again.

—A Life in Folklore

WELL NOW, FIRST START OF MY LIFE, you know, I was away down in Maine, coming across—walking of course, you know—wasn't much way to go, only walk then, had no money. So anyway I thought I seen a kind of a house there and it looked pretty nice, and I thought to myself, "If I can get in there now for the night I'll be all set." So I went in anyway and I rapped at the door and this man come to the door, so I asked him could he keep me all night.

"Well now," he said, "I have seven or eight of a family; I ain't got a bed in the house." I said,

"I don't want a bed, 'long as you put me in, keep me from freezing to death, I'll sleep on the floor."

"Well now," he said. I said, "I got no money. No, and," I said, "I got very little clothes, which I'd freeze to death if I have to stay outside."

"Well now," he said, "come on in and I'll get ye something

to eat." So we come in and we had our supper. He said,

"Lookit," he said, "do you want to make a hundred dollars tonight?"

"Oh," I said, "there's not a man in this country would like a hundred dollars any better than me tonight. I could get away down to Canada if I had a hundred dollars." He said,

"Do you see that house right across the road there?" I said, "Yes."

"Well," he said, "that house is vacant; that belongs to me, and," he said, "there haven't been a soul able to stay in that house," he said, "for five years. That house is haunted." I said,

"What do you mean by a haunted house?" He says,

"You don't believe in ghosts?" I said,

"No, Sir, I do not." I said, "My father and mother taught me that there was no such a thing as a ghost. She says there might be a forerunner before a death, but not after. So," I said, "I don't believe in ghosts."

"Well," he says, "lookit. You'll get a hundred dollars if you're able to stay in that house tonight." I said,

"I'll try her." He said,

"O.K. Now," he said, "all those windows in that house is all shutters on the outside and bolted, and," he says, "when you go in, I'm going to turn the key in the door and remember, you're there for the night." I said,

"O.K." I said, "I'll go." I said, "If there's no man-living-creature in that house to kill me, there'll be no ghosts. Well," I said, "all right." So he took me over about nine o'clock that night and he put me in, which there was no light or nothing, and I went in. He said,

"You'll find a bed right off of the kitchen in the hall," he says. "There's a bed there with mattress on it, and lots of blankets and," he says, "at seven o'clock in the morning I'll come and I'll unlock the door to see are you alive or dead."

Well I went in the house and I lit some matches and I went into every room in that house, even up to the attic—there wasn't one soul in the house. I said, "Boys, this here, these fellas I hear tell of, those fellas from the United States, ghost stories, and I likely have one of them right now," I said. "They don't belong to Canada or they wouldn't be going on this way."

So I laid down, and I had a smoke laying in the bed, and I had been tired traveling all day and anyway, I laid down. A little shivery, you know, but welcome you know that I got in out of the cold in the fall of the year, and I hauled the blanket over me, took off my shoes, and hauled the blanket over me. So I might have been there ten minutes and I felt this cold thing on my back, and it was just like—I don't know, I had a kind of feeling it was—but boys, it started pressing a little tighter and getting kinda bad. Well I commenced to getting a little smaller than I was. So I went to try to turn over, for to see what it would be now, see? But when I'd turn over, there didn't appear to be nothing, but then when I turned back, it would press against me. So I kinda reached around like this, you know, with my left hand, which was my right, and not too much. Well I said to myself now,

"That's imagination. This is what this is. This is imagination now, that there's something here." So by and by it commenced to bury me down, and the first thing it was on top of me, which was crushing me down, and I looked and the body—it's a body—I could feel the shoulders. It left and I felt the shoulders, but no head. There was no head. "Well now," I says to myself, "now it's only about half-past nine now. I'm going to put in some awful night if I'm going to stay here till seven o'clock with this man." Well anyway, when this noise started, it come from the kitchen, so I laid for a while thinking that he's going to kill me anyway; he's going to crush me right to death. Well then there was nothing. So then the noise was in the kitchen, tramping around, thump thump, in and out, in and out.

So I put in the night. He left me around pretty good till about between four and five o'clock, and this racket started. The moans—ooohh—dear, oh looka here, she's getting wooly now boys. She's tightening. Every hair on my head was just tightening boys, I said. So anyway, it was in the bed with me again. So it stayed there for a while and by and by it disappeared again and the thumpin' and the moans, and I was laying there with just kinda one eye shut, ye know and it commenced to break daylight. And I looked out, and the first thing this casket slid right in by the bed. A big black casket, and then the lid, or the top of the casket, stood up, and up sat this man. Well he had no head on. Well I could see what I was looking at then, and I said to myself then,

"I believe there are such thing as a ghost; if I was just clear to here I wouldn't care." And I said to him, I said,

"In the name of God," I said, "what do you want of me?" So the cover went down and there was nothing ever happened. By and by the cover come up again and he sat up again. So I said the same thing, which is about all I could say. So I asked him again. I said, "In the name of God," I said, "what do you want of me?" He said,

"I don't want nothing of you, but," he says, "I was murdered five years ago for my money and," he said, "when they did murder me," he said, "they never got me. They never got the money and," he says, "I'm going to tell you where it is; come with me." Well I looked pretty silly walking alongside of this ghost, and him with no head. So we come out to the kitchen and there was two little sharp boards in the floor which was about three feet long, right in front of the stove. He said,

"Take a crowbar which is standing there, and pull them two boards up, and in between the two floors is me money." So he stood there 'longside of me and I got the money. So I pocketed it all and it disappeared. There was nothing. I went back and laid down and I started to count this money, and I had lots of her then. And I said, "If I ever get to Canada, hello for liquor." So anyway, at seven o'clock the guy come and he took me out. So we went over to give me breakfast. So we sat there and I told him. He said,

"What did you hear and what did you see?" I said,

"I just had the beautifullest night I ever had in my life." See? And he said,

"You never heard nothing?"

"No, my dear man." I said, "The beautifullest home in the

world. But," I said, "I'm going to tell you something. I got to go to the Mounted Police this morning." He said,

"For what?" I said,

"You know what," I said. "There's something on you," I said, "that I don't like about you and," I says, "I might as well tell you the truth. I'm going to the police this morning and you just might as well give yourself up now, for," I said, "you murdered a man five years ago for his money, for he told me." Well him and his wife and the son they flew, and I had everything in my pocket, and I said, "There's the money that you stole, that you was to take from that man, and you never got a cent from him." And I said, "That's why the house is left the way it is."

So I went to the police anyway and I told them the story and there was five thousand dollars reward. Any man could get that. So I give up this money and I got me reward and I landed down here in Chatham and I went away down to Black River and the first thing I fell in was that woman there. She thought a lot of me then, you know. I was only young, and I got around there and she asked me all about this and where I got this money and I told her and I said, "You needn't be scared of ghosts," for I said, "lookit, I was tangled with ghosts," I said, "and it never hurt me one sign at all in the world." I said, "Sometimes I'd just as soon talk to a ghost as anyone else." So that's how I got the money, and how I fell in with that old woman of mine. If I hadn't a got the money, I would never have fell in with her.

[Motifs E231. Return from the dead to reveal murder, E281. Ghosts haunt house, E422.1.1. Headless revenant, and E545.12. Ghost directs man to hidden treasure] *Recorded September 1960.*

DR. EDWARD D. IVES: When Wilmot told the story to Helen Creighton, he told it as something that actually happened; it scared him but he came through it all right, turning it well to his advantage in several ways.... When he told the story to me, he had to manage the rather difficult business of a frame within a frame: he was telling me what he told two impressionable young lads in order to scare them, and he had to keep the two levels of narrative clear in the telling. Thus the storyteller's art is important here too. In addition, so much of the story's effect depends on seeing Wilmot's face go blank with feigned fear and hearing the horror in his voice as he gasps out Bill's last speech (and, of course, experiencing the explosion of laughter at the end), that it may appear a little pointless in print. But my son Steve is a good barometer in these matters: he was right on the edge of his seat all through the story and he simply came unglued with laughter at the end.

—from *Eight Folktales from Miramichi*

63. Woman in Trance Buried Alive

AS TOLD BY WILMOT MACDONALD, NEWCASTLE, N.B.

THIS IS A STORY ABOUT A WOMAN that died. She went into a trance. Well in them times, you know, there was no doctors, all is just dead and buried, that's all there is to it. You died with something. They didn't know what you died with in the first place. But this woman they said dropped dead, and they wakened her three nights and they buried her.

Well her man couldn't sleep; every night she come back to him, and every night she come back. Well this dawned on him and got so bad and he never seen her, only he could hear her moaning, and she come back to him every night. So he told them. The snow was awful deep. So they went about three weeks after and he ordered them. He says,

"We got to dig her up. We got to dig her up for," he says, "I never was left alone since the last night I buried her."

So they dug her up, and when they opened the casket she was on her side in the casket; her hair was about six inches longer than what it really was, and every bit of skin was all tore off her face with her finger nails where she was scratching, all in the casket. But this time she's dead now anyway, so they just covered her up and let her go. *(Laughter.)* And I was standing there when they dug her up and he said, "We might just as well let the tail go with the hide now." *(More laughter.)*

Old Bob Brown when he buried his wife, you know, and the old joke, the old saying then, you know, he said to him, "Mr. Brown," he said, "are you going to take the breastplate off of the casket?" He said no. He said, "What about the ring on her finger?" He said, "No, just let the tail go with the hide." *(Much laughter.)*

[Motifs E723. Wraiths of persons separate from body, S123. Burial alive, and V67. Accompaniments of burial] *Recorded September 1960.*

HELEN CREIGHTON: Speaking of his wife, Mr. MacDonald said: "You know when I'm home, you know, and she'll say, 'I wish you'd get out of the house,' and the first thing I come in and she's got some old record of mine, you know, and listening to me. I said, 'You still just can't leave me alone.'" *(Laughter.)*

64. Woman Buried Alive

AS TOLD BY WILMOT MACDONALD, NEWCASTLE, N.B.

WELL, THIS IS A STORY, and it's supposed to be a true story. If you get it from me it must be true. Now we had an old neighbour who just lived in her own settlement, and him and his sister lived all alone, just the two of them. They never was married, but this old woman was the finest old creature in the world, and every time from the time that I was maybe ten years old, we used to go down there. Our mail never come up our road; we used to have to go down to the corner and get our mail.

Well, in the wintertime when I'd be coming from school this poor dear old lady would come out and she'd call me in. Which I used to do her a few chores 'round the barn, maybe feed the hens or throw the cattle a bite to eat when the old man was in the woods, but she'd always make me this lovely cup of tea. Well now, this run on for years, but finally the poor old creature, she fell out of the bed—she took a heart attack—and the word come up that poor old Tina McLean was dead. Well that day the old man went out and he got her casket. That time there never was no doctor ever come in for to pronounce if it was dead or a thing, so I went down to see me dear old lady that night. So anyway I went down, and I went in to see the remains. Well this poor old lady was in her casket laid out there, all rigged up with her good black dress on and everything, and I was standing there and my brother was 'longside of me, and I said to my brother, I said, I took me elbow and I reached over, which there was quite a crowd in the room, and I kinda nudged him with my elbow, and I says,

"I don't believe the poor old creature's dead."

"Oh oh," he says, "don't say that." He used to call me Bill. He said, "Bill, don't say that." I said,

"Give me that looking glass." So anyway there was some old woman going in and out, so I held the looking glass right down tight on her face, right over her face, for about, oh I'd say half a minute, and when someone was coming in the room I takes it off. The looking glass was wet. So anyway, I went home and I told my mother. My mother was in bed, and my father which was about half past eleven, and I said,

"Lookit, they're going to bury Tina McLean dead." See? Mom said,

"For the love of goodness now, I know you're crazy, but go way to bed," she said. "The poor old soul...." I said,

"Lookit, poor old Tina McLean, I bet five dollars right here that's alive." Well, two days after they buried her, eh? That night, now this. I don't know whether it's imagination, but that night when she was the first night in the grave, which I went to her funeral and was there and watched her being buried, and that night, every time I'd go to sleep this would wake me up. Well it got so bad at the last of it that I just could hardly stand it, but anyway, after she was buried three or four night, there was nothing I could dream about. You know, it was all about her, and I'd wake up in those scares, see? Well anyway, this went on, so the next summer I took me horses and I went down for to cut a piece of hay for the old man, her brother. So whenever he was done having his dinner, he grabbed his pipe and he used to go out on the verandah for to fill his pipe. He had a verandah and he sat there into an old armchair to fill this pipe and smoke, eh? And I was rolling a cigarette, and the first thing I heard this upstairs. Now this is where me old woman took the heart attack. So the first thing I hear is the thump towards the stairs, and then she starts down the stairs. Well, it commenced to tighten boys, and I says I have nothing for to fear about the old woman, so they come right down, come right down, crunch, crunch. Well now, there's one step in these stairs is loose, and it'll go squeak. I showed it to Joe McKay after he bought the property. Well, I said to Joe,

"I heard it." I said, "Right in the middle of the day, and," I said, "I heard nothing at all—I couldn't see nothing, but I could hear it." So this went on, and every time I went into that house till the old man died it was the same, and Joe MacKay bought that house and he told me that he didn't hear it once—he heard it fifty times in the house and it got so bad that they tore the old house down. It's flat now, and he moved down in the front of the place.

So that's what I heard in the line of ghost stories, was that and I believe it was the truth and I still say they buried her alive. Yah, yah. Oh I was young then and I could rough her out, you know I could stand a ghost then, you know. No, I wouldn't like it a little bit now.

[Motifs E322. Dead wife's friendly return, E338. Non-malevolent ghost haunts building, and S123. Burial alive] *Recorded September 1960.*

PART EIGHT

Somewhere to End...

65. Big Claus and Little Claus (1)

AS TOLD BY JUDSON AND ALLISTAIR ARMSTRONG, LEVY
SETTLEMENT

LITTLE CLAUS LIVED IN THE VALLEY, and Big Claus lived on the hill. Big Claus was the rich man, and Little Claus had a home and he started a farm. He wanted to borrow his brother's horses, but the only time he could have them was on Sunday. His brother didn't like him working on Sunday, so Little Claus took his old horse and hooked it ahead of the nice team and said, "Get up, my three horses."

So his brother didn't like it, so he came down and said he'd kill Little Claus' old horse, so he did. Little Claus skinned the old horse and dried his hide and on his way to town night overtook him, so he went up to a farmhouse and he asked the lady if he could stay all night. She said she would keep him if he would sleep on the floor, so he laid the horsehide down and made a bed of it. She said to him,

"My husband's away and he won't be in till late." So in the night he heard something going on in the house. When her husband came in he asked Little Claus what he was doing here. He said,

"I'm a fortuneteller."

"How much would you charge to tell my fortune?" He said,

"A good fortune will cost you two bushels of money." He said,

"In this house is a closet with all kinds of cake and pie, and there's a chest in this house with a man in it." Little Claus got his money and he borrowed his rich brother's bushel for to measure the money and when he took it home he stuck the cracks with silver and he says,

"There's a good sale down there for old horse hides. You get two bushels of money for them." So Big Claus went to work and killed his nice pair of horses and dried the hides and took them to town and couldn't give them away, so he told his brother he was going to kill him. So that night Little Claus changed beds with his mother. So Big Claus crawled up over the porch with his iron bar and came in the window and killed Little Claus' mother, so Little Claus took his mother out of bed and froze her and took her to town. The bar just had opened. He ordered two drinks, one for himself and one for his mother and he told the bartender that she was awful hard of hearing and if she didn't hear him to give her a clout, and he knocked her out of the sleigh. He went in and said,

"I knocked your mother out of the sleigh." Little Claus said,

"You killed her." He says, "It's early in the morning. You give me two bushels of money and we'll call it square. I'll take her down to the wharf and dump her over."

He went back to Big Claus and he borrowed the basket, and when he sent it home he stuck the cracks with silver and said, "There's a good sale down there for old women." So Big Claus goes to work and called his grandmother out to the barn and he cut her throat and he took her downtown and he couldn't give her away. He lost millions of dollars and was beginning to become a poor man.

When this garden got big enough to use, Big Claus comes along with a boy and grabs his brother and puts him into a bag. He says,

"I've got you now; I'm going to drown you." When he started out with him in the wheelbarrow he said, "Now you've got to say, 'How happy I am to enter the kingdom of heaven,'" and on his way to the lake he had to go by a church. The church service was going on so he went in. There was an old fellow coming along with fifty head of cattle. He says,

"I'm an old man and I'd like to enter the kingdom of heaven." Little Claus says,

"Just untie this bag and I'll get out and you get in, but you've got to say, 'How happy I am to enter the kingdom of heaven.'" Big Claus came out of the church and took the wheelbarrow. He wheeled the old fellow down and wheeled him into the lake thinking it was his brother. So when Big Claus came home he had to go by Little Claus' home and he was setting beside the house with fifty head of cattle in his yard. He says,

"I thought I drowned you." He says,

"You did, but I found a mermaid down there and fifty head of cattle." Big Claus said, "I should get some too." So Little Claus said,

"I'll take you down," so he took Big Claus down and put him in the lake and that was the end of Big Claus.

[Type 1535 The Rich and the Poor Peasant] *Collected June 1949.*

HELEN CREIGHTON: There is some doubt whether Big Claus killed his grandmother or his wife's mother.

66. Big Claus and Little Claus (2)
AS TOLD BY DAN MACPHERSON, EAST ERINVILLE, N.S.

THREE BROTHERS LIVED TOGETHER, two together and one alone, the one alone with his mother. The two lived with their aunt. They were all getting along well, but the boy with his mother was getting along better so the others got jealous and were going to kill him. They made up they were going to kill him, so the brother caught on and told his mother he wasn't feeling well, and told her if she'd mind sleeping in his bed. Two brothers came that night and they killed him, but they killed the old lady instead.

Next morning he went to bury her and he put her on his back and went to the nearest village and got to town and he was pretty hungry so he went to get a cup of tea and propped the old lady up at the well and went in and ordered lunch for two. When it was ready he told a little girl to go out and tell his mother to come in. She went out and spoke to her and she didn't answer. She spoke a few times and then run in and said his mother wouldn't answer. He said to give her a little shake and she did, and she fell down the well. So the little girl jumped in the house and he come out and was in an awful way and she was drowned.

They made a collection for him, quite a bit of money, and he went back home. They buried the old lady first and he had his money and he told his brothers,

"You fellows thought you done me a lot of harm last night when you killed my mother, but it was the best thing that ever happened to me. There's great sales for old women. They buy them for gunpowder." So the two brothers went to work and killed the other old lady, their aunt, and they took her in and tried to sell her and they were arrested. So they got back home again after a time and, my gosh, they were wild at their brother and were going to make away with him.

This night they went and they got a bag and put him in the bag and were going to drown him. So they took him down to the shore of the lake and cut the hole in the ice and while they were doing this a drover came along with cattle. The brother was singing a hymn in the bag and the drover heard him. The old drover said,

"What in the world are you doing here?"

"Oh, don't say a word. I'm just waiting for the angels to come down. I'm going to heaven." The old drover got interested, but he said, "Don't talk to me at all, I'm going to heaven." The old drover said he wanted to go to heaven, but he wasn't too anxious to give up his chance. At last he said,

"I might get the chance again." So the old drover took the string off the bag and the brother got out and the drover went in the bag and he tied the string on the bag. Before that he had offered him all the cattle he had if he'd let him go in the bag and the brother drove the cattle home and the other two brothers finished cutting the hole and came back and took the bag and thought it was the brother they had drowned. They walked home. The next morning when they got up the brother's field was full of cattle, and after they drowned him. So they didn't know what to make of it, and they knew he was home again. So they thought the best thing was to get in with him and see what secrets he had about getting along. So they went over and had a talk with him and he said,

"You thought you done me a lot of harm last night. You were going to drown me. I went down to the bottom of the lake last night and there was nothing but cattle there and I took up that many last night." The two brothers wanted to know if he'd do something for them and they'd try to get along together.

"Oh yes, that's the way I'd like to get along. I'd like to help anybody, and if you fellows want to get a stock of cattle like this, there's no trouble. The bottom of the lake is full of cattle." The two brothers wanted to go down that night and see if they could get some cattle. He said yes, he'd go down. They went down to the same hole in the ice they'd dug for him, and he told one of them to go down. He went down, and after a time he come up and he made a kind of gurgle. The other said,

"What is he saying?"

"He says he's got a big ox and he can't take him up alone and he wants you to go down and give him a help." So he went down, and that was the end of that.

[Type 1535 The Rich and the Poor Peasant] *Collected September, 1961.*

67. Big Claus and Little Claus (3)

AS TOLD BY NORMAN MCGRATH, VICTORIA BEACH, N.S.

THERE WERE TWO BROTHERS. One had very good success through life; the other didn't do so well. So they left home and went west, and in the west one had finances enough to get along and get his farming utensils, but the other fellow only had one old horse; a cheap one at that. The other fellow had five horses. The fellow with the five horses was religious and attended church and he made quite a scene through the place. He wanted to be noticed. The other fellow had to work hard every day, even Sundays. So the fellow with the five horses was getting along very well and he would go to church every Sunday, and going to church he would have to pass by the other fellow's farm where he was working, and in his position in life it didn't look very good to see his brother working on Sunday.

So the poor fellow told his better brother if he would lend his better horses to him on Sundays, he would work for him all the rest of the week with his one horse. The one fellow, being very ambitious, agreed to that.

The first fellow was rather a proud man, and he was with a lot of others going to church. The poor brother was very proud to be having all those horses, so he said,

"Get up, all my six horses, get up, all my six horses." So after church the brother came to him and says,

"I don't want you to say that. Five of those horses are mine. It don't sound very good passing to church on Sunday." So he says to him,

"Now don't do that any more or I'll take my five horses from you and kill your one horse and you won't have any."

He promised he wouldn't say it any more. He had the horses the following Sunday but, being a little anxious to boast, he had to keep up, "Get up, all my six horses." The brother went and killed his one horse that night as he told him he would, and took his own five horses from him.

Well, he didn't know what to do, so he skinned the horse and went to town with the skin. He thought he might make money by pretending to make fortunes with this thing, and he went into a barn because a woman wouldn't let him stay in the farmhouse all night.

He went in the barn, and in a lot of the farmer's beams there were pigeon holes. He laid up in the hay, and he was watching and waiting for her husband to come home, and he thought that when he came he might get lodging there all night.

During the time he was watching, he saw from the barn in through the window a man there, and he saw the woman spread a table with all kinds of food, and then she took the cloth and put it in a brick oven and hid it there. When the farmer came home he went back to the house, and the farmer said he could stay there for the night.

They sat down to the table and they just had common food, so this feller says,

"Why should we be eating common food when there's so much better to eat?" The farmer says,

"No, this is all we can afford to eat and I don't want to hear any remarks."

Before this he had put the horsehide under the table and he stepped on it and it made a peculiar sound. He looked down and said,

"Say you, shut up. Nobody's talking to you."

The farmer wanted to know what he said, and the man told him it was a fortunetelling machine, and he wasn't asking for the information but the fortuneteller butted in himself. Then the farmer was very anxious to know what it had said. He says,

"It doesn't matter. I won't be offended. If he says there's better food in the house than this he must be lying. I'm a poor man." The man says,

"This fortuneteller never lies."

"Then ask him where the better food is." So he stepped on the horsehide again and the horsehide says,

"Well, the food is in the brick oven over there." So the farmer opened the oven and, sure enough, there was a big tablecloth with all kinds of food wrapped into it. Then he made it talk again.

"What's he saying now?"

"I wouldn't dare tell you."

"You've got to tell me."

"Well, you go upstairs to the room on the south side, and you'll find the devil inside the chest." So up went the uncle and raised up the cover, and there was a man. He came down as white as a sheet and said,

"Can you take the devil out of the house with that?"

"Oh yes, I can do anything with it."

"I'll give you five hundred dollars if you can take the devil out of the house." So he took the chest and the money and went away. When he came back after selling his horsehide for a good price, he went for his brother to see if he could borrow a measure. In those days they measured their money instead of counting it. His brother wondered what he wanted of that measure, so he smeared a little grease around it so that whatever he measured would stick to it. He wondered how his brother got such a price for his horsehide that he would have money to measure, so he went over and asked him. He says,

"You weren't measuring money?"

"Oh yes, I was. I was measuring money I got from the horsehide."

"Well," the brother says, "you must have an awful lot of money that you had to measure it for that one horsehide." He says,

"Yes, I never saw such a demand for horsehides."

"Well," says his brother, "I will go and kill my five horses and I'll have five times as much as that." So he kills his five horses and takes them to town and he kept singing out in town,

"Horsehides for sale; horsehides for sale; who wants to buy horsehides?" So he came out of the tanner's and he found they were only a few cents a pound. It made him very mad and he went home and saw his brother and asked why he did that. He thought he wanted to get him on a level with himself, so he said,

"I'm coming over tonight to kill you."

The other brother was living with his mother-in-law, and she was a very old lady at that time. He thought he could arrange it to get his mother-in-law to sleep in his bed, and he could sleep in some other bed. He did that, and the other brother went over and clubbed her to death, thinking it was his brother. In the morning this fellow found that his mother-in-law was killed instead of him, so he would have to do something with her.

He borrowed one of the neighbour's rigs and he set the dead woman up on the seat beside him. It was a horse rig. He started very early in the morning. It was a cold day. Passing by a saloon he thought he'd go in and have something hot to drink and the man at the inn claims,

"Wouldn't that old lady like to have something warm to drink?" He says,

"Yes, you might take her out a glass of something warm." He says,

"She's very hard of hearing. You'll have to speak very loud to her." So he gets in on the other side by the old lady.

The man came in with the drink and said to the old lady,

"Here's a hot drink. It will do you good this morning." The brother says,

"You'll have to speak louder than that. She's very hard of hearing." So he put the glass up to her and spoke very hard and had put it against her, when the brother gave her a little push and she fell out of the wagon. He says,

"Oh, you've killed me mother-in-law."

"Well, what arrangement can we make for it not to be known? I'll do everything." So he told him the only thing that would settle it would be about five bushels of money. So he takes the old lady away with him, and takes the five bushels of money home. Then he went over again to borrow his brother's measure. The brother put some grease on it again to see what he was measuring and when it was returned there were some more coins still sticking to it. So he goes to his brother and says,

"Say, I thought I killed you last night." He says,

"No, you didn't kill me. You killed my mother-in-law."

"Well, where did you get all that money that you're measuring?" He says,

"I took my mother-in-law to town and I sold her. I never see such a demand in town as there is now for mothers-in-law."

"Well," he says, "I'll kill my mother-in-law and take her into town." So he killed his mother-in-law and took her to town, and he kept singing out in town,

"Mother-in-law, mother-in-law. Who wants to buy a mother-in-law?" They thought he was some insane person, so he just got away without being arrested.

Well, he rode back to his brother, and he says,

"I will kill you this time. You've ruined me." So the brother put a dummy in his bed and the brother killed him all to pieces and was sure he had him this time, but in the morning he was there again. The next thing he decided was to put him in a bag and throw him over the bridge to make sure of killing him. It was Sunday, so as he was going by the church he thought of a passage where the Lord would lighten his burden. The bag was getting very heavy, so he went into the church. During the time he was in church his brother was singing from the bag.

"Oh, I'm so young and so rich and I'm going to heaven." A stranger who was much lighter came along and said,

"Could I go to heaven in your place?" So he got into the bag, and the brother came out of church he found the bag much lighter, so he says, "I do believe in the Scripture. The word of the Lord has greatly lightened up my burden," and he carried the bag to the bridge and threw it over.

When he got home his brother was there, and with him was a drove of cattle. He went to him and said,

"I thought I threw you over the bridge and killed you."

"No," he says, "I went down there and I never seen so many fat cattle as there are in the bottom of the ocean. I was all alone or I might have got more."

"Well," says the brother, "with as many cattle as you've got there, I'll go down too, but I'll get you to put my wife, myself, and my daughter into the bag and throw us all over the bridge." So he got them all in a bag and left an opening so they could get some air. Then he threw them all over the bridge.

The poor fellow being left alone then with his brother and his brother's wife and family gone, he became heir to all his brother's property, and with what he had got himself through fraud, he became quite a rich man, and his friends in the east considered he had done well to go to the west.

[Type 1535 The Rich and the Poor Peasant] *Collected July 1947.*

HELEN CREIGHTON: Norman McGrath called it a farmer's story. He probably hadn't told his Big Claus and Little Claus for a long time, for he didn't know it as well as his other stories and at the end he was quite mixed up.

EDITORS' NOTE: For yet another version of "Big Claus and Little Claus," this one told by Edward Collicutt, see Helen Creighton's *Folklore of Lunenburg County.*

ALSO AVAILABLE FROM
Breton Books & Music

SILENT OBSERVER
written & illustrated
by CHRISTY MacKINNON
A children's book of emotional and historical substance—the autobiographical story
of a little girl who lived both in rural Cape
Breton and in the world of a deaf person.
$21.50

WATCHMAN
AGAINST THE WORLD
by FLORA McPHERSON
The Remarkable Journey of Norman
McLeod and his People from Scotland to
Cape Breton Island to New Zealand
A detailed picture of the tyranny and
tenderness with which an absolute leader
won, held and developed a community—
and a story of the desperation, vigour,
and devotion of which the 19th-century
Scottish exiles were capable.
$16.25

CASTAWAY ON CAPE BRETON
Two Great Shipwreck Narratives
in One Great Book!
1. Ensign Prenties' *Narrative*
of Shipwreck at Margaree Harbour, 1780
(Edited with an Historical Setting and
Notes by G. G. Campbell)
2. Samuel Burrows' *Narrative* of Shipwreck on the Cheticamp Coast, 1823
(With Notes on Acadians Who Cared for
the Survivors by Charles D. Roach)
$13.00

CAPE BRETON
BOOK OF THE NIGHT
Stories of Tenderness & Terror
51 extraordinary, often chilling, tales,
pervaded with a characteristic Cape
Breton tenderness—a tough, caring
presentation of experience
$16.25

ARCHIE NEIL
by MARY ANNE DUCHARME
From the Life & Stories of Archie Neil
Chisholm of Margaree Forks, C. B.
Saddled with polio, pride, and a lack of
discipline, Archie Neil lived out the con-
tradictory life of a terrific teacher flound-
ering in alcoholism. This extraordinary
book melds oral history, biography and
anthology into "the triumph of a life."
$18.50

THE MOONLIGHT SKATER
by BEATRICE MacNEIL
9 Cape Breton Stories & The Dream
From a mischievous blend of Scottish &
Acadian roots, these stories blossom, or
explode softly, in your life. Plus her
classic play set in rural Cape Breton.
$11.00

DOWN NORTH:
The Original Book of
Cape Breton's Magazine
Word-and-Photo Portrait from the first
5 years of *Cape Breton's Magazine*
239 pages, 286 photographs
$23.50

CAPE BRETON LIVES:
A Second Book from
Cape Breton's Magazine
300 pages of Life Stories • 120 photos
$23.50

HIGHLAND SETTLER
by CHARLES W. DUNN
A Portrait of the Scottish Gael
in Cape Breton and Eastern Nova Scotia
"This is one of the best books yet written
on the culture of the Gaels of Cape Breton
and one of the few good studies of
a folk-culture."— *Western Folklore*
$16.25

• PRICES INCLUDE GST & POSTAGE IN CANADA •

CONTINUED ON NEXT PAGE